Griffin has just popped the q
Michael doesn't have an answei
to see his confidante and son
Will a weekend of beignets and i
knotted-up heart?

Thus begins "Michael's Wings," the eponymous novella that kicks off the latest entry in Tiffany Reisz's LAMBDA Literary Award-winning* Original Sinners series.

This companion collection to fan-favorite *The Angel* also contains six previously-published stories starring Mistress Nora's favorite angel and Griffin—his master, his true love, and the sexy-as-hell bane of Michael's existence.

❖ ❖ ❖

"I worship at the altar of Tiffany Reisz! Whip smart, sexy as hell . . . The Original Sinners series knocked me to my knees." — *New York Times* **bestselling author Lorelei James**

The King (LAMBDA Literary Award 2015 Winner — Best Gay Erotica)

Also by Tiffany Reisz

Novels

The Original Sinners Novels

The Original Sinners Novellas

The Original Sinners Collections

Tiffany Reisz

MICHAEL'S WINGS

AN ORIGINAL SINNERS COLLECTION

8TH CIRCLE PRESS

LOUISVILLE, KY

Michael's Wings: An Original Sinners Collection

Copyright © 2017 Tiffany Reisz

Trade Paperback ISBN 978-1-949769-27-2

MP3-CD Audiobook ISBN: 978-1541459076 (Tantor Audio)

CD Audiobook ISBN: 978-1541409071 (Tantor Audio)

Cover design by Angelica Quintero

Front and back cover images used under license from Depositphotos.com. Griffin/Michael crest designed by Andrew Shaffer.

"A Better Distraction," "Christmas in Suite 37A," "The Couch," "Gauze," "Griffin in Wonderland," and "The Theory of the Moment" previously published as un-edited rough drafts on www.tiffanyreisz.com

www.8thcirclepress.com

First Edition

This collection is dedicated to all my Angels out there in the rainbow.

I pray you find the love you deserve someday.

CONTENTS

MICHAEL'S WINGS

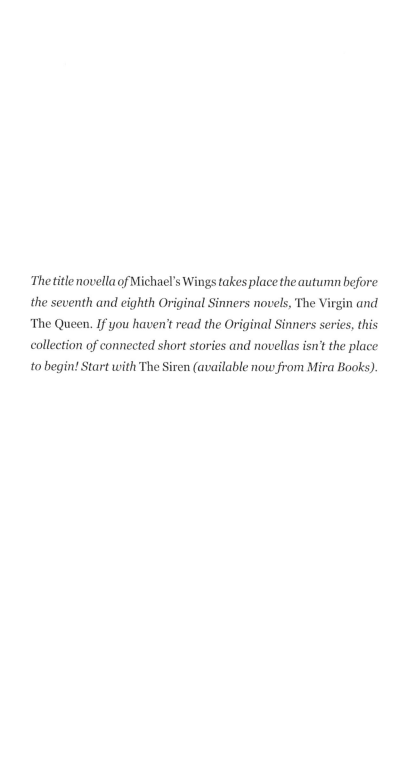

The title novella of Michael's Wings *takes place the autumn before the seventh and eighth Original Sinners novels,* The Virgin *and* The Queen. *If you haven't read the Original Sinners series, this collection of connected short stories and novellas isn't the place to begin! Start with* The Siren *(available now from Mira Books).*

CHAPTER ONE

Saints & Mustangs

I t was like magic.

Michael decided that very morning he would go to New Orleans and by evening he was there.

Although he'd grown up with the Internet in the house, sometimes it still amazed him how quickly things could happen. It really was magical, in a way. He made a wish—*I want to go see Nora*—and ten hours later, the technology gods had answered it.

He'd thought about surprising Nora, but he hated surprises himself and wouldn't wish them on his worst enemy, much less the person he trusted more than anyone else in the world, Griffin excepted. Nora would have probably enjoyed the surprise, but one never knew what she was up to these days. She could have been in France with her new "*Le Boy Toy,*" as Griffin called

Nora's Nico. Michael would have felt like an idiot if he'd showed up on her doorstep only to find she wouldn't be back for weeks.

But she was home. He'd texted her that morning asking if he could come for a quick visit. Yorke's fall break was the third week of October every year. He wanted to spend his long weekend with Griffin but plans changed. Griffin had to fly off to L.A. to deal with some staffing issues at the YMKA—The Young Masters Kink Association—so named because of the old YMCA building that Griffin had taken over. Might as well stay on brand (plus it was cheaper if they only had to change one letter on the exterior). Michael didn't want to go to L.A. if Griffin had to work the whole time. He'd decided he'd stay home at the apartment and do nothing but sleep and read and catch up on his painting.

All rest. No stress.

Then Griffin had to go and be Griffin, and there went that idea.

Michael hadn't slept a wink last night. He probably wouldn't tonight either, but at least he could blame that on his usual trouble with sleeping in new places instead of the real problem, which was he had a big decision to make and he didn't have any idea how to make it.

He wandered through Louis Armstrong International Airport with his blue backpack slung over his shoulder, the only luggage he'd brought. He could feel the steam in the air already, the humidity even though it was October. Nora had warned him October in New Orleans could sometimes feel like July in New York. Michael didn't mind. It had turned chilly in the city faster than he'd been expecting. A few more days of summer, even misplaced in the calendar, might do him some good.

As he walked to the exit, a girl in a green and gold Cabrini High School t-shirt sitting on a bench looked up from her phone. They made eye contact, as people in airports do, and she smiled flirtatiously at him. She was pretty, with dark brown skin and bright brown eyes. She looked about seventeen or eighteen—definitely a senior. If he'd asked her to grab a coffee with him in the airport, she would probably say yes, and when she found out he was twenty and a senior in college, she'd maybe shrug, if that. He was young enough to date a girl still in high school if he wanted.

Crazy, right?

Crazy.

Michael flashed the girl his usual awkward smile and kept walking, head down and earbuds in playing Paramore's newest album. Griffin had tried breaking him of the habit of slouching in public—*You're my sexual property, sub. Hold your head up high.* Griffin's version of a pep talk. And while it never failed to make Michael smile, it didn't quite cure his social anxiety in crowds and around strangers. Luckily, he wouldn't be all on his own in a strange city this weekend. It was just him and Nora, maybe Father S. Maybe he'd see Kingsley and Juliette and Céleste, too. People he knew. People he could relax around. If he could relax. He wasn't hoping for miracles, just distractions. Nora was always good for that.

Outside the airport exit he paused, glanced left and right looking for Nora's little silver BMW. When he didn't see it, he pulled his phone from his pocket and checked for messages warning him she might be late. Just as he glanced down at his phone, he heard a piercing wolf whistle.

Michael stepped to the curb just as a convertible pulled up in the pick-up lane right in front of him. A sleek red Mustang convertible, top down. Behind the wheel sat a black-haired, green-eyed, supposedly grown woman wearing a New Orleans Saints football jersey and cut-off denim shorts.

At the sight of her, Michael smiled for the first time in about twenty-four hours.

"You're a football fan now?" he asked. They knew each other too well to bother with hellos and how-are-yous.

"Gift from a client," Nora said. "He plays for the Saints. I like to torture him by complimenting him on how many 'home runs' his team scored."

"You're such a sadist."

"That's why they pay me the big bucks," she said with a grin. "Hop in, gorgeous. I don't know about you, but I'm starving. Want beignets?"

"What are beignets?"

"Imagine a ball of powdered sugar, fat, and joy."

"I'm in." Michael threw his bag into the tiny back seat and slid into the passenger seat.

"You won't regret it, kid," she said, turning her head to grin at him before putting her eyes back on the road where they belonged. She hit the gas and in minutes they were out on the main road, the airport receding behind them.

"Where's the BMW?" Michael asked. He remembered that car well. Nora had let him drive it home from church one day a few years ago. Now that he thought about it, that little trip marked the beginning of his new life. It was the first time he'd ever heard the name *Griffin*.

"Traded it in last year," Nora said. "It's almost never cold here. If it's going to be seventy in December, I'm going to have a convertible."

It was so warm out he'd already forgotten it was late October. There was a texture to the air, a thickness, and a rich scent like food and sweat and seawater. He relaxed in the heat as the wind tickled his face and sent his hair and Nora's dancing.

"It's nice," Michael said.

"Blondie said it was too 'flashy.' I told him that was pretty rich coming from a Jesuit priest who drives a black Ducati motorcycle."

Out of loyalty to Father S, Michael wanted to take his side but Nora had a point there.

"Plus, this is a Mustang," she said. "Classic American heavy metal. Not much of a back seat but I can fit a linebacker in my trunk."

"You haven't actually done that, right?" Michael asked, not sure he wanted the answer.

"Top secret," she said. "That's for me to know and the inevitable FBI investigation to find out."

Nora winked at him and Michael rolled his eyes and laughed.

"How's Father S?" Michael asked.

"Happy," Nora said. "Which makes me happy. Because when he's happy he's horny."

"Is he not usually happy?" Michael asked. He wasn't going to ask about the horny part of the equation.

"He's better at contentment than happiness, but down here, he's been really good. He's got me close by, King close by. He loves the college professor life, loves his students, loves the city. So do I. New Orleans is the perfect place to be a writer. It's beautiful and wild and old. And it's so hot all I want to do most of the time is stay indoors in my air-conditioned office."

"Very cool," Michael said. He could tell Nora was content. Unlike Father S, she was always good at being happy and terrible at being contented. Maybe finally having Nico, a sub of her own, with Father S as her dominant did the trick. Michael was glad he was just a sub and not a switch. Being a switch sounded complicated.

"He told me to tell you he would have come with me to pick you up, but he's booked tonight," Nora said. "One of his students is a choral singer, practicing for a recital this week. Søren's his accompanist."

"That's nice of Father S."

"Any excuse to play. But you'll see him tomorrow at breakfast. He was glad to hear you were finally coming down to visit us."

"I'm glad, too," Michael said. He was. He would rest here. He would have fun. He would be distracted from the looming decision he had to make. He wouldn't talk about it. He wouldn't think about it. Not tonight, anyway.

"So, Angel," Nora said as she steered them off the interstate and onto a road with the improbable name of Elysian Fields Avenue, "tell me what brings you to my neck of the woods."

Michael answered before he could stop himself, and it was all Nora's fault for phrasing the question as an order. He never could disobey an order.

"Griffin asked me to marry him."

It turned out the Mustang didn't just have a big trunk. It had very good brakes as well.

CHAPTER TWO

Beignets & Secrets

G reat brakes, actually. They didn't even squeak when Nora slammed them and steered the car to the side of the road.

She turned off the engine, turned her incredulous face to him, and said, "What?"

"It's legal in New York now," Michael said, raising both hands and waving them in a sarcastic hooray. "They're recognizing out-of-state marriages, too. I know way too much about it. Griffin spoke to a lawyer already."

"Yes, I know it's legal in the state now. But so is tattooing a purple dick on your face. Doesn't mean you have to do it."

"I know you're not really into the whole marriage thing," Michael said.

"Doesn't matter what I'm into or not," she said. "What are you into?"

Michael sighed, hard. "I . . ." He dropped his head back and stared at the sky.

"You didn't tell Griffin an answer? And you call me a sadist?"

Michael laughed a sad miserable little laugh. "He told me not to answer. He knows me, so he knows I have to think about it. He asked me last night, and he's going to be in L.A. till Sunday. He said to think about it until then, tell him yes or no when he gets home, and if it's a no we won't talk about it again unless I bring it up. I'm following orders and thinking about it until Sunday. I couldn't stand the thought of being alone in our apartment for days obsessing about it."

"So you came here to obsess about it?"

"Exactly."

"All right," she said. "Let's obsess about it. Over beignets."

They didn't talk much more as she drove them into the French Quarter. They had to park a few blocks away from the café, but the walk gave Michael a chance to stretch his legs and take in the sights. The houses fascinated him and he wished he'd thought to bring a better camera than just his iPhone. They were all so brightly colored—pink and red and mint green and blue—and right on the sidewalk. But to make up for their proximity to the general public, they were shuttered in the front so you couldn't see inside the windows. He glanced through iron gates between the houses and caught glimpses of elegant little courtyards with fountains. Everything was old and odd and eerie. No wonder Nora and Father S and Kingsley liked it here so much.

At the café, Nora bought them beignets and *café au lait*, which they carried back to the car instead of eating at the crowded tables.

"You're making me wait for powdered sugar, fat, and joy?" Michael asked.

"It's for the best," she said. "Pro tip from an old pro—let them cool down first. I burned my tongue on a beignet right after we moved here. Couldn't give a blowjob for a week. My priest was pissed." The blowjob comment was made just as they passed a young couple pushing a stroller with a sleeping toddler inside. The father gave Nora a double take, which resulted in him getting a hard slap on the arm by his unamused wife. Nora didn't notice any of it.

"Okay, but coffee at nine o'clock?" Michael asked as Nora passed him his cup.

"You have three days to decide if you're getting married. We're going to need all the caffeine we can get."

Michael sipped at his coffee and studied all the strange buildings they passed as Nora drove them to her house in the Garden District. The architecture major in him was in heaven. The art major was in an even higher circle of heaven. He'd never seen houses like this anywhere in the world. Shotgun houses. Looming Victorians with massive balconies. Iron fences with spiky fleurs-de-lis pointing straight up, defying anyone to jump the gates. They drove past a cemetery in the middle of a residential neighborhood surrounded by high stone walls and filled with aboveground crypts. Actual crypts full of actual human remains and right across the street from a café. A cemetery and a café.

"Nora, this town is weird."

"I know," she said grinning. "I love it."

A few blocks later, Nora pulled to a stop in front of a massive white house, an estate more than a house—grand and gleaming, with stone steps leading to an ebony front door and a black iron fence surrounding the entire property.

"Home sweet home," Nora said.

"This is your place?" Michael asked, staring wide-eyed and amazed.

"Just kidding. This is King's," she said. "Mine's a little smaller. But it's right around the corner."

"It's an upgrade from the townhouse," Michael said, still staring at the white mansion as she pulled away from the curb.

"The best part is that it was a third of the price of the townhouse. That's how insane Manhattan real estate is."

"Wow."

"And my new place was about the same price as my old place in Connecticut *and* it's bigger," she said. "That's mine."

She pointed it out as they slowed and turned into the off-street driveway. It was a red two-story with a big porch and a balcony on the second floor. He couldn't see much else as it was hidden behind a massive oak tree and every lower limb dripped with hundreds of Mardi Gras beads of every color.

"What's with the beads in your tree?" he asked.

"They just keep appearing," she said with a shrug as she parked behind the house. "Sometimes I go away and come home and there's a bunch of new beads that weren't there before. Søren thinks they're a gift from an admirer."

"An admirer?"

"He's old so he says things like 'I think you have an admirer.' "

Michael could hear Father S saying just that.

"He's not that old," Michael said.

"I know, but he's going gray and it's killing me. I've always had a thing for older men. He said if I didn't stop groping him all the time he was going to start using a safeword on me. Rude, right?"

"How dare he," Michael said dryly.

"Thank you, I agree. Come on," Nora said, throwing open her car door. "Let's talk and eat. Not in that order."

She had a small backyard but it was nice. She had stone benches and tropical potted plants here, there, and everywhere, a few small live oak trees, and a little back porch with a swing on it.

Nora let them in the backdoor and tossed her keys onto the kitchen counter. Spacious kitchen, all old hardwood and cabinets painted white.

"Table's there," she said, pointing. "I'll get us plates, napkins, and even more napkins."

"Don't forget the napkins," Michael said as he sat down at her big butcher block table. She set a plate in front of him, opened the beignet bag and out poured five gallons of powdered sugar.

Michael stared at the sugar pile before looking up at Nora. "I'm gonna need a bigger napkin."

As they ate their fried balls of sugar and joy, Nora told him about her house. An Italianate style—hence the big porch—and built in 1910. Three bedrooms—her room, a guest room, and her newly finished private playroom, plus a tiny downstairs office. Almost everything in the house was original except the paint job. She'd painted every room downstairs a different shade of blue and every room upstairs a different shade of red. Her bedroom was scarlet, she said, and her playroom the color of red wine. She said the last part with the tiniest hint of a blush on her face, and that's when Michael remembered her *Le Boy Toy* was a winemaker. He wouldn't mention the blush to Nora, but he might mention it to Griffin.

"How's Kingsley?" Michael asked. "Is he around?"

"He's . . . um . . ." Nora closed one eye, wrinkled her nose, tapped her foot on the floor. "Somewhere."

Michael narrowed his eyes at her. "Somewhere?"

"Somewhere I can't tell you. Under pain of death. But Juliette and Céleste are with him at this undisclosed location. Well, he's with them. He didn't want to go. Juliette made him go. Well, Céleste made him go. He'd only go because of her. He wouldn't have gone if she hadn't begged. You know how kids are: They like what they like, and you can't say no to your kid, I guess. And it's a good time to go what with the weather being a little cooler, and all that."

"He's at Disney World, isn't he?"

Nora exhaled slowly through her nose. "Yeah."

"Thought so."

"Don't tell anyone," Nora said. "He'll really kill us if it gets out. Céleste is going through a princess phase."

"I won't tell if you won't tell anyone Griffin asked me to marry him. I feel bad even telling you except I know Griffin wouldn't mind. I just don't want to talk to anyone about what I've decided until I've told him."

"What have you decided?" she asked.

"I've decided I need to decide."

"It's a good start. Can I ask, on a scale of one to ten, how stressed out are you about all this?"

"Can the scale go to eleven?" he asked. "Thousand, I mean?"

Nora nodded, a little smile on her lips but she didn't say anything else.

They finished their beignets and Nora offered to take him out in the backyard and hose him down. He opted instead to rinse off in her bathroom sink. He splashed cold water on his face, ran his head under the faucet to wet his hair. Nothing helped. It got rid of the sugar, but it didn't take away the buzzing in his brain caused by the question Griffin had asked him. It was a weight on his shoulders. It was a hamster on a wheel in his head. It was a thorn in his side. Being around Nora was fun, but it hadn't cured him of his anxiousness yet. Was there anything that could? No. Probably nothing in the world would help. It was a lost cause.

When he opened the bathroom door, he found a note taped to it that read, *Take your shoes and socks off and come to the last room down the hall.*

Intrigued, Michael did as the note told him. Barefoot, he walked down the hall and opened the last door on the right. It was Nora's playroom. In wide-eyed wonder, he glanced around, taking in the black leather St. Andrew's Cross and the rows of floggers and the rows of canes and the rows of whips lining the wine-colored walls. And there was Nora standing in the center in black high-heeled boots, tiny black shorts and a black bustier. She had a flogger in her hand and was casually slapping it against her leg.

"I thought I might try to bring your stress level down a little, Angel," she said with a smile. "If you think this would help."

Michael slowly nodded.

"Yeah," he said. "This might help."

CHAPTER THREE

In the Playroom

J ust standing in that room made Michael feel better. He closed his eyes and took the first deep breath he'd been able to take in twenty-four hours. Some people relaxed in hot tubs. Some people relaxed on their sofas. He relaxed in a dungeon with every known instrument of erotic torture surrounding him.

"Do another one of those, Angel," Nora said as she walked over to him, the thick woven rug under her feet absorbing the sounds of her booted heels. She put her hand flat on his stomach and the other flat on his back. "Breathe."

He did as ordered. Who knew whether it was the breath or the order that did it, but he felt better.

"You need a beating?"

"Yes, ma'am."

"Same rules as usual?" Nora asked.

Michael nodded and he took another long deep breath. Griffin had very strict rules for Michael's body. Rule number one: No one penetrates Michael but Griffin. No oral sex. No anal sex. No tongue kissing. Simple. Rule number two: Beatings were allowed only by Griffin and whoever Griffin was supervising. Nora was the one exception to this rule because Nora was the one exception to *every* rule. Rule number three: No damaging the property. Beatings were allowed as long as the skin wasn't broken. If anyone was going to break Michael it would be Griffin.

As for the rest, it was all on the table. Including a good hard flogging from the best dominatrix in the business.

Luckily he happened to know the best dominatrix in the business. She was playing with his hair at that very moment.

"I do like the shorter hair," Nora said, running her fingers over his scalp. He'd let his hair grow a little on top until it started to curl. Griffin liked having enough hair to pull and Michael liked having it short enough it didn't fall in his face while working. And Nora apparently liked it because she found it "very sexy."

"Thank you, Mistress," he said, falling into the old routine with her like he'd never left. Stepping into this room reminded him of his study-abroad semester in Italy. All day long he'd struggle to communicate in his bare-bones Italian. But in the evening, he'd return to the house where he and the other art students were staying, and he could finally understand and be understood. In this room, this beautiful room, he and Nora could speak in their native language to each other.

"I remember the first time I saw you," she said, her voice soft and soothing. "You were sleeping on the bed in the white room of the club and your hair was down to your shoulders and you had a hole in your sock. Søren gave you to me."

Michael laughed to himself. He didn't mean to. It just happened.

"What's that laugh about?" she asked. "Something funny?"

"That's not what happened," Michael said.

"It isn't? Then what did happen?" she asked in her low sensual voice.

"He didn't give me to you, Mistress," Michael said. "He gave *you* to *me*."

She kissed him on the mouth and whispered, "He gives good gifts."

Nora slipped her hands under the front of his t-shirt and placed her palms on his bare stomach. He quivered under her touch. Then she lifted his shirt and pulled it off of him.

"Much better," she said. "New ink?" She touched the gryphon tattoo on his ribcage. The head of the beast was on his stomach and the tail on his back.

"I got it last year when Griffin and I were going through our break. I wanted him to know that even when we were apart, I was still in love with him."

"You could have sent a postcard, you know," she teased.

"I like more permanent ink," Michael said.

"It's beautiful," she said. "A perfect target. I can't wait to slap your little gryphon's ass with my flogger until he begs for mercy."

"He can't wait, either. He's as much of a pain slut as I am."

She jerked her thumb at the St. Andrew's Cross. Michael walked over to it and waited while Nora hooked her flogger over her wrist and went digging through a dark wood cabinet for cuffs.

It was then he noticed the little sign with gothic lettering hanging on the wall between the upper bars of the St. Andrew's Cross. It was a slogan he'd seen on t-shirts, but it seemed far more appropriate in this setting than any other.

THE FLOGGINGS WILL CONTINUE UNTIL MORALE IMPROVES.

His morale had improved already.

Nora walked toward him, black leather cuffs in hand.

"Face the wall. Arms behind your back. You know the drill."

He knew the drill.

He leaned forward and let his right cheek rest against the cool smooth leather of the cross. Heaven. Ice cream on a hot day. A back rub right on the sore spot. A kiss on the boo-boo. Who needed a day at the spa when he could have a night in a dungeon?

"When was your last good beating?" she asked, pulling his arms behind his back to buckle the cuffs on his wrists.

"Not for a while," Michael said. "It's been pretty crazy at home."

"Did something happen?" Nora asked.

Michael nodded. "We've had a hard couple of weeks."

"You're going to have a hard hour," she said. "Then you're going to tell me everything that happened. And maybe by the time we leave this room, you'll know what to do."

From anyone else such a bold claim would have sounded arrogant. But Michael remembered his first night with Nora. In one hour with her, his life had changed course. She'd turned his fate like a captain turns the wheel of his ship. She'd steered him out of the rough waters that were threatening to tear his little boat apart and sailed him into the safest of harbors.

Griffin's bed.

And if anyone could steer him toward safety again, it was Nora.

Nora lifted his arms over his head and secured his wrists high on the cross. He felt his muscles stretch and pull, his back straighten and his lungs expand. Nora kissed his shoulder blade, and Michael took a deep breath again.

"You know Sheridan was the most recent victim to hang on my cross," Nora said.

"Sheridan?" He tried to sound innocent and casual and failed miserably.

"My Little Miss? Angel's face, demon's libido?"

"We've met," Michael said. He and Griffin had played with Sheridan one amazing night over a year ago. His cock still remembered it very fondly.

"You know she's got a crush on you."

"She's, uh . . . really sweet," Michael said. Sheridan was one of the few people he'd bonded with at the club. At first he'd been intimidated by the pretty—and famous—blonde actress, but she'd taken a shine to him when she learned he was also one of Nora's pets. Sheridan called him "Ol' Blue Eyes," and whenever she saw him, she hugged him and kissed him a few hundred times. One time Griffin tried to extract Michael from one of her passionate octopus hugs, and Sheridan hissed at him like an angry cat. She was, in a word, adorable.

"Sheridan comes to visit me about once every six weeks," Nora said. "We had a little party in here last time she visited. I cuffed her to the cross, stuck a vibrator deep in her, and flogged her. I didn't let her off the cross until she'd come in the double digits. She'd want you to know that. And picture it. She told me so."

Michael made a sound. It wasn't a whimper . . . but it was close.

"Kingsley was nice enough to help. He held the vibe in her," Nora said. "In case you were wondering how it stayed in there while I was flogging her."

"I was wondering, yeah," Michael said.

"Then King flogged Sheridan," Nora said. "Shirtless. I mean, Sheridan was naked and Kingsley had no shirt on. He does the most gorgeous Florentine flogging. It was August and it was so hot in here, Kingsley was dripping sweat all down his back and chest." Michael made another sound. "What was that?" Nora said, her tone taunting, teasing. "Did you say something?"

"I feel funny in my tummy," Michael said to make Nora laugh. It worked.

"You're about to feel funny in your back, kid. Now close your eyes," she said. "And . . . scream."

The first strike was hard. He didn't scream but he wasn't silent either. The second strike was even harder. He liked that. He liked that Nora respected him enough not to pull her punches. She didn't coddle him. She didn't treat him like he was new at this because he was not. He'd been doing kink longer than some people he knew twice his age. He could take pain and lots of it, and even more, he wanted pain and lots of it. He had no time for any dominant who wasn't going to take him and his love of pain seriously.

Nora took it very seriously.

She spared no inch of his exposed flesh. She struck his shoulders, his upper arms, his back and sides—especially the black tattoo of the gryphon, which was sensitive to even the lightest of touches. Hers were not the lightest of touches. His skin was ablaze. Sounds escaped his lips—grunts of pain and gasps of pleasure. He was hard, very hard, painfully hard and the pain of the arousal aroused him even more.

It was a rough flogging. It hurt. He loved every second of it.

And just when he thought Nora was almost done flogging him . . . she switched from the suede flogger to a much thicker, harder, sharper leather and went at him again, flogging him like he had a demon inside him, and she had no recourse but to beat it out of him. The demon never stood a chance.

The beating was so thorough and brutal and long that for a moment Michael simply ceased existing. It happened sometimes when he fell into deepest subspace. A human being was a matrix of wants, needs, and desires, but when the pain reached its peak, Michael wanted nothing, he needed nothing, he desired nothing and so he became nothing. It was the purest peace. What little was left of his consciousness floated near the ceiling and watched the show. Nora was a savage goddess, glowing and grinning at her own sadism. He was a body on a cross and nothing more.

The last few strikes of her flogger were so hard they jarred him back into his body. Nora always did like to end on a high note, and that high note tonight was Michael crying out in bliss-filled agony.

Then it was over.

He sagged in his cuffs, letting them hold his full weight. He felt something . . . Nora's hand, maybe. It was on his back, rubbing the legion of welts, pressing them and caressing them.

"Red, red, and more red," she said. "Red's my favorite color for a reason."

"How bad is it?"

"You know what a marble floor looks like, right?" she said. "Imagine blood-red marble."

"Good," he said, panting.

If Nora kissed his back again, he couldn't feel it. He couldn't feel much of anything. Not his hands or his feet or his back or his sides. And he couldn't feel his fear anymore or his anxiety. He couldn't even feel Nora unhooking him from the cross.

"Let's go sit down," she said. "You need to rest after that."

He let himself be led to a black leather chair in the corner of the room, in front of the window with the deep-red curtains drawn. She lit a red altar candle and set it on the table by the chair, and set a velvet cushion on the floor for him. He sank to his knees. She went to a small black refrigerator and took out a bottle of water, which she poured into a wine glass and held against his lips to drink. *Oh, Nora, never change*, he thought. She could make the simple act of drinking water an erotic act of submission. A drop of water remained on his lips when she took the glass away, and she wiped it away with her thumb.

After she took a seat in her chair, she tapped her lap and Michael rested his head against her thigh.

"Your back is red," she said. "And your front is white. I like my subs to match," she said, lifting the red altar candle off the table. "While I decorate your chest to match your back, you're going to tell me everything that happened. You understand?"

He nodded. "Yes, Mistress."

She dug her left hand into the back of his hair and pulled hard enough to tilt his head back.

"Begin," she ordered.

The first drop of wax landed in the hollow of his throat.

He began.

CHAPTER FOUR

The Phone Call

W hen the phone rings after midnight or before eight in the morning, Michael's mother had said more than once, you can bet money somebody died.

The call came at 12:17 am.

Friday nights were Michael's favorite nights. He spent every week playing a normal college kid at Yorke, living in a dorm room, going to class, eating shitty cat food and studying with friends in the library. But Fridays . . . Fridays he went home. And home meant Griffin and their apartment in the Village. His friends at school thought it was hilarious that Michael led this odd double life. His freshman year he hadn't told anyone about Griffin. He'd wanted to, but working up the courage took a little while, especially after living his entire life afraid of his conservative, judgmental father. Griffin had understood and hadn't forced himself into Michael's college life. Michael just let everyone think he was a momma's boy who went home every weekend. By sophomore year Michael started to hint to his friends that wasn't quite the case. He wasn't sure how to tell people at school. Just tell them? Or should he invite Griffin to school to meet them and let them figure it out? The decision was made for him the awful week he came down with a vicious case of strep throat that required more medical attention than the school clinic could give. His mother had been out of town visiting his grandparents, which meant Michael had to bite the bullet and call Griffin to take him to the doctor. Griffin had come immediately. And he'd come in his Porsche since it was faster, he claimed, than the far more subdued Range Rover he also owned. He'd pulled up in front of Michael's dorm and emerged from the car looking like an off-duty rock star in ripped jeans, sunglasses, and a black t-shirt clinging to his broad chest and tattooed boxer's biceps. Michael had watched from his dorm room window as Griffin ran up the steps, two at time, as a couple of Michael's friends who were on their way to class stared in wide-eyed wonder at the visitor. By the time Michael was back at school a week later, he had gone from being a regular student—quiet, studious, with a handful of friends and good grades—to something of a legend. It wasn't the money so much. There were other students who came from even wealthier families than Griffin. It was that nobody would have suspected in a million *billion* years that quiet, studious, and incredibly boring Michael Dimir had a rich, older boyfriend, especially one who looked—as Michael's friend Astrid had said—"Like THAT." Luckily his confused friends got over it fast, especially when they got to know Griffin, got to talk to him, and found out how chill and funny and down-to-earth he was, even if his father was the former president of the New York Stock Exchange and Griffin could have bought the school with his trust fund had he wanted to.

Still, when Michael threw his stuff in his backpack every Friday after his last class was over, there were a few people who smirked knowingly as he headed out his dorm's side door to catch the bus that would take him to the train station. A few looks, a few smiles, sometimes a few eyerolls. Whatever. It didn't bother him anymore. How could it when he had just gotten flogged and sucked and fucked—the Friday night special?

Griffin was sitting up against the padded leather headboard on their bed and Michael lay draped over Griffin's hip with his back up while Griffin rubbed his favorite Vitamin K goo into the welts. They were both naked and smiling and tired and happy.

"So," Griffin said, running the flat of his hand over Michael's naked hip, "how was school this week, dear?"

Michael laughed at Griffin's attempt to sound like his mother.

"It was fine," Michael said. "I passed my Astronomy midterm. Sun's the big yellow one. Moon's the little white one."

"The moon's my favorite," Griffin said before slapping Michael on his moon. "Did you miss me?"

"You know I missed you. I always miss you." That was the game they played. Of course they texted every single day they were apart. Texting, Skyping, and talking on the phone a couple times a week, too, but they always acted like the five days they'd spent apart was five weeks.

Griffin squeezed a bit more goo onto his fingertips and rubbed it hard enough into one particularly nasty bruise under Michael's shoulder blade that Michael groaned.

"Slut," Griffin said, laughing softly.

"I can't help it," Michael said. "It hurt. Good hurt."

"I already let you come twice tonight, Mick," he said. "I'm not going to let you come again. You know what the Bible says—spoil the rod, spoil the child."

Michael lifted his head and looked at Griffin.

"Spoil the rod, spoil the child?"

"Yeah," Griffin said, shrugging. "If I spoil your cock, you'll get spoiled."

"It's 'spare the rod, spoil the child.' And the rod is not a cock, it's a rod rod. Like a cane."

"I think my interpretation is the correct one."

"I'm calling Father S," Michael said.

"Call anyone you want, but I'm not letting you come again until tomorrow."

Michael dropped his head down. "You're mean."

"I'm mean? Me? Mean?" Griffin sounded aghast. Michael loved making Griffin aghast. "That's backtalk. I will show you mean."

"Oh no," Michael said. "Anything but that."

"That's it, sub. You're getting it this time."

Michael tried to make a break for it, but Griffin was too fast for him. Before he could even slide off the bed, Michael was trapped in Griffin's arms. Griffin threw him onto the covers and wrestled him down onto his back. Because it was obvious from Griffin's smile—and his erection—that he was enjoying this play fight, Michael kept it up and had almost squirmed out of his ridiculous master's iron grasp before Griffin got a good hold on his wrists again and pinned him down to the bed, hands over his head.

"Submit, sub," Griffin ordered.

"You'll never take me alive," Michael said.

"Are you dead?" Griffin asked.

"No, sir."

"I want to take you, but if I can't take you alive and you're not dead . . . either I'll have to kill you—gross—or you'll have to let me take you alive. What'll it be?"

Michael turned his head to the side, tapped his foot, wrinkled his nose.

"Mick?"

"I'm deciding," Michael said.

"You brat," Griffin said. "That's it. Dead or alive, you're getting it. And if you come, you're in trouble, and not the good kind of trouble."

Griffin reached over Michael's head for the under-the-mattress strap he used when he wanted to tie Michael to the bed. It was a perfect moment and Michael knew it. Griffin was happy and horny. Michael was happy and horny. They were happy and horny together and alone and in their bed, which was the most comfortable bed in the universe.

It was right at the moment when Griffin was about to enter him that the phone rang.

They had a landline phone in their room, a weird relic of their pre-war building. Usually the only people who called them on it was the doormen to let them know they had a visitor or a delivery in the lobby, and sometimes Griffin's mother when she couldn't get Griffin on his cell.

They both turned their heads simultaneously to the ringing black phone on the side table. They hadn't ordered take-out, and it was way too late for visitors.

"Shit," Griffin said, immediately unbuckling Michael from the bondage strap.

"Your dad?" Michael asked.

Griffin's eyes were wide with fear. A week ago his mother had taken his father to the hospital with chest pains. The doctors said it was only severe indigestion, but Griffin had been on edge ever since.

He answered the phone.

There was a pause, a short one, and then Griffin said, "Dad's okay?"

His shoulders slumped with relief, and Michael exhaled the breath he'd been holding.

"Okay," Griffin said. "What's the number again?"

He pulled a pad of paper out of the drawer and scribbled a number on it with a pencil.

"You don't know?" Griffin asked and Michael knew he was talking to his mother. Whatever it was, it didn't seem to have anything to do with Griffin's father. But that didn't mean they were off the hook. Something was definitely up.

"I'll call right now. Thanks, Mom. Love you."

Griffin hung up.

"What is it?" Michael asked. Griffin had grabbed his jeans off the floor and was yanking them on. If he was getting dressed, it meant Griffin was worried he'd have to leave the house in a hurry. Michael threw on his clothes, just in case. Where Griffin went, Michael went, too.

"I don't know," Griffin said. "A friend of a friend called my old house number. Mom answered and took the message. They didn't say what it was. They just asked me to call this number right away. I need to find my cell."

"It's on the kitchen charger," Michael said. Griffin nodded, his face blank with worry. Michael followed him from the bedroom to the kitchen. He picked up the phone and dialed the number. Michael tensed, not sure what to do or say. Someone on the other end of the line answered quickly.

"Hey, this is Griffin Fiske," Griffin said. "Someone told me to call?"

Silence followed.

Michael watched Griffin's face, his eyes. At first they flashed with shock and then his brow furrowed as if he'd felt a pain in his stomach.

"Fuck . . ." Griffin breathed. "I'm sorry. Yeah, of course . . . Right. No, I never . . . Definitely. Yeah, definitely, I can do that. Eleven? Right. Okay. Thanks for letting me know, Jay. You, too. If you need anything, you know . . . Right."

Griffin hung up.

"What?" Michael asked.

Griffin swallowed visibly as he put his phone down onto the counter.

"You remember my friend Adam, from rehab trip number two?"

"The guy with the beard we met for dinner last year?" Michael asked. "Yeah, he was hilarious." Adam was a comedy writer who wrote for one of the only two shows on TV this season he had any desire to watch. He had a quick cynical wit and knew all sorts of Hollywood gossip. Michael had liked him immediately.

"Was that him on the phone?"

"That was his husband, Jay. Adam had a relapse."

"Oh, shit," Michael said. "Is he in the hospital? Or back in rehab?"

Griffin shook his head and that's when Michael knew his mother had been right about phone calls that come before eight in the morning or after midnight.

"He died."

CHAPTER FIVE

The Question, Part 1

M ichael didn't know what to do and he really
didn't know what to say. This was the first death
they'd ever dealt with together. Michael stood
frozen on the kitchen's black and white tile floor and just
stared.

"I better call Mom," Griffin said. "She'll, uh . . . she'll want
to know. She's met Adam a couple times."

Griffin dialed his mother's number and while they were
on the phone Michael texted his own mother. He told her
everything he knew about Adam—that he was the one friend
Griffin had made at his second stint in rehab, that Adam
worked in Hollywood, that he'd struggled with heroin
addiction on and off for years, but when they'd seen him last

year he'd seemed fine. It was a long message but she wrote back quickly.

Mom: **I'm going to call.**

Michael: **Now?**

But it was too late. The phone rang in his hand.

"Hey, Mom," Michael said.

"Hey, sweetheart. How is he? Shocked or sad?"

"Freaked out," Michael said.

"Can he talk now?" Her voice was soft and calm, her professional seen-everything nurse's voice.

"He just got off the phone with his mom."

"Put me on speaker with him, okay?" his mother said.

"Griff," Michael said. "Mom wants to talk to you."

Griffin nodded. His eyes were hollow and his face was still a blank. Michael hated seeing him like this especially since he had no idea how to help.

Michael put his phone on speaker and set it on the kitchen table.

"Okay, Mom," Michael said.

"Griffin?" she said. "Can you hear me?"

"Yeah. Hey, Melissa."

"This isn't going to happen to you," she said.

Griffin's eyes widened at her words, and then he slowly sank down into the kitchen chair. With his hands over his face he wept silently.

"This isn't going to happen to you," Michael's mother said again and then one more time for good measure. "I know that's what you're thinking, isn't it?"

Griffin nodded slowly, then whispered a rasping, "Yes."

"It's not. It's absolutely not going to happen. Your friend OD'd on heroin, yes?"

"Yeah," Griffin said.

"Listen to me. I've worked in the ER a long time," she said. "I know some things, which is why I know this is not going to happen to you. You did club drugs and you drank too much and sometimes you snorted coke, right?"

"Right, but not that often," Griffin said. "It was mostly alcohol, pot and mushrooms. My overdose was on E. Never took that shit again."

"Heroin?" she asked.

"Not once. I don't do needles except for tats."

"Good. Look, you did some stupid, dangerous stuff when you were younger, kid, and I'm not going to sugarcoat it. But you're not going to relapse, and you're not going to die and leave Michael alone in the world."

Griffin rubbed tears off his face. "But what if I do?" he said.

Michael was weeping, too. He couldn't help it. Seeing Griffin so scared, so undone, undid him.

"If you get hit by a bus tomorrow," Michael's mother said, "Michael will miss the hell out of you for a very long time. But he'll have me and his sister and all his friends to love him and take care of him, and eventually he'll be okay again. He won't hurt himself. He'll live his life in a way that honors how much you two loved each other. That's what'll happen if something happens to you. Got it?"

"You won't let his father near Mick, will you?" Griffin asked.

"If it takes a pack of wild dogs and a shotgun to keep my ex-husband away from him, I'll do it," she said. "But that's not something you have to worry about. You've been completely sober for almost . . . how long?"

"About ten years," Griffin said.

"Ten years is a long time," she said. "Even longer in recovery years. Michael's not ever going to have to make the phone calls your friend's husband is making tonight. By the time you keel over at ninety, we won't even be using phones anymore. We'll all have telepathy."

Griffin laughed. "Thank you, Melissa."

"No thanks necessary. I'm telling you the truth, okay? As a medical professional, I am telling you, this is not going to happen to you."

"Can you say that one more time?" Griffin asked. She did. She said it slowly and she said it kindly and by the time she was done saying it again, Griffin looked a little more like himself.

"When's the funeral?" she asked.

"Visitation is tomorrow from eleven to two. Funeral on Sunday at five," Griffin said. "Jay said Adam's family might not show up—they weren't on great terms. He's hoping to get as many friends there as he can."

"Then I'm coming with you two, okay?" she said.

Griffin swallowed visibly. "Thank you," he said again.

"Your friend's death was a tragedy," she said. "But his life wasn't. He was your friend, so you know what a good person he was. Focus on that."

"I will. You're the best, Other Mom," Griffin said.

"Back at you, Other Son," Melissa said.

They talked a few minutes more and then she told them both she loved them and hung up. Michael walked over to Griffin still sitting at the table. Griffin pulled him close and wrapped him in a strong embrace. For at least five minutes, Michael just stood there by Griffin's chair holding and being held. They didn't talk. What was there to say?

The funeral was hard but it was made bearable by the presence of Griffin's entire family, who were doing their part to make up for the lack of people from Adam's. Griffin's parents came, all of his brothers, their wives and even some of the older kids. Michael sat next to Griffin and Michael's mother sat next to him. Griffin's mother spoke for nearly half an hour with Jay, Adam's husband, while Michael's mother stayed close to Griffin's side.

When they met Jay, all Michael could think to say was, "I'm really sorry." Jay shook his hand and looked between him and Griffin.

"I'm just glad we'd gotten married last year," Jay said. "I had to fight like hell as it was to get the funeral home to let me make all the decisions. His parents were just going to cremate him, no funeral. They had the gall to ask me if Adam left them any of his money in his will."

"I hope they got jack shit," Griffin said.

"Jack shit and nothing else," Jay said. Michael could tell Jay was running on pure anger and adrenaline. The poor guy couldn't have been over thirty but his eyes looked eighty. Apparently Adam had relapsed twice before while trying to get sober. They'd both been working on getting jobs back in New York. Hollywood held too much temptation, too much pressure. Griffin's dad had offered to set up some interviews for Jay when he was ready. Sometimes Michael forgot what good people Griffin's parents were, even if they were insanely intimidating.

"You two should consider getting hitched," Jay said. "I wouldn't have made it if I had to sit on the sidelines while I watched Adam's family erase him from existence. We need all the laws on our side we can get, right?"

"God bless Cuomo," Griffin said

He and Jay hugged goodbye. Michael shook the man's hand again and turned back to Griffin, who was staring across the room at his own mother and his brother Lucas.

"Griffin?" Michael said. "You okay?"

"Just thinking . . . I was with Mom when Lucas got engaged," Griffin said. "I was in the backyard, and I heard this shrill piercing scream. I thought Mom had seen a rat or something in the house. Or someone was trying to kill her."

Michael smiled. Griffin's mom Alexis was a screamer.

"I ran into the house," Griffin said. "Mom was on the phone sobbing. She looked at me and said, 'Lucas and Lily are getting married!' Her hands were shaking, she was jumping up and down . . . He's her stepson, Mick. She was that crazy happy when her *stepson* got engaged." Griffin fell silent for a moment. "She'd probably faint dead away if I ever got engaged. Woman goes nuts at weddings."

"We have good moms," was all Michael could think to say. He had never imagined marrying Griffin. They were as together as two people could ever be anyway. Sure, there was no red tape around their relationship, but who needed red tape? Marriage was a money thing and Michael didn't want or love Griffin for his money. And his mother was right—Griffin was probably never going to relapse. His situation was very different from Adam's. They didn't need to worry about stuff like hospitals and funerals and inheritances. And their families loved and accepted them as a couple. Why get married for the legal protections when they didn't need any, right?

Griffin didn't say anything else about it that day or any day after. He was quieter than usual. Not his typical exuberant self. When Michael went back to school, they talked on the phone, but they didn't exchange their usual goofy text messages all day every day. Instead of running in the park, Griffin went to the gym and lifted weights until he was miserable with exhaustion. And then a week and a half later, last night when Michael came home for his four-day fall break, Griffin said to him over dinner at their favorite small Italian restaurant, "Don't answer me until Sunday because I know you, and I know you'll need to think about it, but I want us to get married after you graduate in May."

"Wait . . . what?" Michael asked.

"I'm asking you if you'll marry me," Griffin said. "But don't answer me until Sunday. Got it?"

Michael didn't say anything, not a word. He could only stare in shocked silence. Griffin pointed his fork at Michael's entrée.

"So," Griffin said. "How's the lasagna?"

CHAPTER SIX

The Red Cord

"So how was it?" Nora asked.

"What?"

"The lasagna?"

Michael stared at Nora.

Nora kissed him. A quick gentle kiss on the lips and all was forgiven.

"That's rough, Angel," she said, stroking his hair again. "No wonder you're stressed to the power of eleven."

"It's humiliating," he said, resting his head again on her thigh.

"What is? Being proposed to? I was proposed to and survived it. Barely."

Michael had red candle wax all over his shoulders, throat, chest, and stomach. The red streaks looked like a wolf had clawed the front of him from shoulder to hip. Nora was a genius. Michael knew he'd never be able to get through telling that story to her if it hadn't been for the comfort of physical pain distracting from the heartache.

Michael smiled and shook his head. "Not being proposed to," he said. "I mean . . . not knowing what to do when Griffin's friend died."

"I'd say you handled it pretty well."

He looked up at her through narrowed eyes. "Nora, I called my mommy. I felt like a five-year-old kid, not an adult. Five-year-old kids don't get married. Adults get married."

She grinned at him. "Your 'mommy' is a nurse who works in the ER. She's had grief training, addiction training, and she knows Griffin's history with drugs. She was exactly the right person to call. Asking for help from someone who knows more than you do doesn't make you a kid. It's a sign of maturity."

Michael took a deep breath, so deep the congealing wax on his chest cracked in places.

"I felt so . . . dumb," Michael said. "Young and dumb."

"I was in my early thirties when Søren's mother died. I didn't know what to say to him, what to do to make it better. I did the only thing I could do which was be with him. And that is the only thing you can do because there is no making death better. You didn't run away from Griffin or try to force him to cheer up, and you didn't tell him everything was fine when it wasn't. You called a professional to talk him through it. You went to the funeral with him. You stayed by his side. You didn't rush him into acting like his old self while he was grieving. I hate to tell you, Angel, but you handled it better than a lot of people my age handle this sort of stuff. So if you're using that as your excuse to not get married, it's not a very good one."

"I'm not looking for excuses to not get married," he said.

"Good," she said. "Because you don't need one. You get married because you want to get married. You don't get married if you don't want to get married. Why am I not married? I don't want to be married. Marriage would chafe, like too-tight lace panties, the kind that are like sandpaper on your asshole. But that's me. Marriage might be a better fit for you."

"It never occurred to me he'd want to get married," Michael said. "It's so . . . vanilla."

Nora cackled at that, head back and smile broad.

"Now you're laughing at me," he said.

"Some of the filthiest, kinkiest people I know are married," she said.

"Are they straight?" Michael asked.

"Most of them are."

"I'm not," Michael said. "We're not."

"True, but same-sex marriage is legal in New York now."

"Great," he said. "They finally let us into their little clubhouse. Maybe I don't want to be in their clubhouse."

"That's fair," Nora said. "I can't argue with that. Despite the old joke, I wouldn't want to be a member of any club that wouldn't have me as a member."

"You get married," Michael said, "and people don't believe you're bi anymore. If you and Father S got married, they'd see you as a straight couple."

"Horrifying."

"If Griff and I got married, they'd see us as a gay couple, and we're not."

"Then they'd be wrong," she said. "People are wrong all the time. It's kind of what people are known for. All you can do is correct them the first time they get it wrong and kick them out of your house the second time."

"I'm too young to get married," Michael said.

"Me, too, Angel," Nora said. "Me, too."

"You shouldn't get married just because you're scared one of you is going to die."

"Is that why Griffin asked you to marry him?" she asked.

Michael sat up straight.

"You know, I didn't ask," he said. "He just brought it up and told me not to answer until Sunday when he got back from checking in with the L.A. club."

"Just a thought—maybe ask him why he wants to marry you," she said. "Throwing that out there. It might not be for the reason you think it is. I know for a fact Griffin already put you in his will, so it's not like you have to get married to inherit from him if a bus does hit him. Although, being New York, it's more likely going to be a taxi that gets him."

"I don't want his money," Michael said.

"Fuck, I do."

Michael groaned.

"Go on," Nora said. "What else?"

"He thinks I'm perfect," Michael said, "and I'm not. And if we get married after I graduate, we'll be together all the time. Every day. Every night. He's going to get sick of me. I don't want that to happen. I don't want to disappoint him. And I know I will. When

I do, I don't want him feeling like he's stuck with me just because of the red tape and paperwork."

Nora kissed his cheek.

"You aren't perfect and he knows that," Nora said. "And you will disappoint him at some point in the future whether you marry him or not. Søren's disappointed me in the past. I've disappointed him. It happens to everyone. That being said . . . you'll amaze Griffin some days. And you'll delight him on others. And some night you'll make him furious to the point he's got to walk away before he says something he regrets and maybe he doesn't walk away in time and he does say it, or you say it, and the next day you'll make up and you'll have sex so good you'll think, 'Ah . . . we should fight more often.' You'll have a ton of inside jokes no one gets but you two. I can make Søren laugh just by saying the word 'diphthong' and I will go to my grave before I tell you or anyone else the story behind it. You'll never lack for someone to go for dinner with. You'll always have someone to call in an emergency. There's a lot to be said for getting married. Then again, there's a lot to be said for climbing Mount Everest, but you don't see me doing that either."

She tugged his hair playfully, hard enough to make him gasp.

Michael laughed and stretched out across Nora's lap. She leaned over and rested her face against his still warm and welt-covered back.

"Tell me the truth," she whispered. "Tell me why you're afraid of saying yes to something you and I both know you want."

There it was. Leave it to Nora to say the thing he didn't have the guts to say. Yes, he did want to marry Griffin. And for no other reason than . . . he wanted to marry Griffin.

"It's . . ." He shook his head. "Stupid. Awful. Awful and stupid."

"I won't judge you. That's not what happens in this room. Just say it."

"If Griff and I get married, that's it," Michael said. "I'll be dead to my father."

"I thought you hated your father," Nora said.

"I do," Michael said. "But he's still my father."

He fell silent and Nora didn't push him to say more. She just stroked his hair and waited.

"He asked Erin about me the other day," Michael said. "Just 'How's your brother?' She told him I was fine. He said, 'Good.' That was the whole conversation apparently. And you know what? When she told me he asked about me . . ."

"You were happy?"

"I was," he said. "Stupid fucking happy that my fucking awful father asked my sister how I was. And I hate that. I hate that I still give a shit about his opinion of me. I hate . . . I hate it. All of it. But it's there. I marry Griffin and that'll probably be the last time Dad ever acknowledges I exist."

Nora was quiet a long time.

"I don't know what to tell you," she said finally.

"You always know what to tell me."

"Not this time. This time it's not for me to tell you what to do or think."

"Could you maybe try please?"

Nora laughed her big sexy laugh and it made Michael feel better to hear it. Things couldn't be too bad if Nora was still laughing.

"Okay, I'll try. Well . . . you know, my mom never understood me, was always angry at me for the kind of person I turned into, but . . . the minute I got the phone call that she was dying, I was out of the house in five minutes on my way to see her."

"Why can't we cut the cord?" Michael asked.

"Because the cord is made out of the same stuff our hearts are made of," she said. "That's why it's red."

"That explains it."

"Earth is just an island in space," Nora said, "and we're all stranded on it. There came a time I had to ask myself who did I want to be stranded on this island with? Someone who wanted to change me or someone who wouldn't change a hair on my head . . ." Nora held out her hands, palms up, and lifted them up and down like they were two sides of a scale. Very quickly one side won that battle. "I'm not telling you that you should marry Griffin. What I will tell you is that I know you, and I know your heart. If your dad called and said he was sorry, that he wanted to start over with you, you'd give him a chance, right?"

"In a heartbeat."

"So the ball's in his court then. It's up to him to make that move. You marrying or not marrying Griffin has nothing to do with it. Your father is in the wrong. Only he can make it right. Not you. You're already in the right. So you might as well do what you want to do."

Michael turned his head and pressed a kiss on her thigh. She couldn't give him the answers he needed, but he worshipped her for giving him the question he needed to ask himself. If he had to choose between Griffin and his father, well, that question answered itself.

After all, Griffin would never ask him to make that choice.

But his father would.

"What are you thinking about right now?" Nora asked, gently stroking his cheek with her knuckles.

"I miss Griff," Michael said. "I wish he was here."

"Why don't you call him? It's eleven here so it's . . . what? Only nine in L.A.?"

"Do you mind?" he asked.

"I'll leave you alone in here to call him. He'll get a kick out of you calling him from my dungeon."

"He definitely will," Michael said. "He'll want pics."

"Better send them then."

Nora took his phone out of her bustier, where she'd stored it for safe-keeping.

"I'll be back in ten minutes to clean you up," she said. "If Griffin can't tell you in ten minutes or less why he wants to marry you, then neither of you needs to get married."

CHAPTER SEVEN

The Question, Part 2

Nora patted Michael's face, and he sat up to let her stand. On her way out of the playroom she stopped by her chest of drawers where she kept all her little toys—cuffs and collars and dildos and talons and the like. She opened one small drawer and took something out and tossed it at him. "Maybe marriage is red tape," she said. "But there's a lot to be said for red tape."

She left him alone in the room holding a roll of bondage tape, the kind that sticks to itself but not the skin.

Bright red bondage tape.

He'd worn this tape before. Griffin used it on him more than a dozen times when they were on trips where they couldn't easily bring lots of kink equipment. He remembered one particular weekend they spent at Griffin's parents' beach cottage in the Hamptons. Mr. and Mrs. Fiske would be sleeping in the very next room so Griffin had left the spreader bars and floggers at home. But with one little roll of bondage tape, Griffin had been able to blindfold Michael and tie his wrists to the bed frame. Those three nights at the beach house ranked among their most intense, their most intimate, as they could only speak to each other in whispers during sex. And the things Griffin had whispered in his ear—sexual fantasies, kinky fantasies, things Michael had never known Griffin dreamed about . . . Michael couldn't remember those whispers without his blood burning and his cock stiffening. He could still feel Griffin's fingers clamped on the back of his neck and the tape wrapped around his head covering his eyes as Griffin fucked the life out of him, and all with nothing but a thin wall between them and Griffin's sleeping parents.

If marriage meant red tape, sign him up for a lifetime of it.

Michael called Griffin.

The phone rang only once before Griffin answered.

"Mick?"

"Hey, sir. You'll never guess where I'm calling you from," Michael said.

"Do I get a hint?" Griffin asked.

"I'm wearing bondage cuffs, and I'm covered with welts and red candle wax."

"I know where you're calling from—my dreams."

Michael dropped his head to his chest. "You are so corny," Michael said. "Sir."

"Love makes a man say corny things," Griffin said. "I'm guessing you're with Nora? You better be if you're covered in welts."

"Her new playroom. It's kind of amazing here."

"She was starting to put it together when I was there last year. Look good?"

"It's fancy," Michael said. "Too fancy. Who is she playing with in here? I mean, other than me and Sheridan? She doesn't see clients here, does she?"

"She's got another place for her clients. She said her home playroom is mainly for her and Søren since he had to give up his dungeon at the club when they moved down there."

"I thought it might be for . . . you know," Michael said, lowering his voice on the off-chance Nora was standing outside the door. "Nico."

"I don't think he visits her there," Griffin said. "She only goes to visit him, not the other way around."

"Makes sense," Michael said. Nora's unconventional love life was one of their more enduring topics of conversation.

"Has she said anything about *Le Boy Toy* since you got there?" Griffin asked.

"Nothing."

"Have you ever seen a pic of him?" Griffin asked.

"Just the one of him holding Céleste that Juliette showed me last year. He's kind of . . ." Michael exhaled, loudly.

"Right?" Griffin said. "Kid burned my retinas he's so hot. No wonder Nora keeps him on the DL. She's probably afraid someone will steal him from her."

"She is really private about him, which isn't like her. I wonder why."

"Probably out of respect for King as he's King Junior, and that's gotta be weird. It drives me nuts though," Griffin said. "I want all the gossip about those two, and I can't get any out of her other than they are a thing, everyone is cool with it, the end."

"I'll see if I can find anything out."

"Report back to me *immediately* if you do," Griffin said. "That's an order."

"Yes, sir," he said. If they'd been together, Michael would have saluted. It felt so stupid good to be having this conversation with Griffin. This was them, every day, every night, being goofy and corny together, gossiping about the wild lives of their friends, making dumb jokes. If this phone call was anything like what the rest of their lives would be like together, then he had no fear of the future.

"How's L.A.?" Michael asked before he said something rash like *Yes, I'll marry you.* He was under orders not to give Griffin an answer until Sunday night and Michael always obeyed orders.

"Hot and weird. How's New Orleans?"

"Hot and weird. How are you?"

"Hot and weird," Griffin said.

"So your usual self?"

"Ah," Griffin said. "Getting there. I'm sorry I've been kinda out of it the past couple of weeks."

"The guy who helped you get through rehab died," Michael said. "You have the right to be out of it."

"I'm getting okay again," Griffin said. "I'll be back to my old self when I get home Sunday."

"Good," Michael said. "Nora's a great sadist but she doesn't have your magic touch."

"I have a magic touch?" Griffin asked. "What's so magic about my touch?"

"It's you doing the touching," Michael said.

"Who's corny now?" Griffin teased, but Michael could tell he was happy.

Michael heard voices in the background, laughter and a squeal. Good chance Griffin was at the club overseeing a play party.

"I should let you go," Michael said. "I know you're busy."

"Never too busy for you. Did you call just to say hi?"

"I kind of wanted to ask you a question."

"Ask all the questions you want, Mick. I asked you a big one."

Michael took a deep breath. *Here goes.* "It's just . . . I was kind of wondering, why did you ask me to marry you?"

"That's the question?" Griffin sounded surprised but not insulted.

"I thought maybe the only reason you did it was because of what Jay said at the funeral. You know, about needing legal protection in case something happens."

"It has nothing to do with that," Griffin said. "I've got paperwork on us already."

"Oh."

"I only asked after Jay said that to us because you didn't seem freaked out by the idea when he mentioned it. I've been thinking of it for a long time."

"Like . . . how long?" Michael's voice went up a few notes at the end of the question.

"Um . . ." Griffin paused as if counting. "Three years? Yeah, about three years."

"Three *years*?"

"That's . . . a little embarrassing to admit, but yeah, three years. How long have we been together?"

"Three years and about two months," Michael said. "Not counting the three month break last year."

"Okay, so three years is probably accurate then."

"That's insane," Michael said.

"Yeah, I know. Sorry. At least I didn't ask three years ago. I realized it was my cock doing the talking then."

"And now?"

"My cock is still talking," Griffin said. "But other parts of me are, too. You really want to know why I asked you?"

"I'm kind of curious," Michael said. An understatement. A *massive* understatement.

"For starters," Griffin began, "because I love you. I love you, and I want to own you for the rest of my life. I'm happiest when you're tied to the bed and can't go anywhere. I bought you from your dad with a check for sixty-nine thousand dollars and if you'd cost a million times that I would have found a way to pay it even if I had to break into Fort Knox and Dad's wallet. So that's why I want to marry you. Metal chains, cuffs, collar, leash, harness and d-ring, rope and wedding ring, I don't care. If there's even the tiniest way of making you more mine, one more way of owning you, one more way of keeping you tied to me, I want to do it, and I want to do it yesterday. I know that sounds possessive, but that's kind of our thing, right? But you're smart, Mick. You know you own me as much or more than I own you. And that's exactly how I want it."

There followed a long pause.

"So does that answer your question?" Griffin finally said.

"Yeah," Michael said, blinking tears out of his eyes. He'd melted like candle wax into the floor at Griffin's declaration of love, lust, and ownership. "It does."

"Good. Now hang up and text me pics of Nora's wax job. You always look so hot covered in wax."

CHAPTER EIGHT

Good Ideas

Michael took his wax pictures and finished right before Nora stuck her head in the door and asked, "So . . . are we going wedding dress shopping tomorrow or not?"

"I am not wearing a wedding dress."

"It's not for you, it's for me," she said.

Michael stood up and met her eyes.

"Calling Griffin and asking him was a good idea," he said. "Thank you."

"I have so many good ideas. For starters, all porn websites should be .cums, not .coms. Second, femdom should be taught in public schools. Third—"

"Nora."

"So are you getting married or not?"

"I'm . . . going to talk to Griffin about that on Sunday. And only Griffin."

She waved her hand. "Fine, be coy. I won't pry. I'll find out soon enough anyway. If it's a yes, Griffin will call me and crow. If it's a no, I'll hear the weeping and wailing all the way down here."

"Griffin doesn't wail."

"No, but his mother will. Alexis *loooooves* weddings," Nora said, drawing out the "love" to about ten syllables. "She seriously asked me to fake-marry Griffin just so she could plan the wedding."

This fact about Alexis Fiske did not shock him. At all. "I guess you said no?"

"I said yes, but only if I could wear a red latex catsuit in lieu of a wedding dress. She dropped the subject after that."

While he was on the phone with Griffin, Nora had run a warm bath for him. He stripped and got in the water while Nora dug through her linen closet for towels and a sponge. She was one of two people he felt completely comfortable being naked in front of. Michael had a feeling she was on a lot of people's "I can be naked in front of this woman with no problem" lists.

Nora knelt by the bathtub and gently scoured the dried candle wax off his chest and stomach. He could have done this himself, but he never refused an opportunity to indulge himself in some of Nora's world-class aftercare. She'd put music on her iPhone, some gorgeous soft jazz piano he'd never heard before. The lights were low in the bathroom and the water the perfect temperature.

"This music is pretty," Michael said.

"Keith Jarrett's 'Köln Concert.' Søren played it for me years ago. Love at first listen."

Michael watched her face as she spoke.

"You smile when you say his name," he said.

"Keith Jarrett is *very* talented."

"That's not who I meant," Michael said and knew she knew that, too.

"When Søren isn't making me smile it's because he's making me scream . . . for many various and sundry reasons."

"What about Nico?" Michael asked.

Nora blinked. "What about Nico?"

"Just seeing if you smile when you talk about him," Michael said.

"Do I?"

"No, but you blush a little."

Now Nora smiled.

"How is he?" Michael asked.

"Nico? He's wonderful," she said. "And . . . full of wonder."

"I guess you're kind of a . . . new thing for him?" Michael said, trying to be as tactful as possible.

"You could say that," Nora said. "He's never had a domme before me. He's a very eager student."

"He has a good teacher," Michael said. "I guess you, um . . . miss him?" He needed some good gossip for Griffin and he needed it stat.

"I do. But I get to see him next week. We're going to Salem together for Halloween."

"Ah, cool."

Michael waited. Nora said nothing else about it. Subject closed. At least he'd gotten a few words of gossip about Nico for Griffin. Mission accomplished.

"Do I smile when I talk about Griffin?" Michael asked.

"No, but you do something better. You get all . . ." She fluttered her hands like a nervous butterfly.

"He's kind of sexy." Michael pictured Griffin the last time they saw each other. Yesterday, at LaGuardia, Griffin wearing his "big boy" clothes as he called his black Tom Ford suit with a white shirt and an open collar. His dark hair was slicked back and he looked dapper and dangerous and way out of Michael's league. And yet they must have been in the same league because Griffin kissed him goodbye right there two feet away from the security checkpoint with a hundred people to witness it.

"Some days, I just can't believe he's real, you know," Michael said. "And he's mine? That's crazy. Well, he's not *mine*."

"You're his," she said.

"Yeah," Michael said. "I'm his."

"And he has back dimples."

"He does," Michael said. "I didn't know I needed those in my life until him."

"So . . . you got everything figured out?" she asked.

"Almost everything," he said.

"What's left to figure out? You already have your answer for him, right?"

"Right, but . . . there's the answer and then there's how to tell him."

"I was thinking earlier," she said, "about how hard it must have been for Griffin to ask you in such a low-key, no pressure way. It's a miracle he didn't hire a skywriter or ask you at a Mets game in front of forty thousand people."

"Mets didn't make the postseason."

"Griffin would have found a way."

"I was kind of thinking that, too," Michael said. "He did it for me. He knows I freak out under pressure which is why he . . ."

"Reined himself in?"

"Yes, that. Exactly. Probably killed him to do it," Michael said. "He likes to go crazy with the big gestures. He almost bought me a pony once."

"A pony?"

"Don't ask."

"You can't mention ponies and then say, 'Don't ask about the pony.' I'm going to ask about the pony," she said.

Michael groaned. "We went to a fair, they had ponies. I said they were cool. Griffin almost bought me a pony. I reminded him we can't have ponies in our apartment, and that is the only reason he didn't buy one."

"I would have let the man buy me a pony."

"What would you do with a pony, Nora? Seriously?"

"Pony play," she said pertly.

"That's a totally different kind of pony," Michael said. He was starting to figure out that in the world of kink, all dominants were a little nutty. The only sane ones were the subs who had the thankless job of trying to rein in their doms without their doms catching on they were being reined in by their subs.

"What are you planning?" she asked. "You think since he asked you small you should answer big?"

"I think it should be kind of . . . special, right?"

"I think Griffin would appreciate that. He always tries to make things special for you. I remember when he got your wing tattoos." She lifted his hand out of the water and kissed his wet wrist right on the black wing tattoo Griffin had given him as a gift to cover up the scars from his suicide attempt. The beauty of the gift had broken Michael apart. He'd spent weeks trying to convince himself he wasn't in love with Griffin but that did him in. He'd had to stop lying to himself and to Nora and definitely to Griffin. It had all come tumbling out, and all because of those two black wings on his wrists, the perfect gift as they came with pain and, in a way, branded him as Griffin's.

He needed to give something like that to Griffin, something like his wings but not a tattoo. They'd already done that. What could he give Griffin that would say what he needed to say, but in a way he hadn't said it before?

"Sit up a little," Nora said, the order intruding on his musing. "I need to scrub my initials off you."

"Your what?"

He sat up and saw what she meant.

Nora being Nora had, of course, dipped her finger in the still wet candle wax and spelled her initials—*NS*—onto his stomach.

"Dominants," Michael groaned. "Always marking your territory."

"I know, we're as bad as dogs sometimes. At least I didn't pee on you. This time anyway."

"This was good candle wax," Michael said. "Didn't smell like the other kinds."

"I get the candles sent to me from the Dungeon Outfitters in Midtown."

"Dungeon Outfitters? It's actually called Dungeon Outfitters?"

"They outfit dungeons," Nora said. "They have these special candles just for wax play. It gets really warm, but not too hot that you can't play with it. No perfumes or weird chemicals. They're made for kink."

Michael watched her fingers as she scraped off the red wax from his skin.

"The good news is," Nora continued, "your welts are already fading and the wax doesn't leave residue behind. By the time Griffin gets back on Sunday, you'll be a blank canvas again."

A blank canvas.

That was it.

He knew.

He knew then exactly how to tell Griffin what he needed to tell him.

If . . .

"Nora, does this place in Midtown have all colors of candles?"

"Not all colors but they have the basics. Red and white and—"

"Black?"

"Yeah, they have black. You can get the black in four packs. Tell the guy at the counter Mistress Nora sent you and you'll get ten percent off."

"Good," Michael said. "I'm going to need a lot of black candles."

It was after midnight by the time he was cleaned up and ready for bed. He lay, not sleeping, in Nora's luxurious guest bed and remembered that Griffin had slept in this very same bed last year. Griffin had escaped to New Orleans to spend time with Nora after Michael had asked for a break while he was studying for a semester in Italy. At the time it had made perfect sense. Griffin had a possessive streak a mile wide. Usually Michael loved that about him, but not when Griffin tried to make him transfer schools so they could spend more time together. Michael had been only nineteen and all of a sudden he'd felt trapped in a very adult relationship with a wealthy man, twelve years his senior, with a large family and serious adult responsibilities. Griffin had stockbrokers, lawyers, and fiduciaries—whatever the hell those were—while Michael had . . . a part-time job as a math tutor and a credit card Griffin gave him and ordered him to use. At yet another too-fancy party Griffin had dragged him to as part of Griffin's attempt to make up for his "fuck-up years" to his parents, Michael had overheard two guests implying the only reason Michael was with Griffin was for his money and the only reason Griffin was with Michael was that Griffin clearly had a thing for teenage boys. That was it, the last straw. Michael left the party without Griffin and asked for the break the next day.

And now . . . one year later . . .

Michael thought of Griffin lying in this same bed and wondering what the future held for them. It held this—Michael lying in the bed and smiling at the thought of telling Griffin that yes, he would marry him. Michael had originally planned to stay in New Orleans until Sunday morning. Before letting himself sleep, he got online and rebooked his return flight so he'd leave tomorrow.

He had things to do.

CHAPTER NINE

The Answer, Part 1

Nora hadn't been kidding.

He really did get ten percent off his black candles when he mentioned "Mistress Nora sent me" to the guy at the counter. He bought a dozen, which he hoped would be enough for what he had in mind. Then he returned to their apartment and went into the little art studio Griffin had set up for him in the spare bedroom.

Time to work.

It took all of Saturday and even Sunday morning before he was finished. Griffin wouldn't be home from his trip until about ten o'clock, and it would probably take until then to get everything set up just the way Michael wanted it. Good thing he'd slept so well the past couple of nights. Even alone in their big bed, Michael had rested well, having already made up his mind. He considered that a good sign, that his decision was helping him sleep better, not worse. Usually he took the train back to school on Sunday nights, but this wasn't an ordinary Sunday night. Griffin could drive him back tomorrow morning. If he bothered going back tomorrow. He'd only miss two classes and there was a lot to be said for spending the entire day in bed with Griffin.

At half past ten, Michael started getting nervous. He tried walking the nervousness off by pacing the apartment. Crazy that he'd lived here with Griffin for three years and he still couldn't completely accept this was his home. It was on the top floor of a tall Art Deco building in the Village and everything in it was fashionably old or brand new. Stainless steel appliances and hundred-year-old fireplaces. Everything Wi-Fi-enabled and original exposed brick walls. He loved the place, but when he gave people his address, he felt like he should put an asterisk by it. He hadn't paid for it, not a penny, and if Griffin kicked him out, he'd have nothing to do but leave. Once they were engaged maybe that "yours" versus "mine" feeling would turn into "ours." And maybe that was part of why Griffin wanted to get married, so Michael would start feeling less like a foreigner and more like a native.

Even now the apartment seemed different somehow. The light from the street streamed in the windows and set the rooms glowing. Everything the light touched spoke to him in memories. The leather sofa, which was the cause of his first fight with Griffin . . . and also the scene of their first time having make-up sex. Over the fireplace hung the flat-screen television where they'd watched a thousand terrible movies together. Griffin particularly loved watching bizarre foreign films—"The Frencher the better," Griffin would say, while Michael preferred campy sci-fi flicks. Didn't matter what they started watching. Griffin could never get through an entire film without forcing Michael to make out with him like they were kids on their first date in the back row of a movie theater. It wasn't even sexy making out. It was just ridiculous, Griffin yawning and putting his arm around Michael's shoulders. Michael inching away, playing hard to get, until Griffin leapt onto him like a feral animal.

They'd had a small dinner party here one night, a double date with Nora and Father S, which sounded weird in theory but ended up being one of the more fun evenings of Michael's life that didn't involve sex and kink. He got to see his priest for the very first time hanging with Nora outside of church, see how relaxed he was around her, how much they made each other laugh. Griffin made them all play Cards Against Humanity and Father S, seemingly so serious and intellectual, had wiped the floor with them all. He'd won on a killer hand. The question was "How did I lose my virginity?" Father S's winning card was, "The Make-A-Wish Foundation." Griffin laughed so hard he slid off the sofa onto the floor and took Michael with him. That night had been a blessing. It had been Father S giving Michael and Griffin his blessing. Later that night when they were alone, Michael had confessed to Griffin that a little part of him wished it had been his parents hanging out with them at their place, eating dinner with them, playing games. "Your dad doesn't know what he's missing," Griffin had said. But Michael knew.

Michael walked to the kitchen for a glass of water. His mouth was dry with nervousness. The gray granite countertops in the kitchen reminded Michael of all the Sunday breakfasts he and Griffin had cooked together. Neither one of them had been naturals in the kitchen, but eventually they'd figured out eggs and bacon and toast. Kingsley had even taught them one morning how to make his lighter-than-air pancakes. He'd never teach them how to make crepes though. He said he could not share the recipe with anyone not-French as it would be an act of treason.

Michael went to the bedroom he shared with Griffin, stood in the open doorway, and stared into the shadowy room. Saturday morning before his flight back to New York, he'd had breakfast with Father S and Nora. They'd eaten al fresco on Nora's back porch—shrimp and grits that had blown his mind—while Michael told Father S what was happening. He had simply nodded his noble head and said, "I'll pray for God's blessing on your home."

Michael closed his eyes and prayed his own prayer. It wasn't a prayer asking for blessings on their house or that he and Griffin would have a happy life together or for protection from harm or evil or anything like that. He just prayed Griffin would hurry up and get home. Michael missed the man.

The front door rattled with the sound of a key in the lock. The door opened. Prayer answered.

Michael stepped into the hallway. Griffin had on his ripped "holey jeans," his Mets jersey—#43 for R.A. Dickey, Griffin's all-time favorite Met—a baseball cap on backwards, and a five o'clock shadow. His usual long-flight ensemble. Michael was wearing his old standby of jeans and a plain black t-shirt, because he hadn't known exactly what one should wear when getting engaged. Dress up? Dress down? Wear nothing?

They met halfway down the hall. They didn't say anything. They hugged each other for a long time, that's all. No kissing at first, only holding like they were holding on for dear life.

Then Griffin kissed him. Michael initially thought this would be a normal kiss—lips on lips, tongues just touching, sexy without requiring sex before, during, or after. That's how it began. It didn't stay that way. Griffin's hands came up to Michael's neck as the kiss went deeper. Before Michael knew it, his back was against the wall right outside their bedroom, Griffin's tongue was inside his mouth. Two strong thumbs pressed into the hollow of Michael's panting throat. Michael was hard and wished they could skip over the formalities and get right to the kink and the sex. But they had things to say to each other that couldn't wait, not even for kisses. Griffin seemed to know that, too, because he broke off the kiss and put a little space between them. But not much. He placed both his palms on the wall on either side of Michael's head. Their bodies barely touched. While the touch made it heaven, the *barely* made it hell.

"What's the verdict?" Griffin said, his first words since walking back into the house after leaving it four days earlier.

"I can't tell you," Michael said.

Griffin cocked an eyebrow at him.

Michael smiled. "But I can show you."

"I like the sound of this," Griffin said. "Show me."

An order was an order. Michael ducked under Griffin's imprisoning arm and slipped into their bedroom. He found the lighter on the bedside table and lit a candle. Griffin waited in the doorway as Michael moved around the room lighting candle after candle until the room glowed with soft flickering fire.

"I know it wasn't easy for you," Michael said as he finished lighting the candles. "You like to do things big and I like things small. So instead of asking me to marry you with a flash mob or skywriting . . ."

"I was seriously considering a scavenger hunt," Griffin said.

"You just asked me here at home alone and you didn't make me answer right away," Michael said. "But since you were nice enough to do that for me, I thought I could do this for you. If you're going to get engaged, it should be kind of a big deal, right? So I made this for you."

Michael had lined up the candles on the bedroom's low fireplace mantel and placed a two-by-three-foot canvas on top. Griffin walked over and stood in front of the painting which was part acrylic paint and part candle wax for added texture.

Griffin stared at the painting for a long time.

Michael took a deep breath and began to speak. "You're the only adult I know who owns a pogo stick," Michael said. "And you hop around the apartment on it sometimes, which is hilarious and insane just like you are. And you look as good in a suit as you do dressed in your roller derby gear. And when you're in your roller derby gear, you always let me blow your whistle and you don't let anyone else blow your whistle. You make me get out of the bed on Saturday mornings to go to the gym with you, which proves you're the sadist of my dreams. There's all these huge tough weightlifting bros at the gym and if I weren't there you'd fit right in with them except you don't because you hold my hand in front of them sometimes, kiss me in front of them sometimes, and I don't think you're telling the world we're together to spite them or piss them off or anything, I think you just like holding my hand in public. You learned to make really good scrambled eggs because those are my favorite and you came to rescue me at school when I was sick and you treat my friends like they're your friends. You're amazing at flogging and even better at fucking and you kiss me like you had Navy SEAL training in kissing." Michael took a step closer to Griffin. He didn't realize he was doing it until he'd done it. "You bought me from my Dad with a check and you threw him against a wall to protect me from him. And you got me these," Michael said, holding out his hands, wrists up. "Tattoos make scars and I already had scars on here from when I tried to kill myself. It doesn't make sense that putting scars on top of scars can make something this beautiful, but it did. And that's kind of what we are together, you know. My scars and your scars and together they're . . . wings. So since you gave me wings, I thought I'd give you wings."

The painting on the mantel was of black wings. Michael had spent hours upon hours texturing those wings, using the tip of a knife to cut through the wax and black paint. From a few feet away the lines in the wings looked like brushstrokes from the paintbrush, but close up, if one looked carefully, as carefully as Griffin was looking at it right then, one could see it. The wings were made up of teeny tiny little words. One word, actually, repeated over and over again a thousand times or more.

Yes.

CHAPTER TEN

The Answer, Part 2

" Yes?" Griffin repeated.

"Yes," Michael said. "I'm saying yes. I'm saying it about a thousand times. And I'm saying it in words and in paint and in wax, and if you want me to get a 'yes' tattooed on my body, I'd say it in permanent ink, too."

Griffin pointed at the painting. "No, this'll do."

His voice was thick with emotion. Michael wanted to touch him but he still had something left to say and he needed to say it before Griffin kissed him again.

"I have a question to ask you," Michael said. Slowly Griffin tore his gaze from the painted black wings on the wall and met Michael's eyes.

"What's the question?"

"You asked me, so I'm asking you," Michael said. "Will you marry me?"

Griffin gave him a look like he was about to burst into laughter. It was a pretty silly question considering they were now already engaged. Griffin pointed at the mantel.

"Are those the good candles?" Griffin asked.

"You mean the wax-play candles?" Michael asked. "Yeah."

"Good. Get your collar."

Michael walked straight to the bedside table, opened the bottom drawer, and took out a black-velvet drawstring bag and passed it to Griffin.

"Shirt off," Griffin said. Michael almost reminded Griffin that he hadn't answered the question yet, but he had a feeling he was going to get his answer soon enough. He just had to be patient—not easy when Griffin was looking at him like that, like he hadn't eaten in weeks and Michael was a feast fit for a king.

Michael let his shirt fall on the floor. Griffin stepped close and wrapped the collar around Michael's neck. It was the same one Griffin had given him during their silly sexy collaring ceremony held at The 8th Circle over three years ago. Griffin had offered to get a new one now that this one was so lived-in and starting to fade. But Michael hadn't wanted a new one. Nora told him she still wore the same collar Father S had given her almost twenty years ago. That was Michael's dream, that even in ten and twenty and forever years from now, he'd still belong to Griffin, even if their love did get a little lived-in, worn out and faded.

Maybe it was just a submissive thing, but Michael always breathed better with a collar buckled round his neck. Especially when Griffin tilted Michael's head to the side so he could press hot slow kisses along the edge of the leather, under Michael's ear and over his shoulder. Griffin's fingertips lightly scoured Michael's bare stomach causing him to inhale sharply at the twin sensation of tickling and teasing. Griffin unbuttoned Michael's jeans, slipped one hand inside and stroked upward with a firm grip.

"I missed your cock," Griffin said into Michael's ear. He had one hand down Michael's jeans, another hand on his neck.

"I—"

Griffin pushed his thumb into Michael's mouth.

"No talking," Griffin said. "You asked a question. I'm going to answer it. My way."

Michael liked Griffin's ways.

"God, you're hard," Griffin said as he stroked Michael. "Nora didn't let you come when you two played?"

Michael shook his head.

"That sadistic bitch," Griffin said. "I'm so much nicer than she is. I'll let you come . . . eventually."

Michael started to growl—Nora had taught him how effective a good growl could be against an intractable dominant—but he stopped when Griffin shoved his thumb a little deeper into his mouth and pressed it against his tongue. There wasn't much in the world that made Michael feel more like a piece of property than when Griffin put his thumb in this mouth like this. It aroused him as much as it infuriated him and it infuriated him because of how much it aroused him. Even more arousing was the pressure of Griffin's hand on his cock, pulling and rubbing. Griffin's body was hot against him. Although Michael wasn't the same skinny teenager he'd been when he and Griffin fell in love, Michael still wasn't as heavily muscled or broad-shouldered as Griffin, so when Griffin pushed Michael down onto his knees in front of him, Michael went down without a fight.

Griffin didn't have to tell him what to do. They'd played this game a thousand times before. Michael opened Griffin's jeans and wrapped his mouth around Griffin's beautiful cock. As always, Griffin cupped the back of his head, tangling his fingers in Michael's hair and holding him in place while Griffin fucked his mouth. Griffin was big all over and his cock nudged the back of Michael's throat. In the beginning, it hadn't been easy for Michael to take Griffin like this, but time and Griffin's patience had trained him well. Now he craved being used like this and would have asked for it if it hadn't been more fun to wait until Griffin ordered him to do it. God knew, he never had to wait long. He spent half his weekends with Griffin's cock in his mouth and that was fine by both of them.

"My beautiful sub," Griffin said, tugging Michael's hair. "Mine, all mine."

Griffin released Michael's hair but only to take off his shirt. Griffin's jersey landed on the floor next to Michael's t-shirt. Michael decided he'd be a happy man as long as his clothes and Griffin's clothes ended up in the same pile on the floor for the rest of their lives.

Slowly Griffin started to pull out of Michael's mouth, something that did not make Michael happy. Griffin laughed at how Michael instinctively tried to stop him from moving with two hands on Griffin's hips.

"Cock slut," Griffin said. "You'll get it, don't worry."

Michael wasn't worried. He was horny. There was a difference. But an order was an order so Michael let Griffin go. He sat back on his knees and with the back of his hand wiped at his wet lips.

Griffin stared down at him.

"There, right there," Griffin said. "The way you're looking at me right now . . . that look that says you want it, you need it, and you need it from me because nobody else knows you the way I know you . . . that's my whole life right there, Mick. You on your knees in front of me with that look on your face. That's my whole damn life."

Michael was sure he'd never seen Griffin looking so possessive of him in their three years together. And that was saying something.

"Get up," Griffin said. "On the bed. On your back."

Michael almost jumped to his feet before he remembered his training from Nora. *Slow down,* she'd said. *Put on a good show for your owner. They deserve it.* Instead of rushing, Michael tucked his bare toes underneath him and rose off the floor in one straight smooth motion.

"God, you're good at that," Griffin said. "Sorry. Forgot I was the dom there for a second."

Michael laughed but he did so very quietly and respectfully. When he was younger, he thought kink was all dark and scary and dangerous. He'd been drawn to that darkness and drawn to that danger. But with Griffin it wasn't like that. Instead of being scared, he felt safe. Instead of being dark, it felt like this, like being in a room full of burning candles. It wasn't dark like evil is dark. It was dark like night is dark and night was beautiful, his favorite time of day. He'd always preferred moths and moonlight to sunshine and butterflies anyway.

Michael lay on the bed as ordered. Griffin knelt next to him and roughly yanked his jeans off and sent them flying to the floor. Then Griffin straddled Michael's stomach, grabbed his wrists, and pinned Michael to the bed, hands over his head.

Strong as Griffin was and as big as his hands were, it wasn't hard for Griffin to hold Michael's wrists by one hand while he reached for a candle on the side table with the other. Michael braced himself as Griffin held the candle over his panting chest.

"You asked me a question," Griffin said, staring down into Michael's eyes. "Here's your answer."

The wax fell onto Michael's chest, a steady scalding drip right on the center of his stomach. Griffin went slowly, carefully, as he let the wax fall and congeal into messy letters. Three letters.

Y-E-S.

That made it official. They'd both asked. They'd both said yes.

They were getting married.

The reality of it seemed to hit them both at once. Griffin put the candle back on the table and released Michael's wrists. He dragged Michael into his arms and they held each other while they knelt together and it didn't matter who was kneeling to whom. They both owned each other tonight.

"I love you, Mick," Griffin said.

"I love you, too, sir."

"I want to fuck you as much as I want to cry," Griffin said.

"I know the feeling."

"You don't get to fuck me," Griffin said. "I'm the top."

"You know what I mean, you insane dom."

They were crying and laughing at the same time, which made them laugh all the more. They were getting married. It was real. They were really getting married. Michael wanted to stand on the rooftop and shout it to the world. But that could wait. They had to celebrate together and alone first.

Griffin took Michael's face in his hands and kissed him hard again, hard and deep, deep and long. It was only seconds before Griffin had pushed him flat on his back on the bed again. Their cocks rubbed together as they kissed with abandon.

"Are you ready for me?" Griffin whispered into Michael's ear. Michael had never been readier. He'd anticipated sex tonight so he'd prepared himself in advance like the good little cock slut he was. Griffin gently eased out the butt plug that Michael had put inside himself earlier and massaged him inside with his fingers. It felt so good, too good to stay silent, and Michael moaned as his shoulders came off the bed.

"This is the real reason I'm marrying you," Griffin said. "Good power bottoms are so hard to find these days. I gotta lock you down."

Michael would have laughed if he hadn't been too busy writhing and panting. Griffin fetched the lube from the drawer and slathered it all over both of them. He took his time, no rushing, which added to the torture, which added to the pleasure. Slowly Griffin pushed Michael's knees up and into his chest, opening him for penetration. Griffin rose up on his knees and pushed his jeans down his hips before bracing himself over Michael to enter him. The first thrust was careful and the second thrust deep. By the third Griffin was fully inside him and Michael was as happy as he'd ever been in his life. When Michael tried lifting his hands to Griffin's shoulders, Griffin caught his wrists again and pushed them down into the bed. Michael lay there, pinned to the bed, impaled by Griffin's cock and wallowing in love and pleasure.

They fucked in silence; the only sounds in the room were their breathing and the quiet creaking of the bed beneath them. Michael was about to lose himself in the moment, but before he did he looked at Griffin, at this man over him, on him, inside him—the strong tattooed arms, the hazel eyes glowing in the candlelight, the sweat on his skin and the slightly parted lips. He'd remember this night on his last day on earth. Then Michael closed his eyes and surrendered his body to Griffin. There was no reason to surrender his heart to Griffin. He'd already done that long, long ago.

Griffin's thrusts were measured and restrained, but only at first. The minutes passed and his self-control waned, and soon he was giving everything to Michael and Michael was taking everything he was given. He loved being penetrated, impaled, taken and made into Griffin's slave. Even when it hurt. Especially when it hurt. Not that it hurt tonight. He could have taken a brutal fucking tonight and not flinched and that was a good thing because Griffin was fucking him brutally. The bed rocked and the room swayed and Michael's vision swam. His back arched off the bed and Griffin wrapped an arm around his waist, pulling him so close they were one flesh for one perfect second.

Griffin lowered Michael back to the bed. He wrapped his hand around Michael's cock and stroked it while they fucked.

"Come with me," Griffin ordered.

Michael was too far gone to speak so he merely nodded. He was there already, in that place where not even a train crashing into their apartment could stop him from coming. Griffin stroked him inside and out, with hand and cock, and brutal biting kisses on his chest and shoulders. It was painful to hold back but he did. He held back and waited until Griffin put his mouth to Michael's ear and whispered a hushed, harsh "Now."

Michael stopped holding himself back. He came in a hot rush all over his stomach and chest and Griffin's hand. The orgasm was blinding, and Michael was barely aware of Griffin coming inside of him. He only knew it was happening because of the unbearably erotic sounds Griffin made when he came—a sort of almost-silent groan that ended in the filthiest grunt ever heard by human ears.

Griffin slowly pulled out but didn't let Michael up from the bed. They stayed where they were, Griffin pinning Michael down and Michael happy to stay there forever.

"Last question," Griffin said. "What made you say yes?"

"Easy answer," Michael said, a sleepy smile on his face. "You."

CHAPTER ELEVEN

Michael's Wings

They lay entwined for a long time on the bed, kissing and touching and dreaming of the future. Michael had Griffin's come inside of him and he wanted for nothing more to make him happy.

"Engagement rings?" Griffin asked.

"Nah," Michael said, tiredly, blissfully lying on Griffin's chest as Griffin stroked his back with his fingertips.

"Engagement . . . cock rings?" Griffin said.

"Talk me into it," Michael said.

"Big wedding? Little wedding?"

"Little wedding," Michael said.

"Okay. We'll keep it small. Two-hundred people."

Michael lifted his head and looked at Griffin.

"That's small?"

"Size is relative."

Michael glared at him.

"Hey, you're lucky I'm not ordering you to marry me in the middle of Times Square, sub. We could project the wedding on the big screen. Invite the whole city as guests," Griffin said.

"No, no, sir. Hard no, sir. Wings. Safeword. Red."

Griffin's chest moved underneath Michael's head with quiet laughter. "Fine, no Jumbotron. We'll figure it out. We got time. You don't graduate until May anyway. And you'll be twenty-one by then. That's a respectable age for getting married."

"In 1952 maybe," Michael said.

Griffin slapped Michael's ass.

"You fell in love with an older man. You have only yourself to blame," Griffin said and pressed a kiss on the top of Michael's head.

They lay in contented silence for a few minutes before Michael posed an important question:

"When are we going to tell people?"

"Oh . . ." Griffin said with a sigh. "I don't know. Whenever."

"You're dying to call your mom, aren't you?" Michael asked.

Griffin ran a hand through his hair and stared up at the ceiling. "It's like a stick in my back and it won't stop poking me until I call her," he said, miming a poking action with his finger.

"It's not midnight yet," Michael said. "She's probably up." Alexis was a bit of a night owl. Griffin got that from her.

"You wouldn't mind?"

"I wouldn't mind."

"Sweet!" Griffin threw Michael off of him, and started to run out of the room.

"Pants!" Michael yelled after him.

"Pants. Right. Calling Mom. This is why I keep you around."

Alexis had discovered FaceTime recently and there was nothing more awkward than getting a FaceTime call from one of the moms while bare-ass naked. Griffin grabbed his jeans off the floor and raced to find his phone he'd apparently left somewhere in the living room. Nothing surprised Michael about any of that except Griffin had used his feet to get to the living room and not the pogo stick that was propped by the bedroom door. Well, it was a little late for pogoing. They did have downstairs neighbors to think about. The Nussbaums were very nice people after all, and they needed their sleep.

At a far more sedate pace, Michael pulled on boxer shorts and a t-shirt and followed Griffin to the living room. Griffin sat on the edge of the couch, phone to his ear, waiting for an answer.

Michael found his own phone on the coffee table and sent his mother a quick text to see if she was up.

"Mom," Griffin said. "Don't panic. There's nothing wrong."

Michael smiled. Griffin looked at him with bright eyes, happy eyes.

"No, it's good news this time," Griffin said, grinning. "Mick and I . . . we're getting married."

Griffin had to immediately hold the phone two feet from his ear. The scream was so loud Michael heard it on the other side of the room.

Michael's phone beeped in his hand.

Mom: **What's up, kid?**

Michael: **You busy?**

Mom: **At work but I have a second.**

Michael: **Don't freak out but Griff asked me to marry him. I said yes.**

A pause followed, but not a long one.

Mom: **Not freaking out. Not even surprised. I'm just smiling. I'm happy for you.**

Michael: **You are?**

Mom: **You're too young but when has that ever stopped you before?**

His mother made a fair point.

Michael: **Thanks, Mom. Love you.**

Mom: **Love you, too. Wish I could talk now. Call me first thing tomorrow morning. I want to hear everything.**

On the couch Griffin was grinning broadly as he tried to talk his mother down off the ceiling.

"Mom, calm down. We're getting married in May, not tomorrow," Griffin said. "We've literally been engaged an hour so we haven't figured out the guest list yet. Why didn't I call you an hour ago? We were, ah . . . a little busy, okay? Don't be gross, Mom. I'm a virgin. What?"

Griffin listened.

"Mom wants to know what you're wearing for the wedding," Griffin said.

"A red latex catsuit."

Griffin raised his eyebrow. To his mother he said, "We haven't figured that out yet."

"Can I tell Nora?" Michael asked. Griffin gave him the thumbs up. He sent Nora a text message.

Michael: **So . . . you want to be my maid of honor?**

Nora: **Me? A maiden? Have you met me?**

Michael: **Matron of honor?**

Nora: **Do I look matronly to you?**

Michael: **Mistress of dishonor?**

Nora: **Now we're talking.**

A few seconds later came another message from Nora.

Nora: **I'm so happy for you both.**

Michael: **Thanks. This is the right thing, right?**

Nora: **Are you happy?**

Michael looked at Griffin, who was currently discussing various castles in Europe that his mother deemed acceptable for a Fiske family wedding.

Michael: **Very happy.**

Nora: **Then it's the right thing. Also, your priest sends his felicitations.**

Michael: **He actually said "felicitations"?**

Nora: **He's so weird.**

Michael: **Is he happy for us?**

Nora: **He must be. He just did a cartwheel. Pretty impressive move for someone his height.**

Michael: **You're an adult.**

Nora: **There goes the ceiling fan!**

Michael: **Bye, Nora.**

Nora: **Love you, Angelface. You two are going to be insanely happy together forever.**

Michael: **Yeah, I think we are.**

Nora: **Ahem . . .**

Michael: **Yeah, I think we are, MISTRESS.**

Nora: **Better.**

Michael sent her a kiss emoji as a sign-off. He went over to Griffin and sat next to him on the sofa. Griffin immediately threw an arm around Michael's shoulders and pulled him down and across his lap. Michael closed his eyes, exhausted and spent and sleepy. Griffin hung up on his mom and called his butler and then his brothers to give them the news.

Curled up on Griffin's lap with his fiancé's hand caressing his back, Michael looked at the black wing tattoos on his wrists and wondered what he would do if, by some strange magic, his wings turned from flesh and ink into feather and bone. Michael didn't know what he would do with his wings if he had them, but he did know the one thing he would never ever do.

He would never fly away from Griffin.

GRIFFIN IN WONDERLAND

"Griffin in Wonderland" takes place approximately seven years before The Angel, *well before Michael came into Griffin's life.*

The last thing he remembered was the sound of shattering glass. Shattering glass . . . and then nothing.

Griffin started to open his eyes but the slight influx of light sent searing pain into the back of his skull. So instead he kept them closed tight while he ran an inventory on his body. Everything still seemed to be there—feet, legs, arms, hands, head, the other far more important head . . . Nothing broken. Perhaps just bruised. Although he did feel an unpleasant weight on his chest like something was stabbing the very center of it.

Griffin sighed . . . Twenty-two years old and he was having chest pains? That couldn't be good. Maybe leaving rehab a week early hadn't been the best idea after all.

Slowly, very slowly, Griffin opened his eyes again and saw the source of his chest pain. A pair of leather riding boots crossed at the ankle rested on the center of his sternum. He stared at the boots a moment and tried to make some sense of them. They seemed to belong to a pair of long male legs in dark gray trousers. And the long male legs seemed to belong to a dark-eyed, olive-skinned man with shoulder-length dark brown hair sitting in a chair and sipping what appeared to be a cup of tea.

"Pardon me for saying this," the booted man said in a rich French accent as he set his teacup down on the table next to him, "but I think you need a new hobby."

Griffin rolled into a sitting position as the booted man removed his feet.

"Pardon me for saying this," Griffin said, "but who the fuck are you?"

The booted man crossed one ankle over his knee and gave Griffin a smile. Despite the aching in his brain, Griffin couldn't help but notice the man's undeniable handsomeness. Not his type really. When he went for guys, they were usually about his age or younger. This guy appeared to be in his mid-thirties, although his clothes looked like they belonged on some duke or earl from two hundred years ago.

"My name is Kingsley Edge. And it is a pleasure to finally make your acquaintance, Monsieur Griffin Fiske. *Comment ça va?*"

Griffin looked up at him sharply.

"Kingsley Edge?" he repeated, the name sending a fissure of nervousness down his spine.

"*C'est moi.*"

For a moment Griffin considered asking if he was *the* Kingsley Edge. But what was the point? In New York there was just the one and only Kingsley Edge—King of the Underground.

"How do you know who I am, Mr. Edge?"

"Call me Kingsley. I think we should be equals, Griffin. Or will be once I'm finished with you. And I know who you are because I own this club. And I've been watching you. You broke my mirror, by the way."

Kingsley nodded toward the bar where the shattered remains of a mirror and a few thousand broken liquor bottles littered the counter, wall, and floor.

"Shit. I did that?"

Smiling, Kingsley picked up his teacup again and took another sip. "You did."

"I'm sorry. I can pay for it."

Kingsley shook his finger at him. "You don't remember how you broke it, do you?"

Groaning, Griffin slowly got to his feet and collapsed into the chair across from Kingsley.

"Bar fight?" Griffin guessed.

"Something like that. One of the patrons last night started to assault Scarlett. He grabbed her off the stage and groped her. You took him by the neck and threw him over the bar and into the mirror."

Griffin's eyes widened. Now he vaguely remembered the event. He'd come to the Möbius Strip Club with a few friends last night. As usual he'd gotten wasted as quickly as possible. In his mind he could make out the outline of a beautiful girl with dark red hair dancing on stage in black jackboots and a black thong . . . and nothing else. And he remembered a scream as some jackass grabbed her ankle and yanked her off the stage. Some kind of animal rage had welled up in him. He'd ripped that asshole's hands off the girl and dragged him by the neck to a clearing by the bar.

"I punched him first. Didn't I? Or am I making that up?"

Kingsley grinned again.

"Ah, *oui*. You fractured his jaw. He attempted to return the favor. That's when you sent him flying. You're a very strong young man, Griffin."

"I lift weights."

"I can tell. I think something else in your system last night might have added to your powers."

Griffin didn't answer right away. Last thing he needed was his parents or anyone else on the face of the earth learning that his rehab vacation hadn't stuck as well as they'd hoped it would.

"Cops coming?" Somewhere in his cell phone Griffin had the number for the family attorney. After all the hell he'd put his family through, he should have that shark's number tattooed on his forearm.

"I've taken care of everything. The patron will not press assault charges against you."

"I broke his face."

Kingsley merely shrugged. "I can be quite persuasive. And I have friends in interesting places. The police did come but your name was not mentioned. By anyone."

Crossing his arms over his chest, Griffin stared at the remnants of the mirror scattered across the black and white tile floor of New York's most infamous strip club.

"Thanks for that. Last thing I need is to piss off my parents. Again. If you know who I am you know I can pay for the damage. I can write a check or bring you cash. I'm guessing since you're you, you prefer cash."

"I do know who you are," Kingsley said, standing up and looking down at him. "Your mother is Alexis Fiske, formally Raeburn. Still one of the most beautiful women in the world."

"She might be an ex-model but she's still my mother, okay?" Griffin's stomach turned when men talked about how hot his mom was. Just weird.

"*Bien sûr*. And your father's empire . . . worth at last estimate approximately one billion dollars. Congratulations to him. I hear he was just elected president of the Stock Exchange."

"He was?"

Kingsley nodded again.

"Haven't talked to him in a few weeks," Griffin said, feeling a knot of shame form in his stomach. This total stranger knew more about what his dad was up to than he did. Another sign maybe he shouldn't have left rehab a week early. "I'll call."

"And you, Griffin Randolfe Fiske. Age twenty-two. Left Brown University for a stint in rehab six weeks ago. Intelligent, very handsome if I may say so, bisexual if the rumors are true, and possibly the most spoiled trust fund baby I've ever had the pleasure of watching pass out in one of my clubs."

Griffin's face warmed at the insulting and unfortunately true description of himself.

"Guilty. Can I go now?"

"*Oui*. But I would like to see you again if I may. There's something I'd like to discuss with you."

Kingsley reached into an inner pocket of his frock coat—frock coat? seriously?—and pulled out a card which he handed to Griffin. Blinking, Griffin studied the card. All black with silver lettering, the only words on the card were for an address in Manhattan. He didn't even see a name—just a little crown symbol with a letter *K* inside.

"Come by the townhouse tonight. We can discuss possibly finding a new hobby for you. Perhaps even a new addiction," Kingsley said. "And don't worry about the mirror. You saved one of my girls from an attacker. I am in your debt."

Griffin only looked at the card a moment.

"But," Kingsley began, "if you come, come clean and sober. Or don't come at all, *mon ami.*"

At that, Kingsley gave an elegant bow and strode from the empty club and into the New York morning leaving Griffin alone with his hangover and the card.

As he stared at the card he held, Griffin couldn't help but look at his hand. Blood from the jackass he'd punched out had crusted and dried across his knuckles. On his palm he had a shallow cut, probably from the broken glass. His hand ached horribly. How hard had he hit that guy? Griffin rubbed his right hand with his left but the pain sent a wave of nausea rocking through his body.

He raced behind the bar to the sink, nearly skidding on the broken glass, and threw up last night's tequila and whatever else was left in his system. He turned on the tap and rinsed the foul taste out of his mouth. With two cupped hands, he splashed his face with the ice-cold water and ran his fingers through his hair.

Rising up he caught a glimpse of himself in one of the shards of mirror still left hanging on the wall. Kingsley called him handsome and he was self-aware enough to know that was a pretty fair estimate of his appearance. His face looked like a male version of his model mother's—strong cheekbones, full lips, classical jawline. But under his eyes he spied black circles. A small bruise had welled up on his cheek. His usually perfectly styled black hair now skewed in all directions. Most days people considered him extremely attractive. Today he looked like shit warmed over.

He had no idea what the one and only Kingsley Edge wanted with him. But he couldn't really argue with the man.

He really did need a new addiction. All his old ones were about to kill him.

Ten hours of sleep, some real food, and an hour-long shower later, Griffin felt and looked much more like himself. He had no clue how to dress for Kingsley Edge's townhouse, so he just put on his usual "fuck me" uniform of black pants and a pinstriped and untucked black button-down shirt. He got into his Porsche and drove to the address on the card Kingsley had given him. Not bad, Griffin thought, as he handed the keys to a valet and looked up at the house. Three stories at least . . . white and black, wrought iron gate. A touch of Empire style, he noted. Empire style? Jesus, he must have actually paid attention in one of his Art History classes.

A woman with a Jamaican accent opened the door for him and let him into the palatial entryway. He was about two seconds away from starting to flirt with the beautiful girl when he heard someone whistling a familiar tune.

"I know that song," Griffin said as Kingsley came whistling down the stairs dressed in an even more elegant suit than he had on that morning. Victorian era maybe?

" 'Alouette,' " Kingsley said as he reached the bottom of the steps. "A French-Canadian children's song."

Kingsley headed down a hallway and motioned Griffin to follow.

"Very cute. I think we sang that song in kindergarten. What does it mean?" Griffin knew a little French but not enough to remember the lyrics of the song.

"It's about killing and plucking a skylark. Have a seat."

Kingsley gestured to a chair in an exquisite if slightly over-decorated parlor. The whole place was lit up by dozens of pale-yellow taper candles. The man seemed to be allergic to modern lighting.

"Nice digs you have here."

"*Merci*. I'm sure it's quite small compared to your mother's home near Guilford."

Griffin swallowed. "I kind of hate how much you know about me."

Kingsley poured a glass of what appeared to be sherry for himself. He pointedly offered none to Griffin.

"I know a great deal about you," Kingsley said as he took a seat on a fainting couch. "It's in my best interest to know everything I can about the people in my world."

"That sounds vaguely threatening." Griffin sat on an armchair across from the couch.

"*Pas du tout*. I use my knowledge to protect my people. The same way you used your strength to protect Scarlett last night. For example . . ." Kingsley paused for a sip of his sherry. "In my world there are those whose professions are considered incompatible with their proclivities. One of the male submissives who frequents my clubs is a rabbi."

"You serious?"

"Quite. And he is the least of the Underground's secrets. But if, perhaps, someone wanted to out this man to his congregation or his family, I might have, perhaps, found some information that would dissuade that person from such a course of action."

Griffin shivered at the words. Kingsley spoke them casually, and they sounded almost musical in his masculine voice tinged with the heady French accent. But no one could mistake the threat of violence and blackmail in the statement.

"Information?"

Kingsley swirled the sherry in his glass. "Perhaps I had pictures of a handsome young man with a rolled up hundred-dollar bill snorting cocaine in the bathroom of a strip club. Such a young man—whose family had threatened to cut him off if he was caught using drugs again—would very likely keep whatever he saw at my home or at my clubs a secret, wouldn't he?"

Every muscle in Griffin's body froze. His heart stopped. His breathing ceased. Ten seconds later it all started up again.

"Yes . . . I'm sure he would."

"I would protect you as well, Griffin, if you were to join my coterie. And I do hope you will."

Sitting carefully back in the chair Griffin studied Kingsley for any signs of humor.

"Join? Join what? How?"

Kingsley smiled at Griffin . . . a long, slow, insinuating smile. As he smiled, Kingsley's sculpted fingers danced over the rim of his sherry glass. Griffin had never met a more terrifyingly erotic man in his life. Every move Kingsley made seemed to be designed for seduction. Griffin might have to rethink what sort of guy he considered his type from now on.

"You, young man, are at the mercy of your desires and impulses. You drink too much and abuse drugs because you are bored. Everything comes too easy for you. You are spoiled and you are pampered and you have no self-respect. You need something in your life to give you purpose."

"And you're going to tell me what that purpose is?"

"I am." Kingsley took another sip of his drink before setting it aside and leaning forward. "I think you have all the makings of an excellent dominant."

Griffin's eyes went wide. "Dominant? Like a whips and chains dominant? No, not my thing."

Kingsley didn't seem bothered by his answer. "Have you ever tried it? Dominating someone in the bedroom? A man or a woman?"

"No. I mean, with guys, I always, you know—"

"You're a top. You don't have to mince words with me."

Griffin nearly blushed again. He had sex all the time with women and men. Just yesterday he ended up fucking some girl he met standing in line at the bank. But he wasn't used to talking about it so frankly. Who was this guy?

"Fine. Yeah, with guys I'm a top. But that's just sex. Not *topping* topping."

Kingsley laughed and that warm rich sound had one or two muscles in Griffin's thighs tightening.

"Perhaps you would like it if you tried it."

"I don't know. Seems like a waste of time. Why bother with all the gear and shit? Gets in the way of the fucking."

Tilting his head to the side, Kingsley seemed to study Griffin.

"Why bother . . . that is a very good question." Kingsley paused and momentarily gazed at a candle burning on the table at Griffin's left. The fire from the candle flickered and danced in Kingsley's dark eyes. "You are a wealthy man, Griffin Fiske. Perhaps even more so than I am. And you've had scores of lovers. Perhaps even more than I've had."

Griffin highly doubted that last part.

"But," Kingsley continued, "I have something you do not."

"Yeah, and what's that?" Griffin asked. "A better tailor?"

Kingsley gave a low laugh. "Power, Griffin. All the money in the world can't buy you the sort of power I have. And I am not talking about the power to blackmail someone or to buy their loyalty."

"I threw a guy over a bar and into a mirror last night. That's not power?"

"That is violence, which is a sort of power. But the kind I have is far headier, far more beautiful, and so much more . . . addictive than the power to hurt someone against their will. I have the power to hurt someone with their permission. *Vous comprendez*? You understand me?"

Griffin shook his head. "Not at all."

"Then perhaps I shall have to show you."

Kingsley stood up and led Griffin from the candlelit parlor down a shadowy hall illuminated only by wall sconces.

"Where are we going?" Griffin asked, nervous excitement gnawing at his stomach. He hadn't felt this alive in years. He'd been such a hard partier for so long that he couldn't remember the last time he'd felt anything like a real adrenaline rush, one not created by the artificial chemicals he sometimes ingested.

"I want you to meet a friend of mine. I think you will like her."

At the end of the hall they paused in the open doorway of another parlor—a smaller, more intimate one. Griffin nearly swore audibly when he saw the inhabitants of the room. The young woman didn't shock him except maybe with her beauty. A little thing, she had wavy black hair and wore a white skirt, white corset, and something around her neck. Not quite a necklace, it looked more like a white dog collar. She sat at a small table across from a man wearing black. The man had been the one who'd nearly set Griffin to swearing. Handsome in a severe sort of way, the man wore all black apart from a square of white at his neck. A chessboard sat between him and the girl. She turned her head and grinned broadly at Kingsley, and Griffin suddenly had a little trouble breathing.

The man who was apparently a priest leaned back in his chair and raised an eyebrow at Kingsley in a manner both condescending and familiar.

"*Pardonne-moi, mon ami,*" Kingsley said to the blond priest. "Might I borrow your pet for a few minutes? *S'il te plait?*"

"*Oui, emmène-la. Elle perd le match exprès à nouveau,*" said the priest in what sounded like flawless French to Griffin. He wasn't quite fluent but he understood most of the sentence: *Yes, take her. She is losing the game on purpose. Again.*

"Elle?" Kingsley said and crooked his finger at the girl. "*Viens ici.*"

The girl stood up and leaned across the chessboard to give the blond priest a quick kiss on the mouth. He whispered something to her against her lips, something that made her smile. She whispered something back to him and he nodded his approval.

"Thirty minutes," the priest said. "Be a good girl for Kingsley, Eleanor."

"Yes, sir." The girl Eleanor came to Kingsley and curtsied.

Kingsley patted her on the cheek and started up a set of back stairs. Griffin and Eleanor followed, and Griffin noticed the girl casting as many curious glances at him as he did at her.

"I'm Griffin," he said to her. "Griffin Fiske." Usually he never told people his last name. Too many people in town knew he had money the second he said it. But for some reason he wanted to impress this girl.

"Griffin. Cool name. You must have played lacrosse."

He laughed softly. Smart girl. Knew her preppy rich kids when she saw them.

"You don't look like an Eleanor," he whispered, not sure why he felt the need to keep his voice low.

"I hate my name. Change it for me," she whispered back with a grin. She had a gorgeous grin, wide and fearless when she smiled, some dangerous kind of light sparked in her eyes like struck flint.

"How about just Nor? Or Nora? It's sexier."

She nodded. "I like it. I'll go to the courthouse tomorrow and get it changed. If Blondie says it's okay, of course."

"Blondie? The priest downstairs?"

"Uh-huh. He makes the decisions. All of them."

"He's . . . a priest? Like a real priest?"

"He is."

"You know Catholic priests aren't supposed to kiss drop-dead gorgeous girls like you."

"Okay," she said. "You go and tell him that."

"Ah . . . none of my business, I guess," he said. "I'm not Catholic."

Eleanor laughed. It was low, throaty, and even sexier than Kingsley's laugh. Griffin had a sudden vision of pushing her against the wall, slipping his hand under her skirt, and becoming her clit's new best friend.

"Smart man," she said. "But this is Wonderland, anyway. The rules don't apply in Wonderland. Like it here so far?"

"This is Wonderland?" Griffin asked, glancing around the well-appointed hallway. "Does that make you Alice?"

"Nope, you're Alice, newbie," she said.

Once more Griffin looked her up and down, taking in her killer curves encased all in white.

"Guess you're the White Rabbit then," he said, deciding then and there he'd follow her little tail anywhere.

"*Non.* I'm the White Rabbit." Kingsley opened the door. "She's the Jabberwocky."

Eleanor playfully bared her teeth at Kingsley right before disappearing into the room.

Was he really in Wonderland? Griffin asked himself. *Or hell?*

Griffin entered the room after them and froze in his tracks.

Definitely hell.

"Oh, holy shit," Griffin breathed as he gazed around the room. He'd expected a bedroom—and in the middle of the room he did see a wrought-iron four-poster bed draped in red and black silk sheets—but this was no bedroom. Along the walls of the room hung floggers and whips, canes and paddles. He'd heard of places like this, but never guessed such a posh Manhattan townhouse had its own dungeon.

The three of them stood in silence a moment. Griffin got the feeling Kingsley and Eleanor were enjoying his wide-eyed astonishment. No one made a sound until Kingsley raised his hand and snapped his fingers in Eleanor's ear. At that she turned to Kingsley and stood in front of him with her eyes lowered.

"Griffin, you asked me why bother with all of this. Allow me to show you. I may, at some point, need your assistance."

Assistance? With that gorgeous girl? "Yeah, sure. Anything you want as long as she's fine with it."

Kingsley laughed and cupped Eleanor's chin. "She's fine with whatever I tell her to be fine with. Isn't that so?"

Eleanor nodded into his hand. "*Oui, Monseiur.*"

"*Très bien.* Now undress, but . . ." Kingsley looked down. On her feet Eleanor wore white go-go boots. "Leave the boots on."

Immediately Eleanor raised her hands to her breasts and began unhooking her corset. Her sheer white blouse came next, and she shed her skirt and white panties with perfunctory quickness. Griffin had seen a lot of naked women in his day, but rarely one with such a naturally beautiful body. Full breasts, round hips, and no shame—the holy trinity of perfection in a woman.

Kingsley seemed to think so as well. He stepped up to Eleanor and laid a kiss on her neck where it met her shoulder. He slipped his jacket off and let it join her clothes on the floor. He spoke an order to her in French, and she moved to the end of the bed.

For a minute or two Kingsley whistled "Alouette" again while strolling the perimeter of the room, examining the various items hanging from the walls or laying on tables. Griffin had heard stories about Kingsley Edge. The man was something of a legend in New York. Everyone knew he ran a stable of the sexiest kinksters money could buy. And Kingsley himself easily ranked as one of the more attractive men Griffin had ever laid eyes on. In his riding boots, fitted trousers, white shirt, and embroidered vest, he looked like something off the cover of those romance novels he saw in airport bookstores. But he doubted the men in those books ever did the sort of stuff Kingsley was supposedly into. If they did, Griffin might have to start reading them.

Kingsley picked up a wicked-looking flogger with long leather thongs and heart-shaped knots at the end. After tossing the flogger on the bed, Kingsley stood behind Eleanor and took her wrists in his hands. Over the end of her right wrist he hooked the end of a black rope.

"These are rope cuffs," Kingsley explained as he tossed the rope over the top bar of the four-poster bed. "Like a Chinese finger puzzle. The more Eleanor struggles, the tighter they'll fit on her wrists."

He cuffed her other wrist. Eleanor now stood with her arms high over her head and secured to the bed. As Kingsley took the flogger off the bed, Eleanor turned her face to Griffin, smiled at him, and yanked down on the cuffs, tightening them on her wrists of her own volition.

"There's a certain technique to giving a good thorough flogging," Kingsley said, taking two steps back from Eleanor's naked body. "When administering a long, sustained beating, it is best to start out soft to desensitize the skin. We don't have that sort of time tonight as our Eleanor is merely on loan. So we shan't bother with the niceties. Eleanor tends to get bored by niceties anyway. Don't you, *chérie*?"

"*Oui, Mon—*" The rest of her sentence was cut off when Kingsley brought the flogger down hard on her back. She flinched and Griffin flinched with her. Redness erupted all over her pale skin between her shoulder blades. Kingsley struck again and Eleanor flinched again. He wielded the flogger with casual power and it whirled nimbly in his hands. The flogging obviously hurt, as Eleanor winced and gasped. But at no point did she say "stop" or "no" or make any sort of protest.

After a few minutes the flogging ceased. Kingsley left Eleanor panting through her pain as he hung the flogger back on the wall. He returned with a riding crop. He spun it in his right hand as deftly as a baton twirler before letting it slide through his fingers. He caught the crop by the handle and raised it.

Griffin had seen enough. "Wait, Kingsley . . ."

Kingsley ignored him and brought the crop down hard in the center of Eleanor's back. He landed five hard strikes down her back from her shoulders to her hips before stopping and tossing the crop aside.

"Now . . ." Kingsley raised his hand and crooked his finger at Griffin. With some reluctance Griffin crossed the room to where Kingsley was standing behind Eleanor. "Let me show you something."

Kingsley tapped Eleanor's thigh and she obediently lifted it, resting her foot on the bed. Griffin inhaled sharply as the angle of her leg opened her body to his view. Blood started pooling in his hips.

"Your hand," Kingsley said and Griffin held it out to him. Kingsley took Griffin's hand and brought it between Eleanor's thighs. "Feel."

Griffin looked at Kingsley and the Frenchman nodded his encouragement. Eleanor made no protest, so Griffin rested his fingers gently at the entrance of her body.

"Fuck . . ." He'd rarely felt such heat emanating from a woman before. He pushed in more and felt her incredible warm wetness. Nothing could stop him from sinking three fingers into her all the way to the third knuckle on his hand. Now extremely aroused, Griffin couldn't stop imagining replacing his fingers with his cock, ramming it deep and hard inside her. A woman like this obviously enjoyed pain, enjoyed being used, and God, he would use her up until she could barely breathe, barely see, barely speak except to say his name.

Griffin moved his hand in her slowly, deeper, pulling out a little before pushing back in again. Through the veil of the black hair that had fallen in her face, Eleanor gazed up at Griffin. Their eyes met and suddenly Kingsley disappeared, the room disappeared, the world disappeared, and it was only Griffin and Eleanor in the whole universe. Then he discovered she didn't have black eyes like he'd previously thought. They were green, dark green and full of wild mischief. He pulled his hand forward into her G-spot until he felt the edge of her pubic bone. Her pulse beat against his fingers. Her eyes closed and her head fell back. Every cent he had, every cent his family had . . . he'd give it all away just to feel her come on his hand.

"Lovely, isn't it?" Kingsley said, forcing Griffin back to reality. "You ask why bother? Feel that heat on your hand, that wetness, and know she could be yours for the taking. She could be at your feet serving you, living as your property. Her body would be yours to take whenever you desired. Anyone has the power to hurt someone. Take a gun, take a knife, take your impressive fists into the street. Beat them, I dare you, and see how long it takes before they beg you to stop. But I promise you won't feel the satisfaction I do right now . . . Eleanor? Do you want to stop?"

"*Non, Monsieur.* Never stop . . ."

"I hurt her. I beat her. And she tells me not to stop. Now that, Griffin, is power." Kingsley kissed Eleanor again on the shoulder. The kiss turned into a bite. "Pardon me, but now I think I need to fuck her."

It nearly killed Griffin to pull his hand out of her, but he wasn't about to argue with Kingsley. Eleanor lowered her leg to the floor as Kingsley turned her toward him. Griffin knew he probably shouldn't be watching this, but he couldn't look away as Kingsley opened his pants and rolled a condom onto one of the most impressive cocks he'd seen in his day. Kingsley grasped Eleanor's hips, raised her up, and lowered her onto him. Eleanor wrapped her white-booted calves around Kingsley's back and arched her hips.

Griffin groaned audibly as Kingsley started thrusting into Eleanor's wet body. His movements were precise and controlled, hard but not without impressive restraint. Eleanor's arms still hung above her head from the bed frame and she used the bonds to lift herself and take more of Kingsley into her. Her breathing turned fast and desperate as Kingsley slipped a hand between their bodies and rubbed her clitoris. With a lusty cry, Eleanor came, her hips bucking into Kingsley's. Griffin waited for Kingsley to start thrusting faster, chasing his own orgasm. But instead he pulled out and untied one of Eleanor's wrists.

"Bed," he ordered. "On your stomach."

Quickly Eleanor obeyed, lying prone across the black and red sheets. Kingsley bound her wrists to the headboard and each ankle to a bedpost. From a bedside table he pulled out a bottle of lube. As wet as Eleanor was, the lube could only mean one thing. Kingsley knelt between her wide-open thighs and with two wet fingers pushed into her. She buried her head into the bed and moaned. Kingsley pulled his fingers out and inch by torturously slow inch pushed his cock into her.

With long controlled thrusts, Kingsley moved in and out of her. Griffin had more than one threesome under his belt, but he'd never just stood in a room and watched a Frenchman beat and fuck a beautiful black-haired girl up the ass. He could get used to this.

Kingsley raised a hand and snapped his fingers at Griffin.

"*Assistance, s'il vous plaît,*" Kingsley said and Griffin came to the side of the bed. "If you would see to her."

Kingsley's left hand grasped the back of Eleanor's neck while his right hand tapped her hip. Eleanor raised her hip high enough that Griffin could slide his hand under her. He found her clitoris and began rubbing the swollen knot with two fingers. Kingsley's thrusts grew harder and faster. Griffin envied Kingsley. He'd never done anal with a woman before. No girl would ever let him once she saw how big he was. Either that or they were all using his size as an excuse to chicken out. But Eleanor clearly enjoyed it. Who was this girl who belonged to a priest, got used by a king, and seemed to be having more fun than anyone? He didn't know but he decided right then and there he had to find out.

Eleanor pulled on her restraints as Griffin moved his fingers harder against her clitoris. Kingsley's hand dug deeper into the soft skin at the base of her neck and Eleanor cried out again as she came once more. With a few more near-brutal thrusts, Kingsley slammed into her and climaxed with a quiet shudder.

Griffin gently pulled his hand away and stood up again. Kingsley pulled out of her, disposed of the condom and straightened his clothes. He untied Eleanor and rolled her over into his arms. Even straining his ears, Griffin couldn't make out a single word Kingsley whispered to Eleanor. But whatever he said made her happy, as she smiled broadly at him and kissed him on the cheek. He gave her a sharp little slap on her shapely bottom, and she got off the bed and wriggled back into her clothes.

Eleanor stopped at the door and looked back at Griffin.

"Nice to meet you, Griffin. Thanks for the hand. Hope I get to return the favor someday. Later, King."

With one last smile she left them alone in the room. Griffin sagged against the wall and knew he was more turned on than he'd ever been in his entire life.

"Enjoy the show?" Kingsley asked.

"You fucked her and she came and you didn't." Griffin still hadn't gotten over that impressive performance at the end of the bed, before Kingsley had ordered Eleanor onto her stomach. "That would have killed me."

Kingsley merely shrugged and walked toward Griffin.

"It does take practice . . . self-control. I could teach you how if you like."

"Are all the women in the Underground like her?"

Kingsley took another step forward.

"Find out for yourself."

"Was that," Griffin said, glancing pointedly at the end of the bed, the floggers on the wall, the riding crop on the floor, "as fun as it looked?"

Kingsley gave him a slow, seductive smile as he took one final step forward until their faces were only inches apart.

"More." Kingsley breathed the word into Griffin's ear and every nerve in Griffin's body tingled to life. No drink, no drug, no chemical had ever made him feel as alive as the last thirty minutes with Kingsley and that amazing girl had.

Griffin took a deep breath. "Okay . . . you got me. I'm in."

Kingsley reached behind Griffin and locked the door. In stereotypical French fashion, Kingsley dropped a kiss on each of Griffin's cheeks. But a third kiss he pressed onto Griffin's lips.

"Welcome to Wonderland."

GAUZE

"Gauze" takes place during The Angel, *the second book in The Original Sinners series. Michael and Griffin have just spent their first night together . . .*

Michael fucking hated gauze. But when he woke up it was the first thing he saw. Michael stared at the gauze on his wrists and tried not to remember, tried so hard not to remember. He didn't want to remember, didn't want to see the blood seeping through the gauze and turning the white cloth pink. It happened though, no matter how he tried to fight it. And before he could stop it, he found himself standing in the sanctuary of Sacred Heart again. And again he saw those crazy old bats at church who were pissed off at Father Stearns.

"I don't care how old and valuable the stained glass windows are," Father S had said. "I don't care if St. Peter himself donated them to Sacred Heart; if the glass breaks it's a safety hazard and the window will have to be replaced."

So much huffing and puffing from those old ladies followed. Someone's rich grandfather had donated the windows at Sacred Heart a hundred years ago. How dare Father Stearns suggest replacing the window? They whined so much that Father S had gathered them around and said, with a straight face that should have won him an Oscar, "If God wants the window to remain in the church, then God can heal the cracks in it Himself. If God wants it gone, he'll leave the job to the glazier. Start praying, ladies."

Usually Father S never got involved with such mundane issues at the church. He had a reputation for being a master delegator. But when it came to the safety of children, he always put his foot down. And when the foot of Father Stearns went down, it never came back up again.

Michael had told himself he was only going to look at the window out of curiosity. Father S had said during Sunday Mass that repairmen were coming to replace it that week. If he wanted to see the spectacularly cracked glass, he needed to do it now. His mom had been out in the entryway with Father S, talking to him in hushed and worried tones. Divorce . . . that's what they were talking about. His parents getting divorced. He didn't want to listen, didn't want to hear Father S telling his mom divorce was a sin and should be avoided at all costs. That's what their old priest said in the last town where they lived. If Father S said that to his mom, then maybe his mom would try to make up with his dad. That was the last thing he wanted. He'd rather live in a cardboard box than under the same roof as his dad again.

He'd rather die.

But what if his mom wanted to get back with his dad? She tried so hard, but they fought so much. Fought all the time. And always about him, their son. Maybe he could run away and then they wouldn't fight anymore if he wasn't there. Maybe he could . . .

He stood in front of the stained-glass window and looked at the scene. He'd never really paid attention to this window before the big broken glass controversy. It depicted an angel standing proud and righteous with tall white wings that reached to the top of the sky, a flaming sword in its hands. A pretty scene. Too bad they'd have to get rid of it. A spiderweb of cracks had appeared at the bottom of the window, and one ran up the center all the way to the angel's chest; a six-foot crack had riven the glass. He ran a finger up one of the cracks, flinching as a sharp edge sliced his finger. A spot of blood appeared on the windowsill. For a few minutes, he could only stare at the darkening spot.

Again he touched the window and left a smear of red on the angel's foot. A piece of glass wiggled under his hand. He dug his fingers into the crack and a shard about four inches long broke off. When he looked down he saw more blood . . . not on the windowsill this time, but on the floor. Good thing it was hardwood . . . Should make it easier to clean.

When he looked up from the pooling blood, he saw Father S rushing toward him, a look of pure terror on his face.

Father S? Terrified? That didn't make any sense. Nothing scared Father S.

"Michael . . . stay with me." He heard Father S's voice in the distance, even though he knew his priest only stood a few feet away. "Help is coming. Don't fall asleep. Stay awake. Talk to me."

"I'll clean the floor," Michael said, but wasn't sure if he said it out loud. He looked up and saw Father S holding him by both wrists. Where had all the blood on Father S's hands come from? Had he cut himself on the window, too?

A mile away he heard a woman screaming. He closed his eyes. When he woke up, he saw gauze.

"Mick? Come on, Mick? Come back to me."

He blinked a few times and looked away from the gauze and into Griffin's hazel eyes. Griffin snapped his fingers again and Michael sat up, pulling the sheets up to his hips. He wasn't quite used to being totally naked in front of someone other than Nora yet.

"I'm sorry, sir." The "sir" came easier than the being naked part did. Michael laughed a little and rubbed his forehead.

"Don't be sorry." Griffin put his hand on the side of Michael's neck. "You want to tell me where you were? Your eyes were open and I said your name about twenty times. You scared the shit out of me."

"I'm sorry. Really sorry. I just woke up and saw the gauze . . ." He held up his wrists, freshly tattooed and gauze-covered. "It brought back memories."

"Bad ones?" Griffin furrowed his brow. Michael didn't like that look. Griffin was gorgeous no matter what look he had on his face, but when he smiled, it was like a bomb went off in the room. A happiness bomb. Nervous, worried—those weren't good looks for him.

"Pretty bad. I'm sorry," Michael said again. "This is our first night in your bed together and I'm being all emo again."

"I love my emo-Mick." Griffin bent forward and kissed him. "You can be as emo as you need to be when you need to be. But if I see you disappearing on me again, I'm going to drag you back to me by your hair if I have to. Fair?" Griffin tugged on his hair hard enough to make the point. The fog of the bad memories had already started to dissipate in Griffin's presence.

"Fair." After all, he could hardly linger in the past when the present moment involved him and a naked Griffin in the biggest, softest, most luxurious bed he'd ever slept in. "I'll try not to go back there. Promise."

"Is gauze a trigger?"

Michael shrugged. Griffin rolled his eyes and sighed before smiling again. He reached out and dragged Michael to him and slammed them both down into the bed.

"Repeat after me, sub," Griffin said, dragging Michael back against his chest. "Ready?"

"*Ready.*"

"Smartass."

"*Smartass.*"

Michael cried out in pain as Griffin bit him hard on the back of the shoulder. The pain sent adrenaline shooting through his body and immediately he felt better. He was even a little turned on.

"I deserved that," Michael said as he relaxed into Griffin's arms.

"You did. Repeat after me: 'I am not a clam.' "

"What?"

"Just say it."

Michael exhaled heavily. "*I am not a clam.*"

"I am a person."

"*I am a person.*"

"I answer the questions that my owner, the devastatingly handsome and charming Griffin Randolfe Fiske, asks me to answer . . ."

"*I answer the questions that my owner, the devastatingly handsome and charming Griffin Randolfe Fiske, asks me to answer . . .*" Michael managed to say all of that without laughing, which made him pretty proud of himself.

"Because I am a person and not a clam."

"Because I am a person and not a clam."

"So stop clamming up." Griffin punctuated the order with another bite. This time the pain also sent blood surging through his body. He felt Griffin starting to get hard against his hip. "I own you, remember? This isn't a game. I can't take care of you if you don't tell me what's going on in your head."

Griffin knocked on Michael's skull like it was a door needing opened. Michael laughed and groaned simultaneously.

"Yes, okay. Gauze is kind of a trigger. I'm alright, I promise."

He'd spent all summer working with Nora on some of his fears and bad memories, on coping techniques to deal with his triggers. Nora had even gotten him to the point he could hold razor blades and other sharp objects without feeling freaked out. Before this summer with Nora, even scissors and butter knives had made his hands a little shaky. He'd forgotten to tell her about the gauze.

"No sub of mine is going to let a Band-Aid beat him. Only I get to beat you. Right?"

"Yes, sir."

"Which is why you're going to talk to me about stuff like this all the time. Because we're together now. I own you. So that means I own your stuff. The bad stuff and the good stuff. It's all mine, just like you're all mine. Got it?"

"I got it."

"So give it up."

Michael took a deep breath. He opened his mouth and then closed it again.

"Mick . . ." Griffin nipped at the back of Michael's neck and placed a kiss on top of the bite. "I'm not going to fuck you again or let you come until you tell me what's going on."

"Okay, so the gauze," Michael began, the words rushing out at breakneck pace, "I slit my wrists, both of them. I don't even remember doing it. I only remember the blood and my mom screaming and Father S trying to keep me conscious. I remember waking up and seeing gauze on my wrists. I lived in gauze for months after that. I couldn't even look when my mom changed the bandages. I closed my eyes and turned my head. I didn't see the scars until three months after I got out of the hospital. All I saw was the gauze."

Michael remembered burying his head against his mom's shoulder as she washed his stitches and changed his bandages night after night. She never said anything during those humiliating tortures at the bathroom sink. She'd work in silence, sometimes crying, sometimes not. Only at the end when it was over would she kiss him on the cheek and tell him she loved him. Once his wrists had healed, she didn't have to deal with the wound washing anymore. Michael almost missed it by then. It was the one time of day he felt close to his mom.

"So gauze makes you think bad things?" Griffin asked, running his hand over Michael's arm from shoulder to wrist and back up again.

"It makes me remember. That's all. I'll get over it. Just . . . bad associations."

"Bad associations. I get it. I do. I got alcohol poisoning once on absinthe and—"

"Absinthe? I thought that was illegal?"

"It is. So is coke too, but that didn't stop me from getting fistfuls of it and shoving it up my nose. Anyway, absinthe has this sort of licorice flavor to it. I can't even smell licorice now without wanting to puke my guts out. That's good though. That bad association will keep me from ever drinking it or any other alcohol again. But you just got some serious ink on your wrists so you'll need the gauze for a few days."

"I know. I know . . . I'll be okay." Michael took a quick and determined breath. "I'll deal with it."

"No, *we'll* deal with it."

Griffin pushed Michael onto his back. Michael wound his arms around Griffin's shoulders as they kissed long and deep, their tongues mingling, their hips pressing into each other. Fucking was a much better idea than talking about Michael's bad associations with gauze.

A low rumbling noise emanated from the area of their stomachs and both he and Griffin paused mid-kiss.

"Wait . . ." Griffin pulled up and looked down at Michael. "Was that your stomach growling or mine?"

"I don't know. I couldn't tell."

"Are you hungry?"

"Starving. But I can wait." Michael hadn't eaten since last night, before the big drama explosion with Griffin running off to confront Father S.

Was that just last night? It seemed like another lifetime, like his entire existence needed to be divided into two parts: Before-Sex-With-Griffin and After-Sex-With-Griffin. This morning he'd woken up in Griffin's bed and they'd had sex for the first time. Then the second time. They'd fallen asleep again and when he'd woken up, he'd seen the gauze staring him down.

"You can wait, but I can't," Griffin said. "I turn into a bear when hungry. Wait. Not a bear. Bad choice of words. I don't suddenly look like a huge gay man with tons of body hair, do I?"

Michael pretended to study him. No excess body hair at all and not an ounce of fat on all those muscles. "No, you're good. You still look metrosexual."

"Thank God. I'm a busy trust fund baby without a real job. I don't have time to get my back waxed. Come on, let's get some food. I'll fuck you later."

"But not much later, right?"

"I mean like in half an hour. Can you wait that long?"

Michael mulled it over. "I'll try. No promises," he said with a ragged, melodramatic sigh.

Griffin laughed as he leaned across Michael and hit the call button on his intercom.

"Alfred!" Griffin yelled loudly enough the intercom box momentarily screamed with feedback. "Are you still awake?"

"No," came the response. Jamison, Griffin's butler, sounded irritated and murderous as usual. "I've died and you are here, Master Griffin. I am in hell."

"Good," Griffin said, not sounding remotely insulted by his butler's bad attitude. "Could you run into Hell's Kitchen and make us some grilled cheeses? Like with the fancy cheese? And some fruit and healthy shit?"

"Yes, Master Griffin. I will use the 'fancy' cheese. And rat poison."

"Extra cheese on mine," Griffin said. "Mick? That sound okay?"

"Sounds great." He was hungry enough he'd even eat non-fancy cheese with rat poison.

"Mick's fine with that."

"I'm pleased to hear your infant approves of the midnight snack selection."

"Can we have orange juice, too?" Griffin asked, winking at Michael. The thought of sixty-something Jamison knowing that he and Griffin were in bed together was slightly mortifying.

"No, you may not. Orange juice is liquid candy," Jamison replied.

"It's good for rehydration. I looked it up on Wiki."

"Wikipedia," Jamison began, his voice dripping with disgust, "is not a resource for researching one's moral quandaries. It is pornography for pseudo-intellectuals."

"Make that two OJ's," Griffin said.

"I pray nightly for the end of your tyranny, Master Griffin."

"Thanks, we'll be down in the dining room in fifteen."

Griffin hit the call button again and the intercom went silent. Griffin threw the sheets off and started gathering their discarded clothes.

"Why does your butler hate you so much?" Michael asked as Griffin tossed him his boxers and t-shirt.

"Alfred? He doesn't hate me."

"He acts like it."

"It only sounds like he hates me because he's British."

Griffin pulled his jeans on and buttoned them, not bothering with underwear. Michael experienced a brief and wonderful fugue state as he stared at Griffin's flat and muscular stomach and that little line of hair disappearing into his low-slung jeans. He even had a little hipbone sticking out. Food . . . What food?

"Mick?" Griffin snapped his fingers again.

"I'm here, I swear. I wasn't in a bad place." Michael forced himself to meet Griffin's eyes.

"Where were you?" Griffin sounded suspicious.

"In your pants."

"Oh . . . that's okay then. Dinner?"

"Dinner."

Jamison had their food waiting for them on the table in the dining room. He'd apparently cooked and returned to bed, so they were not greeted by his ever-charming presence.

"Oh my fucking God . . ." Griffin groaned as he finished his sandwich. "I love fancy cheese."

"It's amazing." Michael ate a little more slowly than Griffin. He sipped at his orange juice as he watched Griffin peel grapes off a stem and pop them into his mouth. "Are you sure it's not poisoned?"

"Nope."

"I'm still going to eat this sandwich though."

"I would. I did. I'm going to see if there's any more left."

Michael sat back and pulled his feet into the chair as he peeled the crusts off the grilled cheese. Alone at the table, Michael finished eating. He felt entirely calm now, at peace, contented. He still couldn't believe this had all happened . . . that Griffin had fallen in love with him and they'd slept together and Griffin even seemed determined they were going to be together now and no one could or would stop them. Nora had even left them earlier that day, left them alone, left Michael in Griffin's care. She saw them as a couple. It was real.

"Are you done eating?" Griffin asked from behind Michael's chair.

"Yeah. That was awesome. Even if Jamison did poison the food, it was a great last meal."

"Want some dessert?"

Michael looked up and saw Griffin standing behind the chair with a wicked smile on his face.

"You're not talking about food, are you?"

Griffin shook his head slowly. The smile got wickeder.

"You know I call this the anal table, right?"

"Right . . ."

"You want to find out why I call it the anal table?"

Griffin took a few steps back, shut the dining room door and locked it behind him. He seemed to have something in his hands.

"Clear the table, Mick," Griffin ordered and Michael rose immediately and started gathering all the plates. He stacked them on the sideboard as Griffin stood by the table and waited, watching him. He'd have to get used to this, jumping at Griffin's command to do whatever he was told. He could get used to this. Truth be told he probably already was used to it.

"Good boy," Griffin said once the table was clear and clean. Griffin crooked his finger at Michael and pointed at the table.

Okay, yeah, he was definitely used to this.

He went to the end of the table and waited. Griffin stood in front of him and put something down behind Michael's back. Michael started to look but Griffin raised his chin.

"Your eyes on my eyes," Griffin said and Michael obeyed.

"Yes, sir."

Michael already felt his blood starting to stir.

"Listen to me . . ." Griffin gathered Michael's t-shirt in his hands and lifted, pulling it off and tossing it on the floor. He ran his hands up and down Michael's shoulders, chest, and stomach. "I'm going to tie you up and I'm going to fuck you. And I'm going to use this to tie you up, okay?" He reached behind Michael and held up a roll of white gauze.

"You are?" Michael's stomach tightened.

"I am. You can safe out now and we'll just go back upstairs and fuck in my bed. But if we're going to do it here we'll use the gauze. You need some better associations. I want to give you and gauze one good, long, hard ass . . . ociation. How does that sound?"

"Amazing, sir."

"Good. Get naked."

Michael slid his boxer shorts off and kicked them aside. Griffin pushed him back onto the table. The cool polished wood beneath his back made him acutely aware of his own body.

Griffin went to the sideboard and opened a drawer. He brought a bottle of lube over and set it next to Michael's hip.

"You keep lube in the dining room?" Michael asked, as Griffin started to unwind a few feet of gauze.

"Trust me, the anal table has earned its name." Griffin grabbed Michael by the forearm and wound two feet of gauze around his already-wrapped wrists. "Tell me if anything gets too tight," Griffin said as he wrapped the gauze around one table leg.

"It's good. I promise, I—" Michael said, but Griffin had disappeared. "Wait. Where—?"

"I'm here." Griffin popped up on the other side of the table. He'd gone under it with the gauze to get to the other side. He took Michael's other wrist and wound the gauze around it.

"Pull a little," Griffin said. Michael tugged, feeling the give in the gauze but also the strength of it. He couldn't get out without cutting it. That was fine. He was okay. Not scared. Not scared at all. "Plenty of give?"

"Yes, sir."

"Good. Now stay there." Griffin gave him a wink that caused Michael to melt like candlewax onto the table. "It's good for the gauze to have some stretch to it since I need to move you . . . right . . . here."

With a gentle tug, Griffin pulled Michael by his thighs to the very edge of the table.

"Pull your knees to your chest," Griffin ordered and Michael obeyed, feeling embarrassed and self-conscious as Griffin applied the lube to him. It felt so weird just lying there while Griffin prepped him. This act, more than anything else so far, made him feel like a piece of property, a body to be used by Griffin for his pleasure, not Michael's. And for some reason that made no sense in his mind but perfect sense to his heart and his body. Being used for Griffin's pleasure gave Michael more pleasure, not less. The more he gave up of himself, the more he got in return.

He started to relax as Griffin inserted two fingers and then three, gently thrusting them in and out. Griffin knew all the right ways to touch him inside.

"You're really good at that," Michael said between breaths.

"I've had some practice."

"Have you . . ." Michael couldn't bring himself to ask the rest of the question.

"Bottomed?" Griffin could apparently speak the language of embarrassed. "Yeah, when I was younger. Never really loved it though. Born to give."

"Born to take." Michael smiled at him.

"You're totally thinking about it now, aren't you? Me getting it up the ass?"

"I really am," Michael said as Griffin opened his jeans and freed his erection. He'd seen a couple pictures of Griffin in his teens and early twenties. Just as gorgeous but with a lot less muscle. "Anyone I know?"

"Let's just say the very last time was about seven years ago. I sort of failed Kingsley's 'Have you ever had sex in the back of a Rolls Royce?' test."

"Awesome."

Michael started to laugh but the laugh died as Griffin started to push into him. For whatever reason—the force, the thrust, the type of lube—the sex felt mind-blowingly good, better than it had even the first and second times they'd done this today.

"God . . ." Michael's back arched off the table.

"Told you this was the anal table for a reason. It's got ass magic, I have no idea why."

"I think it's the angle. Good thrusting angle."

"Good *fucking* angle," Griffin corrected and Michael smiled at the ceiling.

He closed his eyes as Griffin started to move in him harder and deeper. Every thrust worked that magic on him. With each stroke Griffin ran his hands up and down Michael's thighs.

Griffin gave a shuddering breath as he dug his fingers into Michael's skin. "You feel so good, this should be illegal."

"What if it was?"

"I don't care. I'd go to the chair for this."

"The chair . . . like for chair sex?" Michael suggested, raising his head off the table to smile at him.

"Chair sex is on our to do list."

Griffin thrust a few more times before pulling completely out of Michael.

"Come here, sub. I want a new fucking angle."

Michael laughed as Griffin dragged him off the table. The gauze stretched just far enough for Michael to stand at the end of the table with his hips against the edge and his chest and stomach flat on the wood. As soon as Griffin had him in place, he pushed into him again.

"God damn . . ." Griffin groaned as he clamped a hand onto the back of Michael's neck and proceeded to shake the table with thrusts.

Michael could do nothing but relax and take everything Griffin had to give him. Through the haze of sex and sweat, Michael stared at the gauze wrapped around his wrists. It was pretty really, the white crisscrossing pattern, the fabric the color of snow. It was soft, too. Every time he saw it from now on he'd think of this moment bent over a table with the sexiest, funniest, most incredible guy on earth inside him making him feel amazing ten times over.

Griffin's breathing grew heavier, more desperate. His hands scored Michael's back. The pain brought Michael nearly to orgasm, but he held back knowing he shouldn't come without Griffin's permission.

The final few thrusts were so hard they almost hurt. Michael closed his eyes tight as he took them. With a soft grunt, Griffin came inside him. He pulled out slowly and Michael did nothing but lay there on the table breathing.

"Okay," Griffin said, caressing Michael's side from his hip to his shoulder. "That was pretty incredible. Was that incredible for you, too? Because I think my cock is ringing. Is that normal? I don't care. Never mind. Rhetorical question."

Griffin brought out a sharp kitchen knife from the sideboard and sliced through the gauze. He did it far away from Michael, a consideration Michael greatly appreciated. As soon as Michael was free he stood up on shaking legs. Griffin stood behind him and wrapped him up in his tattooed arms.

Griffin started to stroke Michael's erection. "I think we forgot something . . ."

"I hadn't forgotten," Michael said, turning his head for a kiss. "My dick won't let me forget something like that."

"We better head to the living room to take care of this then."

Griffin turned Michael to face him and they lost themselves in one more kiss.

"What's in the living room?" Michael asked as Griffin bit and kissed his neck.

"The oral ottoman."

THE THEORY OF
THE MOMENT

"The Theory of the Moment" *takes place shortly after the end of* The Angel.

Melissa hadn't even set foot in the restaurant yet and she already regretted this idea. It had seemed the right thing to do at the time, the motherly thing to do. But now as she walked into Benno's, a restaurant so fancy it didn't even have its name on the outside, she felt foolish and out of place. Less *mother on a mission* and more *lunatic on a rampage*. But she had to do this—for Michael's sake if not hers.

A waiter in all black greeted her with a smile but with some suspicion in his eyes. Could he tell her dress and shoes were borrowed? Even the necklace was a loaner from a friend whose husband made ten times what she did. If the waiter could tell, it didn't seem to matter much as he ushered her to the back of the restaurant to a table where a man already sat perusing a menu.

"Oh hey," Griffin said, standing up. He waved the waiter off as he pulled out her chair for her. "Glad you found the place."

"I would have never found it. The driver did." She sat down and pulled the chair up to the table. "Thank you for sending the car, by the way. You didn't have to do that. This lunch was my idea."

"Yeah, but the restaurant was mine. I'm kind of in love with this guy, and I'm trying to impress his mom by bringing her here. Do you think it'll work?"

Melissa smiled at him. "Fancy restaurants aren't really what works on worried mothers."

"Damn. I should have stuck with plan A: McDonald's."

"I could have at least worn comfortable shoes there."

"Me too," Griffin said, wincing. Even wincing he was still remarkably handsome in a somewhat unconventional way. Longish and spiky dark hair, a good tan, a wicked smile. Erin would faint the minute she saw him. Unfortunately, it wasn't her daughter this handsome older man was dating. "These shoes are killing me. Would they kick me out if I took them off?"

"You'd look a little strange in that suit with no shoes on."

"The suit's weird, too. I think the last time I wore a suit was to a funeral. Or was it a wedding?" He paused and rubbed his chin. "No, it was a funeral. I wore the kilt to the last wedding I went to."

"You wore a kilt to a wedding?"

"I did. Suddenly I was getting invited to a lot of weddings. Even people I barely know. Anyway, shitty shoes or not, you look really nice."

"Thank you, Griffin. I feel a little out of place."

"Don't. You belong here as much as anyone else. The food is great. I always bring my mom here when we're both in town. Thought you'd like it."

"They serve mom food here then?"

"Moms get their own menu." He winked over the top of his menu.

The waiter came by for a drink order. Griffin said he would stick to mineral water.

"Only water?" she asked after the waiter had gone. "I'm Catholic, you know. Mostly non-practicing these days, but you can drink around me." She wanted to see the real Griffin, not a part he played to impress her.

He shook his head. "I don't drink. But you can. Seriously, I hear they've got a good wine menu."

"No alcohol at all?"

"Nope. I had a problem back when I was in college. Partied a bit too hard. I don't do that stuff anymore—any of it."

"I don't know if I'm comforted by that or scared."

Griffin scratched behind his ear and looked appropriately sheepish. "It's okay to be freaked out. I would be too in your situation."

"And what is my situation?" She put the menu down, food the last thing on her mind.

"You're a single mom with two kids, right?"

"Right."

"You have a daughter living in California, yes?"

"Yes. She went to college there, decided to stay there after she graduated."

"She got away."

Melissa swallowed and nodded. "She got away. Ran away. Escaped, really."

"Can you blame her?" Griffin asked, searching her face.

"I did at first. I was angry that she left. I felt abandoned in the house. My husband . . . ex-husband," she corrected, "wanted a son more than anything. He got a daughter and then proceeded to act like she didn't exist."

"Nice guy."

"It gets better. When he got a son eight years later, he was obsessed with him. Father-son everything all the time. Little League, soccer, weekend fishing trips . . . 'Go take Erin and go shopping, honey. Mikey and I are spending the weekend doing guy stuff.' Didn't even once ask if I might want to go with them, or Erin. We were shut out. And then . . . Michael turned twelve and all hell broke loose."

"The perfect son went weird on Dad?"

"Beyond weird. Something just happened. I don't know what but it was like Michael woke up and decided he had to be someone completely different. He grew his hair out to his shoulders, started staying in his room all the time . . . He'd always been quiet but suddenly he completely stopped talking. Whole days would pass without us hearing a peep out of him. He quit Little League, quit soccer, the Boy Scouts. He started skateboarding everywhere. And he started reading—not normal kids' books. Adult books. Books that scared me when I found them in his room. I lost my son overnight."

"That's the thing, though—you didn't lose your son. Your son finally showed up."

"What do you mean?"

Griffin sat back in the chair. A waiter stopped by and they put in their orders. Melissa was shocked Griffin ordered a salad.

"I'm a health nut," Griffin explained. He must have seen the surprise on her face. "I spent age 16 through 22 trying to kill myself slowly. I have a few years of damage to undo."

"It's fine. Just . . . my husband never ate salads. Called them rabbit food. 'Real men eat meat,' he'd say."

"I'm secure in my manhood enough to eat a salad. Your ex-husband's not even secure enough in his manhood to have a son with long hair."

The waiter returned with drinks and Griffin stared at her over his water glass.

"I'm not ignoring your question," he said. "I'm trying to figure out how to answer it in a way that wouldn't make Mick puke if he overheard us talking. I think the last thing he wants is for me and his mom to talk about his sex life."

Melissa raised her hand and closed her eyes. "Talking about my son's . . . sex life," she forced the words out, "is the very last thing I ever wanted to do either. I'm still trying to recover from some of the things I heard in the kitchen."

"Yeah, the 69-ing was probably too much."

"They don't actually make brain bleach, do they?"

"If they did, my parents would own stock in the company. I get your point. No sex talk. Euphemisms will be our friends. Let's not use words like gay or straight or bi or kinky or anything like that for a minute. Let's just say Mick is an alien. He's from . . . pick a planet."

"Saturn?"

"Saturn—safe choice. This conversation was going to get awkward fast had you picked Uranus."

Melissa laughed behind her hand. She'd come to interrogate Griffin. She didn't need to be laughing at his jokes. He wasn't completely in the clear yet.

"Venus didn't seem safe either."

"Great point. Okay, Saturn then. Mick was born on Saturn. He's an alien. Somehow he made it to earth and ended up your kid. What he did was spend the first twelve years of his life trying to assimilate, trying to fit in with all these weirdo earthlings around him that he didn't even begin to understand. He tried to learn the language, tried to breathe the air. By the time he'd spent twelve years on this planet, he was suffocating."

"Suffocating?"

"Suffocating. So he starts to revert back to what he really is—this alien from Saturn. Wonder what they'd be called. Saturner? Saturonians? Saturpudlians? Never mind. The point is that when he became this thing you didn't recognize, that was when he started to become himself again."

"He did seem alien to me then."

"Because he was alien. At least in that house."

"I did everything I could to help him," she said, trying to keep the anger from her voice.

"I know you did. Mick told me. He told me you tried taking him to therapy, talking to him. He said you read at least a million books on the psychology of children and teenagers."

"I'm a nurse. We see someone hurting, we do whatever we can to make him or her better."

"But Michael wasn't sick. That's the thing. You were treating him like he was actually sick instead of what he really was."

"And what was he?" she demanded, curious what this rich boy who'd known her son three months thought he knew about her child.

"He was homesick. That's all. When Mick tried to kill himself, he didn't want to die. He'd spent fourteen years of his life breathing the wrong atmosphere. When he slit his wrists, he was just trying to go back home, back to where he could breathe again."

"He told you all this?"

"Believe it or not, your son and I do more talking than anything else."

"That is hard to believe. He's not a talker."

"He talks to me."

"Why?" She sat her fork down in frustration. "Why you and not me? I begged him to talk to me for years and got nowhere."

"That's a pretty easy answer. He talks to me and not you because I speak his language. You don't."

"I guess you're from Saturn, too?"

"Nope. Born and bred on earth. But . . . even though I'm an earthling, I never felt quite comfortable here. Something was off with me, something wasn't right. I drank too much, did a lot of stuff I shouldn't have done. Anything to drown that feeling that I was supposed to go somewhere, do something . . . I just didn't know what or where. It was like a splinter I couldn't dig out. Then . . ."

"Then?"

"Then when I was about twenty-two, someone from Saturn found me and said I needed to come visit. I went to the planet and decided to adopt it as my home. I've been living there ever since. That's why I can talk to Mick and you can't."

"So . . . do I want to know what Saturn is like?"

Griffin twirled a fork between his fingers. "It's a lot like France actually."

Melissa laughed as she started to pick at her food. "France. Lovely."

"It really is. There are good people there. Complicated but good. A different kind of good than this world is used to. Mick's one of the Saturnites, and they take good care of him there. Things that make him stick out like a sore thumb in this world? Totally normal there. But the most important thing—when he's there, he can breathe."

"I want my son to be able to breathe. I used to . . ." She paused as her voice caught in her throat. "After he tried to kill himself, listening to him breathe became an obsession of mine. You do it when you're a new mother with a baby. Babies . . . they're awful people. They'll stop breathing on you every now and then just to make sure you're paying attention. They go so quiet and still that your heart stops. And here I was with a fourteen-year-old with scars on his wrists and scars in his heart, and the only thing I could do was make sure he kept breathing."

"He's lucky to have you. You cared. You tried. You did everything you knew to do for him. There are kids out there who were just like Mick whose parents didn't give a damn when they were suffocating. They let them suffer, let them die. You kept him alive long enough to find his way home again. You have nothing to be ashamed of."

"You're very kind to say that, Griffin. I want you to know I don't dislike you. In fact, I like you very much. I'm so grateful that you were able to get my ex-husband away from my son and out of our lives. I want to thank—"

"Don't thank me. Seriously. I don't want you to thank me. Listen . . ." Griffin started to take a bite of his salad but he seemed to rethink it. He put his fork down, pushed his food to the side. "You know Nora Sutherlin, right?"

Melissa nodded an affirmative. She hadn't quite come to terms with her feelings about the enigmatic Nora Sutherlin and her place in her son's life.

"I suppose Ms. Sutherlin is also . . . from Saturn?"

"Ms. Sutherlin happens to be the Queen of Saturn. We also have a king and a pope."

"How medieval."

"Very. But we like that sort of thing. Well, about Queen Nora . . . she has this idea. She calls it 'The Theory of the Moment.' She believes that every person is born for one single moment in their lives, born for one purpose. Basically the whole world is a stage, we're all actors, and each one of us has a part in this play. And they're all important parts—even if it's one line or a starring role. She says we all get a chance for our 'moment,' and that moment is the reason we're born."

Griffin stopped and took a sip of his water. He set the glass down and took a quick breath.

"Slamming your asshole husband into the wall to keep Mick from hearing his father calling him a 'fag'? That was my moment. I know it in my soul. I know it better than I know my own name. I was born for that moment in your kitchen two days ago when I paid off your ex and got him out of your life, out of Mick's life. I'm sure that fucker called Mick a fag before. He might even try to do it again. But that day, Mick didn't have to hear it and he didn't have to hear it because of me. I made sure of it. I just thank God I didn't miss my cue."

Melissa picked up her napkin and wiped the tears off her face. "But you've had your moment now. What's left? What now?"

"Everything's gravy at this point. I delivered my line in the divine comedy that is life on earth. So what now? I think I'll just hang out with your son for the rest of my life and watch the rest of the show."

Melissa took a few cleansing breaths.

"Okay," she said, nodding. "My son is dating a man. This is going to take a little getting used to. I can do it. I will do it. It's just . . . give me a little time. We weren't raised to think being gay or bisexual was okay. The Church, you know . . ."

"I know. Trust me, I know. You don't have to think of Michael as gay or straight or bi. He's just . . . he's your son. You're not sleeping with him so why should you care if he's gay, straight or bi?"

"Good point," she said.

"He's dating a guy. That's what you need to know. And I'm the guy. But who knows? He might end up with a girl someday. Probably not though. He finds some women attractive but because of what he is—a Saturner, I mean. A 'normal' relationship isn't going to work for him. And you're going to have to prepare yourself for that. He might get married to a girl someday. Probably not though. He might have kids someday. Probably not though. He might get a buzz cut and a job as a lumberjack or a stock broker."

"Probably not though," Melissa finished for him.

"Right."

"You keep saying 'he might do this, he might do that.' All that stuff he might do . . . he would do it without you. Getting married, falling for a woman . . ."

Griffin pulled his plate back in front of him. If they didn't stop talking, their food would get soggy. Didn't matter really. Melissa cared much more about knowing who her son was than eating.

"I'm not an idiot," Griffin said, wiping his mouth with the napkin. "I'm older than him by a lot. On Saturn, big age difference relationships are pretty standard. Two guys, two women, poly-couples, open relationships, trios . . . We just do things a little different. But I know any couple faces the risk of a break-up."

"I can testify to that."

"Exactly. More relationships end than last forever. My father was married for fifteen years and had four kids, gets divorced and swears off women for the rest of his life. Then he meets my mom who was a nineteen-year-old *Vogue* cover model. Marries the model after knowing her one month, has me a year later. They've been together thirty years and are still happy, still in love, and it's still gross to me. God damn, it should be illegal for parents to make out in front of their children."

"I can't argue with your logic. My ex-husband and I are the same age, went to the same college, dated two years before getting married. We did everything right, everything the 'normal' way, and we see how well that turned out."

"You got Mick out of that deal. You've got nothing to regret."

"I try to tell myself that."

"Listen to me, Melissa . . . is it okay if I call you that?"

"Better than Mrs. Dimir."

"Can I call you 'Mom'?"

"Never in a million years."

"Fair enough. Here's the thing, Melissa . . . I don't know for sure about this but there's a damn good chance that this is your moment. There are kids out there just like your son who get destroyed by living on this planet. They can't breathe the air around them so they find a way to leave this earth. Sometimes it's drugs. Sometimes it's booze. Sometimes it's self-destructive promiscuity. Sometimes they cut out the middleman and blow their brains out on the kitchen floor. I know what I'm talking about. I had a gay friend in high school who came out to his parents. He tried to kill himself. He survived the first attempt. He didn't survive the second."

Melissa stared at Griffin, unable to speak. She heard the warning in his words.

"Look . . ." Griffin reached across the table and took her hand in his. "You have the chance right now to accept your son. I'm not talking about 'tolerating' him. Tolerance is a slap in the face. You tolerate your noisy neighbors. You love your son. You love him, you accept him, you cheer him on, and you don't judge him for one second. You tell him God made him the way he is because that's the part he's meant to play. And when Mick's onstage having his moment, you stand up and applaud. He loves me, he's crazy about me. But that doesn't change the fact you're his mom. This could be your moment."

"You think it is?"

Griffin squeezed her fingers and let her hand go. "Maybe. Maybe not. But if it is, trust me, you don't want to miss it. Because if you hit it just right it feels like the whole damn world is on its feet applauding you. And you get to keep that feeling for the rest of your life."

"I won't miss my cue, I promise."

"I believe you."

"But you have to promise me something."

"Anything."

"You can't hurt my son. You can't break his heart. You can't break his spirit. I know I'm not a big part of the equation of his life anymore. It happened with Erin and now it's happening with Michael. The first few years they can't live without you.

They hit sixteen, seventeen, eighteen, and suddenly they can't live with you. That's okay. Went through it with my own parents. Cycle of life and I know that. I also know if I told Michael he couldn't see you again, he'd cut me out of the equation entirely. He starts college in a couple weeks and he's on a full-ride scholarship. He doesn't even need me to feed him or put a roof over his head anymore. But I don't want to lose him. Two days ago when Michael hugged me and told me he missed me, that was the first time in five years I felt like I had my son back."

"You're not going to lose your son. You and I are Team Michael, okay? I know he's not one-hundred percent. I know he still has nightmares, still has bad days, still has flashbacks and fears. I know he was on meds but stopped taking them because of the side effects. The Prozac gave him insomnia. The Lexapro made him a zombie. It makes me nervous that he's off meds."

"Glad I'm not the only one."

"So I'm going to keep tabs on him. I have the world's coolest therapist. Mick's going to see her once a month just to be on the safe side. I've been clean and sober for over six years and I still go to see her. I got that part covered."

"You go to a therapist?"

"Wasn't my idea. My parents said 'go to her or you're cut off.' They were right to make me go. She's like a priest, you know. You can tell her anything and she just listens. Does it freak you out I have a therapist?"

"Sorry. My ex-husband . . ."

"Let me guess. Thought therapy was for girls and losers."

"Those might have been his exact words."

Griffin leaned forward and rested his arms on the table. Sitting like that, Griffin's already broad shoulders looked even broader, his cocky smile even cockier, his large strong hands even larger.

"One question: Do I look like a girl or a loser to you?"

For a single split second Melissa saw Griffin the way Michael must see him—strong, tough, handsome, and so completely comfortable with himself that every smile practically dared the world to have a problem with him. The world wisely kept its mouth shut.

"That would be a 'no.' "

"Thought so."

"So therapy, that's great. What can I do?" she asked.

"Keep Dad out of his life, out of his face." Griffin leaned back again. "I don't care if your ex-husband starts sniffing around again, apologizing, promising he's changed. It's bullshit and you know it."

"Trust me, I know it."

"You keep him out of Mick's life entirely. If he gives you any trouble, any at all, you call me right away, and I'll call the lawyers."

"I can do that," she said, grateful to have a partner in this fight, someone on her side. Father Stearns had done everything he could for Michael but what would a celibate Catholic priest really know about a kid like her son with his sort of sexual proclivities? "What else?"

"Just love your son. Don't freak out when he talks about me. I'm a fact of his life now. He and I will be spending a lot of time together, going on trips together . . . even if it bugs you, don't let on. Just tell him to be safe and have a nice time. Make it safe for Mick to be himself around you."

"Lot of time together . . . Do I want to know how much time?" she asked.

"He's going to stay with me on the weekends. Every weekend."

"Oh, God—"

"Hey, he could have gone off to college in California like your daughter," Griffin said, giving her a stern look. This was a man staking his claim. "Could be a whole lot worse than Mick on the other side of the country. He'll be in the city with me. And if you want to see him on the weekends, you can as long as Mick wants that. And I'm sure he does."

"Really?"

"Really. I'm not stealing him from you. I'm inviting you into our life. And it is our life and you'll be an honored guest in it if that's what you want, if you can be the cool mom who is okay with her son having a boyfriend. If you can't . . ."

Griffin's voice trailed off and the threat hung in the air between them. If she couldn't accept their relationship then she couldn't see Michael. There it was laid out before her—the choice and the consequences. Michael belonged to Griffin now. She didn't quite understand how or why but she knew it was true. So if she wanted to see her son, she went through Griffin. And that was that.

"I've never been the cool mom."

"Never too late. Look at you. You're a stone cold fox. You look younger than you are, you're pretty and single. I would totally fix you up with my half-brother Aiden in a heartbeat. He's your age, rich, divorced, one kid about to start college too. Super nice guy. He even puts up with me."

"I think that could get . . . weird."

"Weird is my middle name. That's not true. It's Randolfe. But I get it. Offer's always on the table."

"Thank you. I'll keep that in mind."

Griffin paid the check without even looking at the bill.

"Ready? Let's get out of here," he said as they got up and headed to the door.

"It was a lovely lunch. You didn't have to buy. This was my idea."

"I'm twelve years older than your son, and I'm a dude with tattoos and a history of drug addiction. This is only the first of many fancy 'suck up to mom' lunches."

"That's very sweet of you," she said as they stepped out onto the street. Griffin paused and they stood awkwardly looking at each other. She couldn't blame her son for wanting to be around this man all the time, basking in his warmth, his light. She almost envied her son for having this guardian angel around. Angel . . . "By the way, Michael's new tattoos?"

Griffin winced. "Yeah?"

"They're beautiful."

Griffin grinned broadly and for a moment his smile eclipsed the sun.

"See? Now that's what the cool mom would say," he said.

"Trying."

"You're a natural at this."

A cab came by the curb and Griffin waved it off. He snapped his fingers and rocked back and forth on his heels.

"Something wrong, Griffin?"

"Still hungry. Why did I just order the salad?"

"You said you were a health nut."

"Yeah, and I'm full of shit. Ice cream? That's a health food, right?"

"If you get strawberry it counts as a serving of fruit. I'm a nurse. You can trust me. I'm a medical professional."

"Melissa," he said, linking her arm into his as they strode off toward Central Park in search of ice cream, "I think this is the start of a beautiful friendship."

THE COUCH

"The Couch" takes place shortly after the end of The Angel.

Michael blamed the couch.

He couldn't figure out anyone or anything else to blame. He paced around the living room currently devoid of any furniture but for the couch and an ebony coffee table.

Having no experience in these matters, Michael decided to call the most experienced person he knew. He pulled out his cell phone and dialed up Nora. On the third ring she answered in a slightly breathless, giddy voice. Glad someone was having a good evening. His sucked and was getting worse by the second.

"Did I interrupt something?" Michael asked.

"Nah, just reading the dirty parts of *Atlas Shrugged* again. What's up, Angel?"

"Griffin and I got in a fight," Michael confessed immediately, sitting on the floor and pulling his legs to his chest.

"Aww . . ." she said, almost laughing. "Your first fight. This is one for the scrapbook. Please tell me it's about something totally stupid."

"It's about the new couch," Michael said in utter misery.

"Perfect."

"It's not funny, Nora. Griffin walked out. I keep trying to call him, and he won't answer."

The panic in his voice must have gotten to her.

"Tell me what happened."

"Okay, so I had this big Econ test to study for. But Griffin wants to go furniture shopping. So we went yesterday and spent like eight hundred hours picking out one couch."

"Sounds like Griffin. When he and I went shopping for his Porsche, he test-drove every car on the lot. Even identical models. He said he had to know how the different paint jobs felt."

"Right. He's nutty about this stuff," Michael said, glad to know Nora understood. "So Friday was furniture shopping so today was supposed to be me studying for my test. But he wouldn't let me. First he wanted to have sex, which I didn't complain about. Then he took me to lunch. Then we went to Shakespeare in the Park—"

"That's fucking enchanting right there," Nora said.

Michael ignored her. "Then he made me do even more furniture shopping. Finally, I said I couldn't hang out with him anymore today, or I'd flunk my test. He said he didn't understand why I was stressing so much. And I said . . ."

Michael paused and closed his eyes tight. Now he remembered. Wasn't the couch's fault at all.

"What did you say, Angel?" Nora asked gently.

"I said that unlike him, I cared about graduating from college."

He heard Nora's sharp intake of breath on the other end of the line. "Ouch," she said.

"I know." Michael rubbed at his face. He still couldn't believe he'd said that. Griffin was wicked smart. It wasn't the absence of intelligence that kept Griffin from graduating from Brown but the presence of a drug problem, which he'd faced and conquered.

"I only meant that he's, you know, rich, but I'm going to need to get a job someday. He's going to dump me, and I totally deserve it."

"Relax. Griffin's so in love with you he can't see straight. He's probably out there walking, trying to clear his head. That's all."

"What if he's not? What if it's worse than that?"

"Michael, Griffin's been clean and sober for years now. One fight with you is not going to send him racing to an opium den or whatever the hip new drug trend is now."

"I think opium dens went out two centuries ago."

"Really? I thought I was just at one the other night. Or was that a hookah bar?"

Michael opened his eyes. The couch was sitting there, taunting him. Griffin said he wanted something simple. Michael heard "simple" and thought "IKEA." Griffin's version of simple was made of Italian leather and cost ten thousand dollars.

"I still don't get the couch thing," Michael said, staring at the massive black leather work of art sitting in front of him. "It's his money, his apartment. Why does he want me to pick out the furniture?"

"Michael. Darling. Angelfish. Allow me to state the obvious here for a moment. You are a freshman in college with about zero money to your name, yes?"

"Yes."

"And Griffin is a twenty-nine-year-old trust fund baby."

"True."

"Have you considered that maybe Griffin wants you to pick out the furniture for the apartment so it would feel like your home instead of just his?"

For almost a full ten seconds Michael sat in silence.

"No. Hadn't thought of that."

"You know you're Griffin's first serious relationship, right?"

"He's my first serious relationship, too. One of us needs to know what we're doing."

"Nobody knows what they're doing."

"Is there like *Same Sex Relationships for Dummies* out there?" Nora wrote erotica novels. Surely she would have heard of such a thing.

"You don't need it even if there was. Same sex, opposite sex, kinky sex. All relationships are hard. Even the good ones. I know Griffin. I've known that sexy twerp for years. He's out walking right now trying to figure out what to do, and he'll be back any minute. So relax."

"I can't relax."

"You better relax that tight ass of yours. Soon as he gets back you'll spend five minutes talking about it and the next three hours fucking."

"I hope so," Michael said, not feeling the slightest bit sexy right now. But he'd do anything Griffin wanted as long as he walked through that door safe and sound. "He'll probably never forgive me for saying what I did."

"I'm kind of proud of you myself. That's some feisty shit there. Griffin's been handed everything he's ever wanted in his life. Other than getting clean, you're the only thing he's ever had to work for."

Michael shook his head. "I belong to him. He doesn't have to work for me at all."

"Well, for God's sake don't tell him that."

Michael opened his mouth to say something but he stopped when he heard the sound of keys in the door.

"He's home. I gotta go," Michael said, and hung up just as he heard Nora laughing out an "I told you so."

Pulling himself off the floor, Michael shoved his phone back in his pocket and raced to the front door. Griffin let out a surprised sort of "uff" sound as Michael launched himself into his arms.

"God, I'm so glad you're back," Michael said as Griffin wrapped his strong arms around him. "I'm sorry. I'm so freaking sorry. I can't believe I said that. I'm on a scholarship so I have to keep my GPA up. I got stressed out and took it out on you and I didn't mean it. And—"

"Mick, calm the fuck down," Griffin said, pulling back and looking at him. "I'm not mad."

Michael nearly collapsed onto the floor in relief. "But . . ." he sputtered. "I called you like a million times and you didn't answer."

Griffin grinned sheepishly. "Battery died. Forgot to charge my phone last night. Was a little preoccupied."

Michael blushed. Last night Griffin had instructed him in the art of giving a good blowjob. Way more fun than studying Macroeconomics. "Where did you go?"

"Just out walking. Trying to think things out. Look, Mick, I'm sorry for being so demanding. I don't get to see you during the week so I sort of forgot that you don't completely belong to me on the weekends."

Michael shook his head. "I belong to you all the time."

He reached out and gripped the fabric of Griffin's black shirt. Griffin covered Michael's hands with his. "You do, do you?"

"Yes, sir," Michael said. Griffin raised his eyebrow at him. One surefire way to get Griffin in the mood was to call him "sir." Michael called him that as much as possible.

Griffin ran his hands up Michael's arms and grasped him by the shoulders. Michael quickly found his back pressed to the door and Griffin's body pushing hard into him.

Panting slightly, Michael waited as Griffin brought his lips to Michael's mouth and let them hover only a hairsbreadth apart. Griffin, such a master tease.

"I have an idea," Griffin whispered. "Why don't you go get ready for me and meet me in bed in ten minutes?"

Swallowing, Michael felt every muscle in his body tensing. "I have a better idea," he answered.

"Do you? I'm open to suggestions."

"Maybe . . ." Michael said, tilting his hips forward to meet Griffin's. "Maybe we should meet on the new couch."

Griffin's sculpted lips curled into a cocky grin. "See? You don't need to study, Mick. You're already a genius." Griffin pressed his lips to Michael's and slipped his tongue in his mouth. Groaning softly, Michael dug his fingers into Griffin's forearms.

Suddenly Griffin pulled back and chucked Michael under the chin in a way Michael found infuriatingly fatherly and annoyingly attractive.

"Ten minutes," Griffin said.

Michael headed immediately for the bathroom while Griffin went into their bedroom to gather the usual supplies.

Before leaving the bathroom, Michael paused and glanced at himself in the mirror. He dug through a drawer and found the tube of eyeliner Nora had given him as a gag gift when he and Griffin had made their relationship official. As excited as he was, it took Michael a full two minutes to line his eyes without smearing it everywhere. When he finally got it perfect, he took a deep breath and went straight to the living room.

Michael's knees nearly buckled when he saw Griffin. Griffin was lounging on the large black leather couch with one leg crossed over his knee, his arm draped across the back. A dozen or more candles burned on the ebony coffee table. The flickering light danced in Griffin's dark eyes. Griffin didn't smile, only stared at him. Michael could barely feel his feet as he walked toward the couch and knelt on the floor.

"Like the eyeliner," Griffin said, tracing the outline of Michael's face. "But you knew that already."

Michael glanced at the candles. Just seeing them burning on the table ratcheted up his hunger for Griffin even more. Then he noticed the wax from the candles had started to melt onto the new coffee table. "Shit, sir. The table—"

"Don't care," Griffin said. "We'll buy another one."

Michael smiled. Every time Griffin said "we," Michael fell in love with him a little bit more.

"But not while you're studying," Griffin finished. "Right?"

"Right."

Griffin crooked his finger, beckoning Michael to join him on the couch.

As soon as Michael sat on the couch, Griffin grabbed him and pulled him close, kissing him long and deep on the mouth. His lips moved to Michael's cheek, to his ear, to his throat. Michael ran his hands up and down Griffin's back, relishing the feel of his muscles underneath the smooth fabric of his shirt.

Griffin's hands roamed over Michael's chest and arms. Sighing with exasperation, Griffin grabbed a handful of t-shirt and pulled it off Michael.

"Much better," Griffin said as he placed a series of light kisses across Michael's chest.

Michael's erection pushed against the zipper of his jeans. He ached to be naked and underneath Griffin. But he waited impatiently, letting Griffin take the lead as Griffin liked to do.

"Do you want pain tonight?" Griffin asked into the hollow of Michael's throat. "I'll take your cock twitching against my hip just now as a 'yes.' "

"It's a 'yes,' " Michael answered breathlessly.

Griffin unzipped Michael's pants. He pulled them down Michael's legs and tossed them into the corner of the room. Breathing a sigh of relief to be naked for Griffin again, Michael stretched out and luxuriated on the insanely expensive couch. The leather felt like warm supple skin underneath him. Maybe it was worth all ten grand Griffin paid for it.

Dipping his head, Griffin pressed slow sensual kisses across Michael's stomach and hips. Michael didn't even let himself get his hopes up for kisses on other parts. Griffin enjoyed teasing him too much. As Griffin bit lightly at Michael's hipbone, he reached out and picked up one of the candles. Michael tensed in anticipation.

"Beg for it," Griffin said, letting the candle hover over the center of Michael's chest. Michael had strong masochistic tendencies, which Griffin delighted in playing with.

"Please, hurt me, sir," he whispered, nearly choking on his need. Griffin let the first drop of scalding candle wax land on the center of Michael's chest. Michael arched and panted. Another splash landed on his ribcage. Another on his stomach. It burned for only a few seconds before cooling and congealing. But in those few seconds, the agony became ecstasy.

Griffin let a few drops hit his inner thighs perilously close to Michael's testicles. The fear mixed with pain mixed with love and pleasure brought Michael dangerously close to coming from the erotic torture of the candle wax alone. But Michael knew the rule: Griffin comes first. So he breathed deep to calm himself as Griffin wiped the wax off his body.

"Now," Griffin said sitting back at the opposite end of the couch, "you did smart off to me today. Are you sorry about that?"

"Very much, sir."

"Do you want to show me how sorry?"

"Definitely, sir."

Michael crawled forward and started to unbutton Griffin's shirt. With each button he opened, Michael pressed a kiss onto Griffin's chest. Down his chest, down his stomach until he stopped when he reached Griffin's pants. His hands nearly shaking with desire, Michael unbuttoned and unzipped Griffin's pants.

For a second Michael just stared at Griffin's body.

"Something on your mind, Mick?" Griffin asked, and Michael heard the smile in his voice.

"I love your cock," Michael said, taking it in his hands. Not just long but thick, Griffin's cock should have scared the hell out of him. But while Griffin might have a blast inflicting pain on

Michael during their kinky foreplay, he did everything he could to avoid causing Michael any pain during sex.

"It loves you," Griffin said, smiling down at him. Michael bent and took the straining crown between his lips and teased it with his tongue. He tasted a drop of pre-come on the tip and swallowed it eagerly. Slowly he moved down taking Griffin deeper and deeper into his mouth. Griffin dug his hand into the back of Michael's hair.

As Michael kissed and sucked with his tongue and lips, his fingers wandered over Griffin's hard, flat stomach. Griffin's hips rose and fell to the rhythm of Michael's mouth.

"We should fight more often if this is how you behave afterwards," Griffin said, chuckling softly.

"We don't have to fight for me to want to do this," Michael said, hoping they never fought again. Although he had to admit, the making up part made it almost worth it.

Michael ran his hand up and down Griffin's straining shaft, gripping it firmly as he'd been taught to do. He started to take Griffin in his mouth again but a hand on his chin stopped him.

"Now," Griffin ordered and Michael moved into position—on his hands and knees, his thighs apart and his back flat. He closed his eyes and started taking deep calming breaths as Griffin uncapped the lube. Slowly, gently, Griffin worked his fingers inside Michael.

"Relax, Mick," Griffin said, running his free hand over Michael's lower back, buttocks and thighs.

"Trying."

"Stop trying so hard."

Michael laughed a little as Griffin spread his fingers apart inside him. It hurt and felt amazing at the same time. Griffin went back to two fingers and pushed in even deeper. Michael gasped when Griffin found his G-spot and began gently kneading it.

"Oh, God—" Michael's entire back tensed with pleasure.

"Do you like that?"

"Fuck yes."

"And this?" Griffin reached between Michael's legs and cupped his testicles in his large warm hand.

Michael couldn't even answer with anything other than a groan.

"I'll take that as a 'yes' as well," Griffin teased. "You want me inside you, don't you?"

"Yes, sir," Michael panted. "So much."

"On your stomach."

Griffin's fingers slid out of Michael as he stretched out flat on his stomach. Griffin lay on top of him and pulled them both onto their sides.

"Lift your knee to your chin," Griffin ordered and Michael obediently raised his leg. He loved how in charge Griffin was during sex, how experienced. His prowess relaxed Michael more than anything else. Serious relationships might be new to both of them, but when it came to amazing sex, Griffin knew exactly what he was doing.

Griffin rarely gave Michael a verbal warning before penetrating him. Any sort of warning would cause Michael to tense—the last thing they wanted. So instead they just lay spooned together for a few minutes as Griffin kissed Michael's shoulders, neck and back while gently rubbing his cock against Michael's thighs. Michael turned his head and his mouth met Griffin's. Their tongues leisurely intermingled. As Michael lost himself in the kiss, the heat of Griffin's chest to his back, and the comfort of such strong arms holding him, Griffin pushed the crown of his penis into Michael.

Michael closed his eyes tight but refused to let himself tense up. Griffin had warned him the anal sex would take a little getting used to. Michael had loved fucking like this since their first night together. But it wasn't something they could really do hard or fast or particularly spontaneously just yet. Michael would never forget their first time together. Griffin had been so patient with him as he spent half an hour working himself all the way in. The night had been so sensual, so special . . . Now, Michael panted with pleasure as Griffin pushed in deeper—sensual and special, like every time with Griffin.

"Good?" Griffin asked as he pressed in a little more.

"Very good," Michael answered honestly. No pain, no discomfort, just . . . "Holy fuck, that's awesome."

"What is?" Griffin teased. "Me fucking your ass while stroking your cock? Or the couch?"

Michael couldn't help but laugh. "It is a nice couch," he said.

Griffin moaned softly as he bit the back of Michael's neck.

"I love it when you laugh when I'm in you. I can feel your ass tighten around me."

That made Michael laugh even more. As he laughed, Griffin pushed the last few inches up and into him. The laughter stopped as Michael inhaled sharply at the sudden stab of ecstasy.

"I hope you're enjoying this, Mick," Griffin rasped into his ear, "because I'm not going to be able to stop fucking you for about three hours."

"That's fine," Michael said. "I don't need to be able to walk to study."

"Walking's overrated," Griffin said, lightly teasing the tip of Michael's aching cock. "I definitely prefer you on your hands and knees. But maybe we'll do that next."

Sighing, Michael pressed his back into Griffin's chest again as the speed of the thrusts increased. But before either of them could come, Griffin pulled out and put Michael onto his back. Without having to be told, Michael pulled his knees into his chest as Griffin pushed into him again.

Griffin reached over Michael's head and gripped the arm of the couch as he worked his hips harder and faster. Michael briefly wondered if the snooty old lady at the furniture store would have a stroke if she saw how her customers were breaking their new purchase in. She worked on commission, Michael consoled himself. She'd be fine.

Once more Griffin took Michael into his hand and rubbed him in long, firm strokes that left Michael writhing and moaning underneath him.

"Sir . . ." He had to come, needed to come, but wasn't allowed to come until Griffin did. "Please . . ."

"I love it when you beg," Griffin said, smiling down at him. "You're getting really good at it. Say 'please' again."

For all the teasing, Michael could hear the hoarse desperation in Griffin's tone. He couldn't hold back much longer either.

"Please, sir. Come in me," Michael said, too turned on to even blush. Griffin loved making him talk dirty even though it humiliated him. Of course part of Michael loved being humiliated, so really it was a win-win.

"One more."

Michael's back arched off the ten-thousand dollar couch as he cried out another "please."

Griffin's hips pumped into him as his breathing grew faster and more ragged. Finally Griffin pushed in one final time. Michael gasped as he felt the wet heat of Griffin's semen pouring into him. Griffin's orgasm seemed to go on forever. Michael loved hearing Griffin come—his ragged breathing, his shuddering gasps.

Michael wrapped his arms around Griffin's strong shoulders as Griffin assaulted him with kisses.

"You want to come?" Griffin asked into Michael's lips.

"Yes, sir."

"I think you've earned it."

Griffin stayed inside Michael as he sat up on his knees. He rubbed Michael's cock hard and fast. Michael's hips tensed, his legs strained, his whole body went rigid as come shot out of him and sprayed his own stomach and chest.

For the second time tonight his body had been covered with something white and sticky. Except now Griffin didn't wipe it off with his hands. He dipped his head and licked it off Michael's skin.

Michael reached out and twined his hands in Griffin's hair as Griffin's tongue lapped every drop of Michael's semen off his body. He'd never seen anything in the world more erotic than the wicked dirty grin Griffin flashed him just before he licked the final drop off his chest. When Griffin's mouth met his, Michael could taste himself.

Slowly Griffin pulled out of him.

He looked down at Michael.

"Now . . . I think we said something about you on your hands and knees?" Griffin asked.

Michael sat up. He felt tired and languid, the way he always felt after a good orgasm.

Before Michael could move into position, Griffin pulled him close again. Griffin kissed Michael's neck and shoulders as Michael rested his back into Griffin's chest.

"Did you enjoy that?" Griffin asked, as he ran his hands over Michael's thighs.

"You know I did, sir."

"I like to hear it."

Michael grinned as he relaxed against Griffin's muscular frame. "I love it when you fuck me. It feels amazing. I wish we could do it every day."

Griffin laughed in his ear.

"You want to quit college just so I can fuck you more often?"

"I just wish I could switch my major from 'Art' to 'Fucking.' I'll talk to my advisor next week," Michael offered.

"Do that. In the meantime, we'll just keep it as an extracurricular activity."

He could feel Griffin growing hard again.

Michael straddled Griffin's lap and slowly Griffin pushed into him again.

He liked this position, though they didn't do it very often since Michael was usually tied down during sex. On his knees with his back to Griffin, Michael could control the speed and depth of penetration. Michael moved up and down on Griffin's cock while Griffin caressed Michael's back and sides with his fingertips.

"You're beautiful, Mick," Griffin said as he brushed Michael's long hair to the side so he could kiss the back of Michael's neck. "Even if you are a smart-ass."

"I didn't mean to be," Michael protested, half-laughing. "I'm so sorry."

"I'm fucking your ass for the second time tonight. Safe to say 'apology accepted.' "

Griffin grabbed Michael by the hips and pushed him down hard onto his lap. Michael gasped at the sudden depth of penetration as Griffin thrust his hips up and came in him again.

"Hands and knees now?" Michael asked as Griffin panted in his ear.

"Yes. But not you."

Griffin lifted Michael off him and pushed him onto his back once more. They kissed hard and deep as Griffin held himself over Michael on his hands and knees.

Slowly Griffin kissed his way down Michael's body, lingering over his stomach. Michael thought he'd die if Griffin didn't hurry up and—

"Oh, God," Michael said. Griffin wrapped his mouth and tongue around Michael's cock and sucked it in deep. Griffin didn't stop there. He elbowed Michael's thighs open and pushed a finger into him. Michael loved having his G-spot rubbed. And Griffin knew just how to do it—gentle circles, light taps, thorough kneading.

Michael's fingers dug into Griffin's strong shoulders. Even if he failed his test, lost his scholarship, and flunked out of school, he would say the weekend had been a success for the Griffin blowjob alone. God, Griffin was good at this.

Griffin's tongue swirled around Michael's shaft from the base to the tip and back down again. Michael arched into Griffin's mouth and came so hard he nearly slid off the Italian leather onto the floor.

"Wow," Michael said as his ability to see straight slowly came back to him. "I love this couch."

Griffin crawled up Michael's body and collapsed on top of him. "I love you," he said.

Michael smiled tiredly at him. "I love you, too. And this couch."

"We probably should have gotten some leather cleaner at the store," Griffin said. Michael felt a small wet spot of lube and semen underneath him on the upholstery.

Michael shrugged. "We'll flip the cushions."

"I threatened to fuck you for three hours, didn't I?" Griffin asked.

"You did. And it's only been one hour."

Griffin dropped his head and kissed Michael's chest and throat. "I have a better idea."

"I'm actually terrified right now," Michael said, wrapping one leg around Griffin's back.

"You should be. Go get cleaned up and meet me on the couch in ten minutes."

Michael raised an eyebrow, curious what Griffin wanted to do to him now. But Michael obeyed. He grabbed his clothes, went to the bathroom, and took a five-minute shower, making sure to get all the eyeliner off. Once dry and dressed, he returned to the living room and found Griffin dressed now in a white t-shirt and his jeans with the big holes in the knees. Griffin had crazy hot knees.

"What are you doing with my backpack? Need a pen?" Michael asked as he sat at the opposite end of the couch. Michael loved that time right after sex when everything went back to normal, and he could just sit there eating dinner or reading or writing a paper and think, *I have Griffin's come in me. Awesome.*

"I need a Macroeconomics textbook and luckily, I just found one. So what are we studying?"

Michael tucked his long hair behind his ears and pulled his legs to his chest.

"You're going to help me study?"

"It's economics, right?" Griffin asked. "My father is the president of the Stock Exchange. Trust me, I can handle economics. I'm one of three people on the planet who can actually explain what a derivative is while sober."

"Damn," Michael said, impressed. "Okay, well, the test is on the first four chapters. We're supposed to focus on vocab terms and the business cycle."

"Boring. This is why I didn't go into the family business."

"It's a Gen Ed requirement."

"Okay, first question. What are the main points of Keynesian economics?"

Michael laughed. Griffin actually did sound like he knew what he was talking about.

"You know, we can keep having sex if you want," Michael offered. "I've got all Sunday to study."

"We can have more sex later when you're done studying. I know getting good grades is important to you. Although even if you lost your scholarship, I'd pay your tuition."

Once again that night, Michael's heart swelled with love. He had no memory in his entire life of doing anything good enough to deserve being with Griffin. He was just fucking lucky. No other possible reason.

"You already spend too much money on me as it is. Jesus, the computer alone—"

"You needed a new computer," Griffin said, flipping through the pages of the textbook.

"Yeah, but I didn't have to get a seventeen-inch MacBook Pro. It's bigger than I am."

"So am I and you like me."

"I didn't say I didn't like the Mac. But we could have gotten a smaller, less outrageously expensive model."

"You like it."

"It's amazing," Michael said. When Griffin said he was taking Michael school supply shopping, Michael thought pens, paper, and folders. The first stop had been the Apple Store.

"Mick, I'd give every penny I have to make you happy—2K on a computer is just pocket change."

"You don't have to give me anything to make me happy except for you," Michael tried to explain.

"You already have me. And you always will. So shut up and let me buy you stuff. That's an order."

Michael opened his mouth and shut it again. "Yes, sir."

"Now answer the question or I won't fuck you for a week. What are the key elements of Keynesian economics?"

Michael took a deep breath. His boyfriend, his lover, his owner, his crazy, ex-drug addict, drop-dead gorgeous, kinky trust fund baby Griffin was helping him study for his macro test. How. Bizarre.

There was only one thing for Michael to do.

"Keynesian economics stresses a mixed approach to the economy—public and private . . ." he began, settling into Griffin's couch. His couch.

Their couch.

A BETTER DISTRACTION

"A Better Distraction" takes place shortly after the end of The Angel.

Distraction. That's what Griffin needed. Distraction from imagining Mick tied to the bed, naked, and ready for anything. Unfortunately his distraction options tonight were limited to reading through his financial statements. Better than nothing. Certainly better than thinking about the things he didn't want to think about tonight. Bedtime scooted closer every passing minute, and he hadn't yet figured out how to have the conversation with Mick he didn't want to have.

Griffin grabbed his big pillow and picked up the spiral-bound notebook. Even the most annoying tasks became slightly less annoying when done in bed. His financial manager had sent him the latest reports on his investments. Russ wanted to move money, diversify risk blah blah blah. It all sounded fine to Griffin, but Russ couldn't do it without his signature on about ten thousand pieces of paper. If he had to go to all that trouble to put on a suit next week, go to Russ's office on Wall Street, and sign shit until his hand fell off, he should at least read the damn reports first.

"Mick?" Griffin called out as he flipped through the mutual fund statements.

"Yes, sir?" Mick appeared in the bedroom doorway, sketchbook under his arm. He had that nervous wide-eyed look on his face again. Griffin never liked that look. They'd been together a month now. Time for Mick to get over being nervous. Then again, Griffin was nervous tonight so he didn't have much room to talk.

"Do you need anything?" Mick asked.

"Nope. Just wanted to see what you were doing. I get suspicious when you're out of my eye line."

Griffin winked at him to show he was joking, which he probably shouldn't have done. Nora had warned Griffin the worst thing he could do with Mick was coddle him. *Tease him, torture him, drive him up and down the wall until he's ready to wring your neck. That's the only way he'll lose that "deer in the headlights" look. You treat him like he's made of glass? He'll prove you right one of these days by breaking.* Torture Mick? Easy for her to say. She wasn't the proud owner of a baby submissive and masochist who'd only had sex with one person his entire life before Griffin. A baby submissive who had a suicide attempt in his past and the scars on his wrists to prove it. His job was to protect Mick and Nora's big advice was to torture him? He'd asked her if Søren had tortured her as a teenager. Nora responded by saying that Søren annoyed her so much during their early years that he kept a tally of all the times she told him to his face that she hated him. They hit triple digits before she hit nineteen.

I don't want Mick to hate me, he'd told Nora.

Trust me. Subs want to be tortured. "I hate you" is just another way for a sub to say keep doing what you're doing because it's getting to me.

He wanted to get to Mick like that, but couldn't get over his overwhelming urge to shield him from everything, including himself.

"So what are you working on?" Griffin asked.

"I'm trying to figure out what to do for this weird art assignment that's due next week."

"What's the assignment?"

"We're supposed to pick something that belongs to someone else. Then we're supposed to interview that person about that object or whatever and find out how they feel about it."

"Like what?"

"Professor Laird said in class the best one from last semester was a guy who drew his mom with her hair in a ponytail. She always wore her hair back, and when he asked her why she told him this wild story about how she'd gotten her hair caught in a sewing machine when she was eight and that it took police and EMTs and the fire department to get her out because she refused to let them cut her hair off. So she always wore her hair up after that. He never knew this crazy family story until he decided to draw it and ask her about it."

"Interesting assignment."

"Professor Laird wants us to explore the emotional connection people have to objects so we can put emotion into our art. We can't just draw objects. We have to draw what they mean."

"Is it just me or does that sound like something you can do in here?" This avoiding each other jazz was getting old fast.

"Yes, sir. I just didn't want to interrupt your work."

"I'm reading glorified bank statements. For God's sake, Mick, interrupt me."

Griffin patted the bed next to him. Mick hesitated only a moment before obediently sitting where Griffin had indicated. They'd been nervous around each other all weekend. Maybe sitting in the same room would help relax them both.

"You going to Mass tomorrow?" Griffin asked, trying to sound casual.

"Yes, sir. I thought I'd try St. Patrick's. I hear it's nice."

"You can wear these jeans there if you want." He pointed to his pants, his favorite Levis with the big holes in the knees. "They're religious jeans."

"Your jeans are religious?"

"They're holey."

Mick's entire body went limp as he started to slide off the bed. Griffin grabbed him by the arm and pulled him back up.

"Sorry," Mick said, righting himself. "That joke was so bad I lost consciousness for a second."

"Glad you're feeling better." Griffin handed Mick his sketchbook.

Mick had his "starving artist" uniform on as Griffin had come to think of it—ratty cargo shorts, white sleeveless t-shirt, and a blue handkerchief holding his hair back, Captain Jack Sparrow style. He had a Rhodia pencil behind his ear and that lost "thinking of art and all things arty" look in his eyes that he wore when drawing. Better that look than the anxious, wary look he'd been wearing since last weekend.

Griffin picked his financials up and started flipping through them again, finding himself much more interested in the gorgeous teenage boy sitting next to him than the columns of six-digit numbers. These numbers weren't working. He needed a better distraction.

Out of the corner of his eye Griffin saw Mick put his pencil down and start sketching something. He tried to honor Mick's homework time and not demand attention every second they were together. But still, with Mick at Yorke College an hour away in Connecticut every Monday through Friday, the forty-eight-hour period they spent together from Friday evening to Sunday evening was all the time they had alone together every week.

"What is that?" Griffin asked, unable to sit quietly and read numbers anymore.

"Um . . . just trying to get my brain to work. Right now all I'm doing is drawing the bedroom."

"Our bedroom. Say it."

Mick grinned but didn't look up from the page as he kept drawing. "*Our* bedroom."

"I bought this sexy bitch by the train station just for you. You better say 'our' when you talk about it. Got me?" Griffin grabbed a lock of Mick's hair and tugged it playfully.

"Got it."

"Good." Griffin leaned over Mick's shoulder and watched him draw. In a few short minutes Mick had already put down the outlines of the bedroom—the high loft ceiling with the towering windows that looked out from the thirty-second floor onto the city, the sitting area with the two leather club chairs neither of them ever used because they lived in the bed. And he'd drawn the bed too—the king-size bed with the elaborate wrought-iron headboard and footboard, specially chosen because it made it so easy to cuff Mick to the bed.

"This drives you nuts, doesn't it, Picasso?"

"I'm pretending you're not there," Mick said.

"Yeah, I've noticed. You're getting good at it." The words came out in a far more serious tone than Griffin intended to utter them.

Mick turned to him with wide hurt eyes. "Griffin, I didn't . . . I'm just. I thought you were mad at me."

"Why would I be mad at you?"

"Last weekend."

"Last weekend was my fault, not yours. Have you been thinking this entire time I was mad at you?"

"Well . . . yeah."

"Why?" Mad at Mick? It had never even occurred to Griffin to be mad at Mick.

"Because you won't touch me."

Griffin collapsed back on the bed and rubbed his forehead with both hands.

"Mick . . . The only reason I haven't touched you very much since last weekend is that I'm trying to control myself a little here. It's not you, it's me. Me and my cock."

"That's it." Mick looked up from his drawing. "I got it."

"Got what? Why we didn't have sex last night?"

"No, that still doesn't make any sense to me. But I know what I can do for my art project topic."

"The object and the story project?"

"That one."

"What are you going to write about?"

"Your cock."

"Wait. What?" Griffin sat back up again.

"I can write about your, you know, your cock and then do a drawing of you."

Mick flipped to a clean page in his notebook.

"You want to use my cock as homework? You don't think you'll get in trouble for that?"

"Yorke's a liberal arts school. Professor Laird is really—and I mean really—gay. Plus we're doing nudes later this semester anyway. Not *doing* nudes. It's not that kind of school."

"Sounds like a plan then," Griffin said, happy to have an excuse to push bedtime back by another hour or so while he got over his lingering nervousness. The thought of Mick drawing him seemed a little weird but at least it allowed him to do something he'd wanted to do since he was a teenager. "Mick?"

"Yes, sir?"

Griffin rolled onto his side and put his hand on his forehead. "Draw me like one of your French girls."

Mick only stared at him.

"Oh, God, I'm going to feel really fucking old if you haven't seen *Titanic*," Griffin said.

Mick burst out laughing and rolled on his side. God, it felt good to hear Mick laughing, really laughing again.

Mick held out his hand.

"What?" Griffin asked.

"Where's my dime, Kate?"

"Kate? You just called me Kate? Do you want to be caned tonight?"

"Well . . . yeah."

"Tough. We're doing your assignment now."

"Yes, sir."

"So how do we do this?" Griffin asked, quickly warming up to the idea of having Mick's entire attention focused on his naked body. Best. Distraction. Ever. "Tell me exactly what to do."

Mick looked at him with the deer in the headlights look.

"For posing, I mean," Griffin clarified.

"Whew."

Griffin cupped the back of Mick's neck and kissed him on the mouth. "I'd never expect you to top me. Don't worry. I'm not a switch and neither are you."

"You had me worried there a sec." Mick tapped his pencil on the paper, one of his nervous habits.

"But you are the artist." Griffin kissed him again. "And it's your homework assignment. So you get to tell me how to pose and where to sit and then you have to move lamps around and shit, right?"

"Lighting isn't a joke." Mick gave him another hurt look. "It's really important to artists."

"Mick, I'm sorry. I didn't mean—"

Mick winked at him. The bottom fell out of Griffin's stomach from sheer relief.

"You are in so much trouble for that." Griffin threw Mick down and straddled his hips. Grabbing Mick's slender wrists, Griffin pressed him into the bed.

"I want to be in trouble," Mick said.

Griffin felt the first stirrings of an erection. He wanted nothing more than to strip Mick naked and cuff him to the footboard, flog him senseless and fuck him until morning. But that's what happened last weekend that had gotten them into this nice awkward mess. He needed self-control here, and holding Mick down on the bed wasn't helping in that area.

He sat up on his knees and handed Mick back his pencil.

"Where do you want me?" Griffin asked.

"Hmm . . ." Mick sat up and looked Griffin up and down with a detached appraising stare. "Can you stand up?"

Griffin slid off the bed and stood a few feet away. Mick sat on the edge of the bed with his notebook and pencil.

"I don't think I want you completely naked."

"I'm hurt."

"For the drawing." Mick made a few preliminary lines on his paper. "Your overall . . . what's the word?"

"Fuckhotness?"

"That. Your overall fuckhotness would detract from your, you know—"

"My cock."

"Right."

"So partially nude?"

Mick looked down at his sketchpad. "Maybe in those chairs we never use. We should get some use out of them."

Griffin sat in one of the chairs and leaned his head back trying to seem as casual as possible. Mick stood by the chair and studied him, first while standing, then squatting, and then from the other side of the room. Mick held a pencil in front of his face and seemed to be staring through it and at it while making a circuit around the chair.

"Are you trying to find a good angle for the sketch?" Griffin asked.

"No. I'm just trying to see how long I can be weird before you call me out on it."

"I'm calling you out on it, weirdo," Griffin said, laughing at his weird and wonderful sub.

"Are you comfortable?" Mick rearranged Griffin in the chair. He put Griffin's right leg over the left arm of the chair and unbuttoned Griffin's Mets jersey.

"You're unzipping my pants at the moment. Yes, this is something I'm pretty comfortable with."

Mick grinned. "I just want a hint of cock in the drawing which is why you should keep your pants on."

"My cock doesn't hint."

Even during this perfunctory posing procedure, Mick's hands on Griffin had already caused blood to pool in his hips. He wasn't at a full erection yet but he was getting there rapidly.

"Okay, that is perfect . . ." Mick took a few steps back and looked Griffin up and down. Strange to be in this role-reversed situation where he was the object and Mick the one putting him in his place. "Can you stay like that?"

"I won't move a muscle. Except that one." Griffin nodded down at his cock. "I don't have much control over that one. Unfortunately."

"Why do you say that? 'Unfortunately,' I mean?"

"My cock has gotten me into trouble before."

"Can you tell me a story about that? It'll be for the sketch."

"Well, I never got it caught in a sewing machine. Thank God."

He glanced down and saw his cock protruding from his unzipped jeans. He couldn't remember if he'd ever seen anything sexier than that serious studied look on Mick's face as he drew with the grace and ease of a young Picasso.

"Thank God," Mick agreed as he started making a few preliminary lines on his paper. "How does your cock get you into trouble?"

"It's big."

"Again, thank God." Mick glanced up from his notebook and smiled at him.

So his sub liked his size? Interesting.

"It's not always a good thing," Griffin said. "I mean, a lot of gay guys are size queens which works in my favor with them, but it's caused its fair share of problems."

"Like what?"

Griffin cast his mind far back into the past. Better to go back there than deal with more recent examples.

"Like my first girlfriend Linzy."

"First girlfriend or first—"

"First *first*. First person I dated, first person I had sex with."

"How old were you?"

"Fourteen."

"Beat me by a year." Mick snapped his fingers and Griffin laughed.

"Yeah, but you lost your virginity to the most beautiful dominatrix on earth. I lost mine to a fourteen-year-old girl who had no idea what she was doing. Which was fine. I didn't know either."

"What did she look like?"

"Dark brown hair, really long. Soft hair. Big blue eyes. Had a porcelain doll thing going. I really was terrified I'd break her. I guess I did break her."

"What happened?"

"The story, like my dick, is a long one."

Mick looked up at him with a *Did you really just make that joke?* look.

"Don't pass out again, please," Griffin said at the look of amused disgust on Mick's face. "You really want to hear about my embarrassing first time?"

"I want to hear everything about you. But let's start there."

Griffin started talking. He and Linzy met freshman year at their high school. She was friends with a friend of his. It was lust at first sight.

"I should tell you this was in L.A. Did I tell you I lived in L.A. for about five years?"

"You said you were born in L.A. but I didn't know you lived there that long."

"Born there then moved to New York. Back to L.A. when Mom started modeling again. Anyway, back to Linzy . . ."

Griffin killed an entire box of tissues in one week over Linzy before deciding to ask her out. Age fourteen, no driver's license. He had to get creative. Creative for a fourteen-year-old with a twenty-four hour erection meant asking his older brother for rides. Thank God for Aiden.

"Aiden's your oldest brother, right?" Mick asked as he erased a line. Griffin wanted and yet didn't want to know what part of his body Mick just erased.

"Right. Dad was married before my mom and had Aiden, Chris, and Lucas. Dad finds out his wife, their mom, is cheating and has a drinking problem. Crazy blood-in-the-water type divorce follows. Dad swears off women for eternity and that vow lasts until he meets my mom at a charity fundraiser. She was nineteen. He was in his thirties. Love at first sight. I know how he felt."

Even in the low lamplight Griffin could see Mick blushing. For the first time he realized he did know how his father felt. Griffin hadn't dated anyone seriously his entire adult life. The longest relationship he'd ever had lasted about two weeks and was conducted behind the back of the person he was supposed to be dating. His dad had money, lots of it, and three children. The last person his father should have fallen in love with was a nineteen-year-old cover model. The last person Griffin should have fallen in love with was a much younger guy with a suicide attempt in his past and one of the most homophobic fathers in the history of homophobia. The heart wants what the heart wants. And Griffin's heart wanted Mick.

"Anyway, Aiden was old enough during the divorce to know Dad wasn't the guilty party. So he took the lead in making sure Chris and Lucas didn't murder me in my crib when I was born. We're tight now but it was a shaky start. That we all get along so great now is all thanks to Aiden."

"Sounds like a great guy."

"He is. You'll meet him at Christmas."

"I will?" Mick asked with a squeak of panic in his voice.

"Don't stress. Christmas is four months away."

Mick stopped drawing.

"What's wrong?" Griffin experienced a moment's panic at the look of shock in Mick's eyes.

"It's just . . ." Mick smiled. "You're already planning us being together at Christmas?"

"What? Did you think I'd get tired of you between now and four months from now?"

"It crossed my mind."

"Uncross your mind. Jesus, Mick, I've already planned our ten-year-anniversary party. It's in Scotland, by the way. I'm going to have to get you your own kilt. Keep drawing."

"Yes, sir."

He almost told Mick that he was cute when he was insecure about them. Mick worrying about Griffin breaking up with him made as much sense as Mick worrying about gravity being revoked, which he apparently also worried about because he slept every night with his fingers clinging to the sheets. But Nora had told Griffin not to reward Mick for any behavior Griffin didn't want repeated. They were only a month into their relationship and Mick being worried that Griffin would lose interest in him was cute now; it would be heart-breaking a year from now, or two years from now.

"Anyway, Aiden's ten years older than me. He had just gotten married but still made time for his baby brother. Being driven around by parents on a date is humiliating, but when you had a cool older brother who hauled your ass around, it wasn't so bad. Me and Linzy did double dates with Aiden and his wife, who is now his ex-wife."

"What happened with Aiden's wife?"

"He said he and Quinn just fell out of love and no amount of counseling could make it work. He respected her too much to keep her in a loveless marriage. She felt the same. Probably the most amicable divorce in history. Aiden's the one I want to fix your mom up with."

"My mom isn't old enough to date."

"You keep saying that but I will totally make this happen. Did you just whimper like a dying cat?"

"I might have."

"Just checking. So me and Linzy start getting cozy on our dates. Constant making out and fooling around . . ."

They got to second base in a movie theater. He got his first handjob from her in a park. Aiden and his wife would take them somewhere and make themselves conveniently scarce so Griffin and Linzy could be alone together. After a couple months of feverish groping they decided to go for it. Linzy was on the Pill and Griffin had the box of Trojans his dad had given him during their birds and bees talk the year before. Time to bust that box open.

"So what happened?" Mick asked.

"I talked to Aiden about it. He was fifteen when he lost his V-card so he didn't give me any shit for deciding to do it. In fact, he said me and Linzy could use his apartment. He and Quinn would give us the place for a day while they went out. Aiden's got this old-fashioned gentlemanly streak in him. He said Linzy deserved better than having her first time in the back of a car or on a couch in somebody's basement. His two cents was that we should wait a little longer but if we absolutely couldn't, we could use the guest room."

"Very cool older brother. I wish Erin and I talked more."

"Yeah, I need to meet this sister of yours."

"Thanksgiving maybe?" Mick looked up at him with a nervous sort of hope in his eyes.

"Definitely. Thanksgiving with your mom. Christmas with my parents. Cool?"

"Cool. So how did it go with Linzy?"

"Horrible." Griffin could not emphasize the word enough. "First of all, she was terrified. Determined but terrified, which is a bad combination. Second, she was a virgin complete with hymen. Third, even at fourteen I had this." He looked down at his cock.

"Ow."

"That's what she said. We tried to get it in a few times and I'm not kidding, she screamed every time. Screamed. Not winced or flinched or whatever. Screamed. I kept saying we should stop but she wanted to go for it. A girl screaming in pain is all nice and sexy if she's on a St. Andrew's Cross at the Circle and you're flogging her. If you're trying to have sex with her, it's a boner-killer."

"So what did you do?"

"We fooled around some more. I gave her an orgasm with my fingers which got her really wet. We smoked some pot and went for it again. That time we went through with it, because she was wetter and I was more relaxed. Well, stoned. Stoned is the correct word for it. But don't tell Aiden that part. I don't want him to know I did drugs in his house."

Mick mimed zipping his lips and tossing the key away.

"So happy ending?" Mick asked.

"Not really. She bled a lot, which freaked me out. Blood on the sheets was bad enough but I had blood on me. I felt like a bull in a China shop with her, ripping her open. She wanted to have sex again but I couldn't go through with it."

"Did you two break up?"

"A month later. She said she didn't want to be with a guy who was—"

"Scared to break her?"

"I think those were her words exactly." Griffin gazed at Mick across the six feet of space between them. "I made you bleed last weekend," he said. "During sex."

"I know," Mick said, almost solemnly. "I was there."

"I felt like shit about it. I still do."

"I know you did," Mick said. "But you don't have to. I was as into it as you were."

"It's my job to protect you."

"You don't have to protect me from you. It hurt. It healed. I'm fine."

"Glad one of us is."

Mick's eyes flinched, which was a uniquely Mick sort of expression. His entire face stayed calm but his eyes would widen and narrow in a split second.

"I'm sorry. I guess I keep thinking that I know I'm fine and ready for sex. Guess I didn't think you might not be." Mick shrugged and went back to drawing.

"I will be ready again. I'm really sorry I'm like this today."

"Like what?" Mick asked.

"Confused. Scared. That's the last thing anyone wants in their dominant. It's not very, you know . . . dominant."

"That's not true."

"What?" Griffin wasn't quite sure he'd heard Mick right.

"I said, that's not true. I'm a sub and you're not, so in this area I might know more than you do. I get scared and confused so it makes me feel better to know you sometimes feel that way. The last thing I want is a dominant who won't tell me what's going on. It makes me feel freaked out and confused." Mick sketched and talked at the same time. Griffin would have to remember this, that Mick talked more while working.

"On the day of your collaring, Nora lectured me and told me not to coddle you."

"She did?"

"I'm doing it anyway, aren't I?"

"Kind of."

Griffin sighed heavily and looked up at the ceiling. Last Friday night everything had been going so perfectly. He loved making Mick wait until bedtime to beat him and fuck him. Making Mick wait made the entire day buzzing with anticipation. By midnight they were both about to scream from wanting it so much. He'd flogged Mick for about twenty minutes before cuffing him spread-eagled and face down to the bed. He'd been in such a hurry to get inside Mick he'd rushed the prep-time. Not enough lube and too much eagerness . . . bad combination. He thrust into Mick, who cried out in pain and not pleasure and when Griffin pulled out, he saw blood on his penis.

That had been last Friday night. They didn't have sex Saturday or Sunday. All week long Mick had been distant. Usually Mick would text him every morning and all throughout the day, telling him every hilarious or weird thing that happened at school. But this week the messages had been few and far between.

"You know, I thought you were mad at me all week," Griffin said.

"For what? Fucking me? I thought you were mad at me."

"For what? Having the audacity to bleed? I don't think you did it on purpose."

"You didn't make me bleed on purpose."

"I hate it when you have a point, Mick."

"I'll never do it again, I promise."

"Is your drawing done?"

"Yup."

"Yup? Is that how you address me?"

Mick gave him a guilty look. "No, sir."

"That's better."

"Do you want to see the drawing?"

He did want to see the drawing. Definitely. But he wanted to see something else a whole lot more.

"I'd rather see your mouth on my cock."

Griffin raised his hand and beckoned Mick. Mick put his sketchbook aside and started to stand. Griffin shook his head and Mick froze. Griffin pointed at the floor and without needing any words of instruction Mick went down on his hands and knees. He crawled the six feet to Griffin's chair and waited, kneeling at his feet.

Mick bent and took the tip of Griffin's cock into his mouth and sucked on it lightly. Eight whole days without sex had nearly killed him. They could have fooled around and done something other than intercourse last weekend, but Griffin worried if he got too revved up he'd lose his resolve to give Michael time to heal. But he was the dominant in this relationship. How could he expect Mick to trust him if he didn't trust himself?

Sighing with pleasure, Griffin closed his eyes and leaned his head back on the chair again. He needed this, needed to feel this connection with Mick. Mick licked him from the base to the tip and back down again. Mick put his hands on Griffin's bare knees through the holes in his jeans. He loved feeling Mick's fingers on his legs. He knew he wore his holey pants for a reason.

Griffin's stomach muscles tightened as Mick took him deep into his mouth. The wet heat . . . the light scrape of teeth on his skin . . . the soft murmurs of eagerness that came from the back of Mick's throat. Mick slid his hands up Griffin's thighs and pressed his palms flat against Griffin's ribcage. Griffin breathed into Mick's palms in short breathy pants. Mick always kept his eyes closed during blowjobs. He said it helped him concentrate. Griffin didn't mind. It gave him a chance to stare at Mick, his beautiful face with those crazy eyelashes of his and his pale skin and perfect lips that Griffin ached to bite all night long.

He raised his hips as the blood pounded through him. In his last moment of coherence he whispered Mick's name. Griffin didn't come in Mick's mouth—he exploded. His orgasms always caught him off guard during oral sex. He could never prepare himself for the force of them. His climax wracked his whole body as semen shot out of him in wave after wave of release.

Griffin sunk into the chair, eyes closed and body spent as Mick carefully cleaned him with his tongue.

"God damn, I love my sub."

"Your sub loves you too, sir."

Mick sat back on his heels. He ran the back of his hand over his wet lips and Griffin nearly came again simply from the sight of it.

"I feel much better now," Griffin sighed.

"So do I."

Griffin leaned forward, cupped the back of Mick's neck, and brought their mouths together in a long, lingering kiss.

"Show me your drawing," Griffin ordered against Mick's lips.

Mick crawled over to his sketchbook, grabbed it, and handed it back to Griffin.

Griffin stared at the sketch.

"Wow."

"Is that a good wow?" Mick sounded adorably nervous. Griffin decided to make him sweat it a few minutes. He studied the page, shocked by the detail Mick could put into such a quick pencil sketch. Although the drawing and the conversation had revolved around his cock, Mick had focused the most attention onto Griffin's face.

"Is this how you see me?"

"Yeah. But that's how you look."

"I'm this hot?"

Mick nodded. "That hot. And really, it doesn't do you justice."

Griffin closed the sketchbook and set it aside.

"I love you," he said to Mick, cupping the back of his head again. "And I own you."

"I know you do, sir."

"So we're going to wait another week before we have sex again. We're going to wait not because I'm coddling you but because I want to be one-hundred-percent sure you're okay and I'm okay. Tonight we're going to get into bed, make out for an hour. I'm going to make you come so hard you might lose consciousness again. And you're not going to worry about us waiting another week. You aren't going to stress about it. Neither am I. Cool?"

Mick nodded and smiled. "Cool, sir."

"Good. Now get into bed."

"Definitely, sir."

Mick scrambled off the floor and started stripping out of his shirt on his way to the bed. Not a single welt or bruise marred Mick's back. Maybe in addition to the making out and the blowjob Griffin had planned, he'd get out the cuffs and the candle. A little wax-play never hurt anybody. So many options for torturing that boy tonight. He could erotically torture Mick all night long, no cock-in-ass sex necessary. Hell, he even had that new cane, the thin plastic job that stung like fire and left bright red welts. No, he'd save the cane for later. Mick hadn't quite earned that sort of beating tonight. They'd save it for next weekend.

Until then he had a sub to beat and get off.

And a debt to pay.

Griffin dug in his pocket and found exactly what he needed.

"Hey Mick?"

Mick turned around.

"Catch," Griffin said. "For the drawing."

With an impressive display of reflexes, Mick caught the object and held it on his open palm.

"Thanks . . . Kate," Mick said, pocketing the dime.

Griffin glared at Mick.

"That's it, Leo. Get the cane."

CHRISTMAS IN SUITE 37A

"Christmas in Suite 37A" takes place two years and three months after the end of The Angel.

CHAPTER ONE

Blue Christmas

Sunday, December 22
New Orleans, Garden District

T his was going to be the worst fucking Christmas ever.

It would suck—hard—and not in the fun way.

Nora wasn't making it any easier. She had, in fact, ordered Griffin to go to church with her tonight—further proof she was as much of a sadist as Søren.

He said to her request/demand, "I'm a Buddhist," and Nora gave him the pursed lips to end all pursed lips.

"You're wearing a Nirvana t-shirt. That no more makes you a Buddhist than me wearing a catsuit makes me a pussy," she said, poking him in the center of his chest, right in Kurt Cobain's eye.

Hadn't poor Kurt been through enough? "Don't pull that 'I'm a Buddhist' stuff on me. It didn't work on my mother when I said it, and it's not going to work on me."

"You're seriously making me go to church with you? Serious?" Griffin asked.

"Søren only gets to say Mass once a week now that he's not a parish priest anymore. This is a big fucking deal to him, which makes it a big fucking deal to me, and since you're in my house living under my roof it oughta be a big fucking deal to you."

"But—"

"No buts. You listen to me, Griffin Randolfe Fiske. You've been living in my house under my roof eating my food and sleeping in my guest bed for two months now. And this—coming to Mass with me three days before Christmas—is the one and only thing I've asked you to do in way of repayment. One hour of your life sitting in a beautiful historic New Orleans Catholic church listening to Louisiana angels sing sacred Christmas music while the man I have loved for twenty years of my life says Mass and offers Communion to rich and poor, black and white, citizen and stranger in a two-thousand-year-old ritual of thanksgiving that reminds everyone involved that we are all God's children? Is that really so much to ask?"

"Wow. Did you learn how to do a Catholic guilt trip from your mom or from Søren?"

"Neither," she said with narrowed eyes. "I'm a natural."

She was in domme mode and clearly in the mood to out-alpha him. Griffin folded like a house of cards in a stiff breeze.

"Okay, okay. I'll go. I'm going. You know, since you asked so nicely."

"And . . . ?"

"And because you let me crash here for the past two months and asked nothing of me and all that."

"Oh, honey," Nora said, patting his cheek, "you know it's been my pleasure and you don't owe me a thing." She sauntered off down the hall toward her bedroom. Alone in the kitchen, Griffin shook his head. Did mind-fuckers ever stop mind-fucking? How did Nora talk him into this?

Nora was Nora. That's how.

No doubt she had left him to go change clothes before church. She was, after all, still wearing the vinyl catsuit she'd donned earlier that day for a client. His Blond Holiness probably wouldn't appreciate Griffin showing up to church in jeans and his brother's twenty-year-old Nirvana t-shirt either. Although the jeans were his "holey jeans," with tears in the knees so gaping you could stick an arm through them. And sometimes Mick did.

Sighing, Griffin trudged to his room to shower and change into whatever he owned that could pass for "church clothes." Well, it wasn't *his* room he went to. It was Nora's room in Nora's house in the Garden District. It was a nice room. Antique blue patterned wallpaper, carved oak queen-size bed, thick Persian rug, and a set of French doors that led to his own private veranda. As beautiful as it was—this room, this house—and no matter how comfortable he got here, it would never be Griffin's room. Griffin's room was in his apartment in Manhattan, the apartment he'd bought because he wanted a fresh start with Mick—new relationship, new home, new life. Together. Both of them. A new life together. It was all for them. No. That wasn't true. It was all for Mick.

And now Mick was gone.

Not gone, Griffin chided himself as he stripped out of his clothes and stepped into the shower. Mick wasn't dead. Griffin often had to remind himself not to be a drama queen about the whole thing. Mick was spending a semester abroad in Rome. That was all. Mick had gone overseas after saying the six ugliest words in the English language to Griffin:

I think I need a break.

How could his home in New York feel like his home anymore after that?

Ninety-seven days after Mick said those six ugly words, Griffin could still picture Mick's face during that fight, his silver eyes wide and red-rimmed. The expression he'd worn was sad and scared and apologetic. Griffin could understand the sad and scared. They'd been together—lovers, living together, dom and sub—for two years. Mick was sad to have to say those six words and scared of how Griffin would react to them. But apologetic? That made no sense. What did Mick have to be sorry for? Yes, the break had been Mick's idea. The fault, however, belonged squarely on Griffin's shoulders.

And he knew it.

Griffin turned off the water and wrapped a towel around his waist and cinched it tight. When he'd flown down to New Orleans to hang out at Nora's, it had been to get away from his mother's hovering. He certainly hadn't come here to lose any weight. Bodybuilders like him usually wanted to bulk up, not slim down. And he was in New Orleans, where all the good Cajun food and seafood lived. But Søren had practically ordered Griffin to join him for his almost daily four and five-mile runs. Griffin had left his eternally-worried-about-her-baby-boy mother only to be treated like a child by a priest and a dominatrix.

Still, he didn't blame them. Their coddling/care-taking/near-constant monitoring had kept Griffin clean and sober even when everything in him wanted to drown his sorrows with a bottle of bourbon and a fistful of Oxy. A few weeks after the break-up, he'd come *this close* to begging Kingsley for a sleeping pill from his medicine cabinet. Instead, he'd humbled himself to Nora and told her how tempted he was that night to take something, anything, legal or illegal, it didn't matter. She'd kissed him, told him she loved him, and then stripped him naked. This wasn't about kink or sex. She took his clothes and locked them up where he couldn't get to them. She put a basic bondage strap around one wrist and locked him to the bedpost. If stealing his clothes and tying one hand to the bed was what it took to keep him off Bourbon Street, then so be it. All night long Nora had scratched his back and massaged his neck while telling him a bedtime story about when she and Sheridan were hired by a member of the Moroccan royal family to put on a private show for him and his best friend. Griffin had fallen asleep in her lap and woke up the next morning feeling human for the first time in weeks. He'd known then he would make it through this.

Even if he didn't want to.

Griffin pulled on a pair of black jeans and a white button-down shirt. He put on a black tie but kept the knot loose and his collar open. A tie was his version of making an effort.

As he was shoving his feet into his black Chucks, Nora came in the room looking sexy as hell in a black skirt, red blouse, and black boots that went all the way up to her knees.

"Very handsome," she said, looking him up and down. "Then again, you always look handsome."

She ran her hand through his still-wet hair, slicking it into place.

"You're doing the mom-thing again," Griffin said.

"Only because I'm worried about you."

"I'm fine." He kissed her cheek. "Do I need to tuck in my shirt or anything? What's the dress code?"

"Very relaxed dress code in the Catholic Church. Keep your shirt untucked, but put on your jacket. It'll be in the fifties by the time church lets out."

"The fifties. Three days before Christmas and 'the fifties' means it's cold out."

"It got all the way up to thirty in Manhattan today. Practically balmy. Aren't you glad you're here?"

"No," Griffin said, knowing and loving Nora too well to lie to her.

"I know," she said, kissing him on the lips—the kiss of a friend, not a lover. It seemed that part of their relationship was over now for whatever reason. "Come on. We don't want to be late for church."

"We don't?"

Nora answered that question by grabbing his tie and leading him from the guest room like a dog on a leash.

They got in her car—Nora at the wheel, of course—and Elvis's "Blue Christmas" came on the radio. Nora started to switch the station, but Griffin stopped her.

"I can handle a depressing Christmas song, Nor."

"I'm sorry. I don't mean to coddle you."

"You sure about that?" They drove through the narrow streets. Christmas lights were strung along tropical-colored houses and dripped from the leafy green tops of palm trees. Christmas in New Orleans.

"Break-ups are hard and horrible no matter who does the leaving," Nora said. "I've been there. I can testify."

"You think Mick's out there feeling as shitty as I do?"

"I think there's a very good chance he misses you as much as you miss him. But do you really want him to feel shitty right now?"

Griffin sighed. "No. I want him to be happy. But I also want him to miss me so much it hurts. Does that make any sense at all?"

"It makes all the sense." Nora squeezed his knee.

"You want to know something funny?" Griffin asked.

"No, I want to know something horrible and sad."

He glared at her.

"Tell me," she said.

"I keep thinking about that night you and Søren and me and Mick all hung out together at our apartment. It was right after Christmas, that first December me and Mick were together. Remember?"

"That night was so much fun," Nora said. "I can't believe we talked Søren into playing Cards Against Humanity."

"I'm still pissed he won. Beginner's luck."

"Blondie has a wicked sense of humor when he feels like showing it. Remember he won the game on the 'How did I lose my virginity?' card."

"Answer: The Make-A-Wish Foundation," Griffin said, laughing despite himself.

"I still want to write a book about someone who loses their virginity through the Make-A-Wish Foundation because of that game. It's on my to-write list."

"That night . . . It was the first time Mick and I had people over to our new place. And since it was you and Søren, Mick was really relaxed. When we were playing the game, you and Mick were both sitting on the floor between our knees like—"

"Good little submissives?"

"Exactly. It was the best, Mick sitting there at my feet like he was born for it. He wouldn't do that around vanillas, but since it was you all, he just did it like nothing. I just want that again, you know? I want that to be my normal again."

"I know. I want it for you, too. Michael was pretty young when you two got together."

"You were fifteen when you fell in love with Søren."

"Yes, and I broke up with him, remember? But you know what?"

"What?"

"I went back to him, too."

Griffin took those words and held them in his hand, pressed to his heart. Hope hurt, but it hurt more not to have it.

Nora parked her car a block from Søren's new church—Immaculate Conception Jesuit Church. Immaculate Conception had become some sort of inside joke between Søren, Kingsley and Nora. At least Kingsley was always making some sort of joke about Søren and Immaculate Conception and Nora would laugh at it. And none of them would let Griffin in on the secret.

"So, this is how it works," Nora said as they neared the church. "You stand when I stand. You sit when I sit. You sit when I kneel, because you're not Catholic so you don't have to kneel. You can come forward with me during Communion, but you can't take Communion. Only Catholics can. But you can cross your arms over your chest and bow your head if you want Søren to bless you. He'll do that by drawing a little cross on your forehead with his thumb. It's very gentle. Don't be scared. He might pinch your nose also, so fair warning. Or you can stay in your seat."

"I better take the blessing," Griffin said as they passed the life-size Nativity scene set up on the church's lawn. "I need all the blessings I can get."

He stopped in his tracks and sighed. "I'm doing it again," he said. "I'm rich. I'm healthy. My family is healthy and happy. I have the best friends in the world. I am blessed."

"Don't forget you're also gorgeous, and you have a big cock," Nora said as three elderly women walked passed them. They whipped their heads around to look at him so fast it looked like a scene from *The Exorcist*.

He gave the three women a polite smile and a little wave.

Nora took his hand in hers.

"Even blessed people are allowed to want more blessings. Blessings are a good thing. Blessings are love in tangible form. And blessed people are allowed to have broken hearts. Jesus said, 'Blessed are the poor in spirit.' You're in a good place to receive blessings even if it doesn't feel like it."

Griffin looked up at the night sky. It was only half past seven in the evening, but the sun had set hours ago. Yesterday was Søren's birthday and the Winter Solstice. The longest night of the year and the shortest day. Now that winter had come it seemed like night all the time, which made Griffin miss Mick even more. Night was for kink and sex. Griffin had installed a restraint bar in their bedroom the perfect height for strapping Mick's wrists to it for a beating. After he finished flogging, caning, and/or cropping Mick into a state of erotic bliss, he'd tie his beautiful sub spread-eagle to the bed—face down, of course. Griffin would spend the first half of the night inside Mick and the other half of the night holding him while they slept. Winter was a season for people who lived at night. He missed Mick so much it hurt. It was times like this Griffin wished he was a masochist.

"Five years," Griffin said. "You and Søren were broken up for five years. I know why you left him, and I respect your decision. I probably would have run, too. But what I don't know is how he survived that. How? What's the secret?"

"He would tell you it was prayer," Nora said. "I know that's not the answer you want, and I'm certainly not saying it would work for you like it worked for him. But not a day passed when he didn't pray for me, pray that I would come back. Sometimes he would just pray for me, that I was happy and safe. Like C.S. Lewis said—"

"The Narnia guy?"

"The one and only. He said prayer 'doesn't change God. It changes me.' And it changed Søren. By the time I went back to Søren he was a different man than the one I'd left. He was someone I could be with, someone who understood me or at least tried to. And if it makes you feel any better, even Søren fell apart a few times. So did I."

It did make him feel better, that Søren had fallen apart? Hard to believe and yet . . . Griffin knew just how he must have felt.

"You think Søren would pray for me?" Griffin asked. "For me and Mick, I mean?"

"He has," she said. "He and I both have. Together and apart. And often."

"You have?"

"Søren and I don't have kinky sex the entire time when we're alone together. Sometimes we even talk." She gave him a wink.

"I guess God's saying no to me and Mick getting back together then. I mean if Søren prayed for me and it still hasn't happened . . ."

"You don't know that. God has three answers to prayers: yes, no, and not yet. Maybe this one's just a 'not yet.' "

"What do you think God's waiting on?"

"You, maybe?" She shrugged her shoulders. "Maybe He wants you to ask Him? Worth a shot anyway. Wouldn't hurt to try."

"I don't believe in God, you know. I'm not Catholic. Or a Christian. Or Jewish. Or even a theist."

"Surely you believe in something. You go to NA meetings. Isn't the first step at NA and AA something about giving it up to a higher power?"

"Third step—We make a decision to turn our will and our lives over to the care of God as we understand Him."

"So what higher power did you turn your life over to then?" she asked.

"David Bowie."

"Of course you did."

Nora led him into the church, which was as grand and elegant as she promised it would be. Arches reached up to the fifty-foot ceiling. Along the side walls were endless stained-glass windows. The whole sanctuary glowed a golden hue.

"God has a good decorator," Griffin whispered to Nora, impressed.

"The Church has a good decorator," she whispered back. She led them to a pew in front of the same three elderly women who had done the double-take.

"God has a good PR person too," Griffin said, giving her a pinch on the ass as she went to sit down in the pew.

"I'm not in PR," she countered. "Just another satisfied customer."

"You banged a priest last night, didn't you?"

"Yup."

One of the elderly women behind them gasped in shock. Griffin turned around and gave her an apologetic smile.

"She banged a Prius last night," Griffin whispered to her. "Fender bender. She's still a little shook up about it."

The woman exchanged looks of concerned understanding.

Nora apparently hadn't heard the lady's gasp. She was too busy putting the padded kneeler thingie—Griffin had no idea what it was called—on the floor. Then she slid onto her knees, crossed herself, clasped her hands, and closed her eyes. Griffin had seen Nora beating people, fucking people. He'd seen her drunk. He'd seen her high. He'd seen her in handcuffs getting dragged off by cops who mistook her client's screams of consensual pain for screams of the other kind of pain. But he'd never seen her pray before. It was a good look for her—peaceful and quiet and calm. He wished he could feel peaceful inside his heart for a few minutes. It would be nice to have a little vacation from missing Mick. He'd give anything to see him again, to talk to him. Fuck, they hadn't even talked in three months. That had been one of the rules. No phone calls. No texts. A real break. Now Griffin understood why they were called "breaks." He'd never felt this broken.

Griffin glanced up at the ceiling. Three days until Christmas. All Griffin wanted was to see Mick on Christmas. Nothing else. Not a new car, not a new motorcycle, not a new house, not even world peace.

Seriously, fuck world peace.

Even if it wasn't to get back together . . . even if all that happened was Griffin and Mick in the same room again talking. Actually, fuck talking. Just seeing his face would be enough. That face . . . Griffin had Mick's face memorized so well he could recognize it blindfolded by simply touching his lips and nose and jaw. That was all. Mick for Christmas. Just so Griffin would know Mick was okay.

Please?

Nora sat back in the pew as the music changed.

"What did you pray for?" Griffin asked.

"Nothing," she said.

"Nothing?"

"I tried," she said. "But I kept having sex flashbacks from last night. Don't worry. God's used to this from me."

"I prayed for something," he said. The music was loud so he had to put his mouth to her ear so she could hear him.

"What?"

"To see Mick on Christmas."

"Good prayer," she said. "I think God appreciates prayers like that one. Prayers to see someone we love again. He loves us so much, I'm sure it does His heart good to see us loving each other."

Griffin smiled and turned his attention to the front of the church. He watched as Søren bent his head to kiss the altar. It was strangely moving seeing Søren become Father Marcus Stearns before his eyes. Søren had to mean it, the whole priest thing, right? He had to believe it all, didn't he? Why else would he still be a priest when he could be anything else at all? It made no sense otherwise. Of course, Søren was also a sadist, dangerously intelligent, capable of twisting minds and hearts around his little finger like tinsel. Maybe it was for the best he was a priest. Better to have a man like him on the side of the angels.

"The grace of our Lord Jesus Christ, and the love of God, and the communion of the Holy Spirit be with you all," Søren/Father Stearns said, lifting his hands in greeting.

"And with your spirit," Nora and the rest of the congregation answered in a sort of chant.

Mass progressed as Nora had told him it would. There was sitting and standing, readings from three different books of the Bible. Then Søren came to the pulpit and began to speak.

"Christmas is a dark and lonely time," Søren said, and Griffin sat up a little straighter in the pew. Those weren't the words he expected a priest to say three days before Christmas in a church packed to the rafters with believers.

The silence in the church was heavy as a shroud.

Søren continued, "I'm sure there are those of us here tonight in this church who are feeling that—the darkness and the loneliness that this season of lights brings upon the world. I assure you there's nothing wrong with this feeling, nothing to be ashamed of. Light casts shadows. It's only natural some of us will find ourselves in the dark."

Dark and lonely . . . Griffin knew exactly what Søren meant.

"I have no doubt every adult in this church," Søren continued, "could stand up now and tell us a story of a terrible Christmas he or she has survived. It was over ten years ago that someone I loved was suddenly gone from my life, and I had to face Christmas alone."

Griffin glanced at Nora, but she kept her eyes forward, trained on Søren's face. She looked so lovely right now with tears in her eyes and the slightest knowing smile on her lips. How many times had Søren invoked his relationship with Nora in a sermon with her sitting there trying not to giggle or out herself?

"When Christmas is hard for us," Søren said, "we often feel like we're doing Christmas wrong. We are invited to Christmas parties we don't want to attend, hear Christmas music that reminds us of happier times we'd rather forget. We're exhorted to feel joy. Joy to the world even. There's nothing wrong with this either, being happy during this season when we celebrate the birth of our Savior. And yet . . ." Søren paused and looked out on the congregation. Griffin felt Søren's eyes on him for a moment. "And yet, I imagine Mary and Joseph would have found it odd that such a time in their lives would someday turn into a celebration. The first Christmas was hard. Mary was pregnant with a child that wasn't her husband's. Joseph's wife was pregnant with a child that wasn't his own. How terrifying that must have been for them. I can only imagine . . ."

Nora sniggered quietly and Griffin raised his eyebrow at her. She composed herself again. Whatever she found funny about that, she kept it to herself.

"The first Christmas was a terrible Christmas," Søren continued. "Mary and Joseph had to journey miles on foot and donkey to make it to Bethlehem for the census when she was nine months pregnant. They had no family there to take them in. They stayed in a stable, possibly a cave. Mary gave birth surrounded by animals and dirty hay. Not quite the pristine hospitals we're all used to. She had no midwife but her husband, and they had never been intimate as Mary was a virgin. She was also very likely no more than sixteen years old. How embarrassed she must have been, being assisted in the birth by her much older husband? One has to wonder . . . The birth of a child is a fearful occasion under the best of circumstances. But for Mary and Joseph, alone but for each other, it must have been a nightmare. A time of great fear and loneliness. After such promise, after an angel had come to Mary, and Joseph had been visited in his dreams by God . . . nothing. No angel came to carry Mary and Joseph to Bethlehem. No palace was waiting to welcome them when they arrived. No bed of gold and silk to hold her when she had her child. No midwife to assist her. No miracles to take away her pain. How alone they must have felt in that stable. How terribly scared."

Scared? Yes. Griffin understood scared. Yes, he could remember every line of Mick's face right now. But in a month? A year? When would he start to forget?

Søren glanced Griffin's way again.

"That was the very first Christmas. A time of loneliness, darkness, and fear. If that's what you're feeling tonight—disconsolate, lonely, and afraid—then let this comfort you: You are having a truly authentic Christmas experience."

A ripple of laughter trickled through the congregation. Even Griffin laughed. He leaned over to Nora. "Is this why you wanted me to come to church tonight? You knew Søren would be talking about being lonely at Christmas?"

"I never know his homilies in advance. He knows I'll try to re-write them."

"Then why does it seem like he's talking to me?" Griffin asked.

"Because, my darling, the Lord works in mysterious ways."

Griffin smiled and kissed the top of her head. "You are a mysterious way," he whispered.

When Mass ended, Griffin remained in the pew sitting by Nora. She was waiting for Søren to finish giving all his Christmas hugs and handshakes to the parting congregation.

"I didn't know Søren could sing," Griffin said.

"I wouldn't invite him to karaoke, but most priests sing the Mass parts."

"Nice." Griffin had to admit it, Søren could hold a tune in a bucket. "It's really unfair he's that pretty and that talented. Does he have to be both?"

"Well . . . in the animal kingdom there are two reasons animals have attractive plumage. It's either to snare a mate or to snare dinner."

"Which one are you?"

"Both. At the same time usually." Nora rested her head on his shoulder. "You okay?"

"I will be," he said. "One of these days. I just wish I knew what to do. I can't face my family and all the pity. I can't go back to the country house because Alfred kicked me out."

"Again?"

"He said he'd rather be tied up and forced to watch Simon Cowell lance a boil off David Cameron's ass than watch me moping around the house in mourning for my 'teenaged boy toy' like Blanche DuBois. He said I had to take my *Streetcar Named Desire* act somewhere else."

"You know he does work for you, right?"

"Try telling him that. I can't go home to our place in the city either. I slept on the couch for a week after Mick went to Rome because I couldn't stand sleeping in our bed."

"What do you want to do?"

"I want to make Mick spend Christmas with me, by force if necessary. And by 'make him,' I mean I want him to want to spend Christmas with me, and I don't want to have to force him."

"You are the proverbial hot mess, my love."

"Tell me something I don't know." Griffin leaned back in the pew and looked up at the ceiling. "I wish Mick would talk to me."

"Have you forgotten who Mick is? Remember, this is the kid who once told me, 'I don't talk.' Which was a little odd since he said it out loud. Talking has never been his strong suit."

"It was with me," Griffin said. "He always talked to me."

Nora took his hand in both of hers and held it tight.

"I read something once that really stuck with me," she said. "It's God talking in this saying, but I think it applies to other people we love, too. It goes something like . . . *If he approaches Me by a hand's breadth, I draw near to him by an arm's length; and if he draws near to Me by an arm's length, I draw near to him by a fathom. If he comes to Me walking, I come to him running.*"

"That's beautiful," Griffin said, sitting back up again. "What does it mean?"

"I think it means good things will happen if you have the courage to take the first step toward love."

Griffin nodded. *If he comes to Me walking, I come to him running . . .* What Griffin wouldn't give to have Mick run to him . . .

"Is that from the Bible?" Griffin asked.

"No, actually it's a Muslim Hadith. Great and beautiful truths can be found everywhere."

"So you think I should take the first step?"

Nora reached into the pocket of his black jacket and pulled out his phone. "I think if you take the first step toward him, he'll take two steps toward you. In other words . . . call him."

"On the phone? Nobody uses their phone to make calls. If I call him, he'll think somebody died."

"Fine. Text him then."

"Do I have to?"

"Yes," she said. "Does God have to do everything for you? You're the dom. Act like it."

If Nora had said those words once to him, she'd said them a thousand times. He was trying to be the dominant by letting Mick go and being strong and silent about the whole thing. Yes, he'd whined to Nora for weeks about how much he missed Mick, how much he wanted to see him, how much he wanted to drag him home to America by the ear, throw him on their bed, beat him senseless and then fuck him until the cows came home—which would be a long damn time as they did not, in fact, own any cows.

But he hadn't said a word of that to Mick. If Mick wanted time apart, Griffin would give it to him. He'd promised himself when he collared Mick, he would always give his sub what he needed, even when what Mick needed was the opposite of what Griffin wanted.

Griffin typed his passcode and stared down at the keypad. If he was going to finally break his silence, he had to say something good. But what? It had to be right. It had to be perfect. It had to be poetry that would melt Mick's heart while simultaneously giving him an erection.

Or . . .

Griffin: **Hey, you.**

Griffin sent the message before he could talk himself out of it. His hands were clammy. His heart was racing. He couldn't take a full breath to save his life.

The phone buzzed in his hand. He wanted to flip it over and look at the reply. He could. He would. But first he took a moment, just a second, just enough time to remind himself that he was healthy, he had a great family, he had the best friends in the world . . . plus he was gorgeous and had a big cock. If Mick said no, Griffin would survive it. He'd be okay. Eventually he would be okay. He might even love someone else again. A long, long time from now. But eventually . . . yes. He'd be fine.

Once that was established, he turned his phone over and looked at the answer.

Michael: **Hey, you back.**

Griffin might have been disappointed by that message but it was followed by a ":)" which gave him hope.

Griffin: **Are you home from Rome?**

Michael: **Got back a couple days ago. I'm at my grandparents'.**

Griffin pondered that a moment. Mick's grandparents lived in Fall River, Massachusetts. They were the "good" grandparents, his mom's parents.

Griffin: **You want to hang out soon? We should probably talk.**

Griffin wasn't sure about sending that message. Sounded too serious. But he did want to hang out, and they probably should talk. If the break-up was going to be a permanent deal, then they had a lot to talk about. At the very least, Mick would need to get his stuff out of Griffin's place, a prospect so miserable Griffin felt light-headed and sick simply imagining it. He'd have to move. No way could he stay in their place without Mick.

Griffin sent the invitation. The response came a few seconds later.

Michael: **Tell me when and where, and I'll be there.**

Mick included yet another ":)" at the end of that message. Griffin almost shouted a "praise the Lord" to the rafters. The phrase "tell me when and where, and I'll be there" was one Mick had texted many times before. It was his usual reply to Griffin's "I'm dying to beat you and fuck you" message he sent at least once a week.

Before the break-up, of course.

Griffin: **Waldorf-Astoria. Christmas Eve. Dinner at 7?**

Griffin typed the reply instantly without even thinking. After hitting SEND, he stared at the text and wondered why he'd chosen that particular hotel. He knew why, actually. He'd just forgotten about it, about that night at the Waldorf and what happened there and why it mattered so much that Mick know about it. But whatever happened between him and Mick, Griffin needed to tell him about that night and he needed to tell him there. That is, if Mick agreed to it. It had to be the Waldorf and it had to be Suite 37A. If he could talk Mick into going up with him . . .

Michael: **Sounds good. See you then.**

Griffin showed the reply to Nora. "Praise be to Bowie," Griffin said. Nora laughed and kissed him. Outside the church he heard people singing. The church choir was caroling.

Griffin knew this song—"Hark the Herald Angels Sing." For the first time in three months he felt something like joy. Or at least hope. Beautiful bright hope ringing in his heart like a golden bell.

Maybe this Christmas wouldn't fucking suck after all.

CHAPTER TWO

Silver Bells

On Christmas Eve morning, Griffin packed his bags and kissed Nora by the front door. He'd already kissed Kingsley, Juliette, and Céleste goodbye the night before. Céleste he'd had to kiss twice. She wouldn't let him go until he did.

Søren, in his day-off uniform of jeans and a black t-shirt, offered him a handshake—"No kiss?"—and Griffin hugged him just to see the look on his face.

"I believe I liked you better when I didn't like you, Griffin," Søren said. Griffin rested his head on Søren's chest. He felt and heard Søren's sigh.

"Cuddle me, big guy," Griffin said. "Sing me a lullaby with your pretty priest voice."

"I'm discovering a new hard limit," Søren said. "At this very moment, in fact."

Griffin didn't let go of Søren, but he did look up at him.

"Has anyone ever told you that you have resting bitch face?" Griffin asked, tightening his hold on Søren.

"This isn't resting. This is quite active."

"Remember when I'd piss you off at the club, and you'd choke me Darth Vader-style?" Griffin asked.

"I believe that's what's referred to as 'the good old days.'" Søren patted Griffin on top of the head. "Don't miss your flight."

"I'm going." Griffin released Søren, kissed Nora goodbye one more time, and headed to his cab waiting on the curb.

"Griff?" Nora ran from the house to catch him just before he got in the cab. She wrapped her arms around him.

"I'll be fine," he whispered.

"If things . . ." She paused and smiled up at him, a fretful sort of smile. "I'm sure things with you and Michael will turn out right. But just in case . . . if things don't go the way you want, or you need more time, you can come back here. I'm leaving again on New Year's, but you can stay with King and Juliette. They'd love to have you. They told me to tell you that."

"I'm not going to fall off the wagon, I swear," he said. "If things don't work out . . . life goes on, right?"

She put her hand on his chest. "You'll let me know?"

"I'll text you. Thanks for taking me in."

"Anytime. I mean that."

The cab driver knocked on the window.

"I gotta go," Griffin said.

"Safe travels," she said. "Merry Christmas. Love you."

She opened the door for him, and Griffin threw his big black duffle bag onto the backseat.

"Gone again on New Year's, huh? You ever going to tell me where you keep disappearing to?" he asked, looking back at her.

"France," she said.

"France? What's in France?"

"The Eiffel Tower," she said with a wink and shut the door on him. As the cab pulled away Griffin turned around. Nora was still on the curb watching him go, a look of concern on her face.

Women.

He'd gotten a non-stop flight, first class, and three hours after leaving New Orleans, he landed at JFK. A blast of freezing air hit him in the face as he ran from the airport to the car waiting for him. A pedestrian dragging a roller bag walked in front of the car too slowly to suit his driver and was rewarded with a honk and a middle finger.

Ah, New York. Home sweet home.

Luckily Emil, the doorman, was occupied talking to someone else when Griffin walked in the front door of his Village apartment building. Emil gave him a wave but was too busy with the other tenant to interrogate Griffin about where he'd been. Griffin rode the elevator alone up to his floor and hesitated only a few seconds before pushing his key into the lock and opening his door.

The apartment smelled clean and empty, like wood polish and loneliness. It was a Tuesday and the housekeeper always came on Mondays. No one was home to mess the place up, but Griffin kept her on to bring in the mail and keep the dust from piling up.

He dropped his keys in the pewter bowl on the little table by the door where he always dropped his keys when he came home.

They made a terrible metallic clatter, loud enough to wake the dead. If Mick were here, he'd call out from the living room or the bedroom, "I hate that bowl!" Mick had once switched it with a plastic Tupperware container stuffed with cotton balls just to punk Griffin.

Alas, no overly sensitive art students yelled at him about the noise. Griffin was alone.

He walked down the hallway past the living room. He didn't even glance at the leather couch he and Mick had fucked on so many times that they'd already gone through two bottles of leather cleaner.

The apartment was something special. Of course, Griffin could have afforded a two-bedroom or a three-bedroom or a ten-bedroom if he was feeling extravagant. But when it came time to find a new place to live, he'd asked to see only one-bedroom apartments. And when Griffin saw the bedroom in this apartment, he'd said "I'll take it" and started moving in the next day.

He opened the door to the bedroom. Since they'd finished moving in, only three people had crossed this threshold—Griffin, Mick, and the housekeeper when she cleaned. That was it. Their bedroom was off-limits. Not even Nora was allowed inside the room. Any threesomes that transpired (and they did) all took place at The 8th Circle or at someone else's place. The bedroom was for Griffin and Mick alone.

This room . . . God, the memories. So many nights here, so many mornings, so many conversations. So much sex, so much kink. And the last month before the break-up . . . so many fights.

Griffin shoved the memories out of his mind with sheer force of will. If he could have pried them out with a crowbar . . . No, he wouldn't have done that. Better bad memories than none at all.

The bed was a king-size, but the room still dwarfed it. A series of full-length windows lined the wall to his right. Opposite the windows sat the bed. At the furthest end of the room was the fireplace, red brick with one of Mick's abstract paintings hanging over it. A low sofa sat in front of the fireplace. Two chairs on either side of the sofa. The floors were the original hardwood that had been there since before World War II. Griffin wondered how many feet had walked on these dark distressed floors before he and Mick had. The bed he'd bought for them was a big wooden four-poster, the best sort of bed for bondage. He'd also had the softest, thickest rug put in the room under the bed. He didn't want Mick's feet getting cold or tired when he was tied to the bedpost for a flogging.

"You want me to be comfortable when you're beating me?" Mick had asked.

"Right."

"You're weird, sir."

"You know you love me," Griffin had said and kissed Mick until neither of them could breathe.

"I know," Mick had said when Griffin finally let him up for air. "I'll always know . . ."

Griffin ran his hand over the suede slate comforter on the bed. Mick had picked it out because the color of it fell between blue and gray on the spectrum, his two favorite hues. The bed itself was the most comfortable Griffin had ever slept in. When he sat on it and sank down into the sheets it was like he was falling into warm water. He and Mick had fallen into it together time and time again and sunk down to the sea floor, never drowning because when they were together they could both breathe underwater. They were each other's air.

The temptation to lie on the bed and remember every good memory was strong, but the brass clock on the bedside table told him he needed to get his ass in gear.

Griffin exhaled heavily and walked to the closet. He needed to change clothes and get over to the Waldorf. What to wear, what to wear . . . He didn't want to look good. He wanted to look amazing. He wanted Mick to see him and not be able to look away ever again.

Leather pants? No. Not on Christmas Eve. He only ever wore those at the club or alone with Mick in this bedroom.

Holey jeans? Mick loved them but the Waldorf wouldn't.

Tuxedo? Too formal for dinner for two.

Three-piece suit? Griffin could rock that look, but it was a bit too staid for a seduction scene.

Black jeans and a leather jacket? Maybe . . .

Or.

Or . . .

Or?

Desperate times called for desperate outfits.

Griffin pulled a garment bag from the back of his closet, hung it on the door, and unzipped it.

If this didn't do it, nothing would.

Fifteen minutes later Griffin stood in front of the closet mirror in knee-high English white socks, black shoes that laced up his calves, a black tuxedo coat, white shirt, black tie, and a red, green, and white kilt with gold kilt pins. And a leather sporran, of course.

Griffin had every right to wear the tartan. His mother's grandparents were Scottish, and this plaid was the pattern of the clan they were descended from. He only ever wore this particular kilt to family weddings and funerals. Mick had never seen him in a kilt other than the black one he wore to the club sometimes. And if Griffin said so himself, he looked phenomenally fuck-able in plaid. And so he did.

Right before leaving the apartment, Griffin retrieved an envelope from a box in his closet. Couldn't see Mick without giving him a Christmas gift, after all. He debated with himself for five whole seconds before throwing a flogger in his overnight bag with a few other kink toys. With a Tower Suite at the Waldorf Astoria waiting for him, it was only smart to be prepared. Just in case.

He made it to the Waldorf by 6:45 and had a quick talk with the concierge. Everything was as Griffin had requested. Room ready. Reservations locked in. Sometimes Griffin hated being the son of the man who ran the New York Stock Exchange. Other days having Fiske as his last name had its benefits.

After slipping the concierge another hundred, Griffin turned, intending to go to the restaurant and check on their table. But as he walked from the lobby toward the Bull and Bear, he stopped.

Standing in the lobby under the chandelier was his Mick.

Mick hadn't seen him yet, and Griffin froze near a pillar and just stared at him.

He looked older. Three months had passed but the Mick in the lobby looked a year older than the Mick who'd left him in September. Griffin counted that as a good thing. Mick wasn't even twenty yet, and Griffin would turn thirty-two soon. Mick wore part of a suit—navy pants, navy pin-striped vest, white button-front shirt with the sleeves rolled up a few turns. Their first Christmas together, Nora had gotten Mick's hair cut short to make him look older. Since then he'd let it grow out a few inches, long enough he could tuck it behind his ears but not long enough to touch his collar. A perfect length in Griffin's estimation. Short enough he didn't look like a teenaged skater anymore. Long enough Griffin could dig his fingers in it and pull Mick's head back for a kiss or the threat of a kiss.

In that moment, with Mick standing underneath a crystal chandelier in the lobby of the Waldorf-Astoria, Griffin had never wanted anything as much as him in his life. It wasn't even a sexual urge (although that was there, too). Griffin simply wanted Mick. Wanted to have him and own him and be near him and hold him and that was it. Pure want.

Griffin took a deep breath and walked down the steps into the lobby past a string quartet playing "Silver Bells." His own heart rang like a bell inside him. He could almost hear it, a sweet and shattering sound.

Mick spotted him and smiled, a big smile.

The smile turned into a laugh, a big laugh.

Griffin put one foot over the other and made a slow twirl.

"You like?" Griffin asked.

Mick raised his hands and gave him a golf clap.

Griffin took one step toward Mick and stopped. Mick walked the rest of the way to him.

"Fancy," Mick said. "When did you get that?"

"Before your time. I only bust it out for the family weddings, and the Raeburns don't get married very often." His cousin

Claudia had gotten married last year, but he and Mick had skipped it. Mick had his first art show at Yorke that week, and Griffin wouldn't have missed that for all the weddings in the world.

"Red and green," Mick said, eyeing the kilt. "Good call."

"My ancestors were very festive. You look good." Griffin fought the very real urge to grab Mick and drag him into his arms.

"Not as good as you," Mick said.

They stopped talking and Griffin, being Griffin, couldn't bear the silence.

"Are we going to do the awkward thing with each other? Or just pretend everything's normal? Or just figure it out as we go?" he asked Mick.

"I'm always awkward so I guess we'll figure it out? I hope?" Mick said.

"Works for me. You ready for dinner?"

"Ready when you are."

Side by side they walked to the Bull and Bear. The maître d' showed them to their table after giving Griffin only the barest little bit of side eye over the kilt. He was probably just jealous. It was a killer kilt.

As Griffin had requested, they were given a table by the window. Griffin ordered water and coffee, Mick water and tea. Their menus laid in front of them untouched.

"So . . ." Griffin began. "Tell me about Rome."

Mick nodded. "Pretty amazing city. I filled up ten sketchbooks."

"Ten? Did your hand fall off?"

"I thought it was going to. Still here." He held up his hand and wiggled his fingers. Griffin had something very inappropriate to say. He kept it to himself.

"I'd love to see some of your sketches."

"I'll show you after dinner," Mick said. "I have some in my bag."

Mick had brought his backpack with him, but Griffin knew better than to get his hopes up over that. The backpack might contain a change of clothes because Mick planned to spend the night. Or it could just be his sketchbooks and laptop. Mick never went anywhere without his backpack.

"Can't wait. I guess we should order then," Griffin said when he noted their waiter circling round their way again. "You know what you want?"

"You decide," Mick said, his menu still closed in front of him. "You know this place better than I do."

Griffin raised his eyebrow at Mick, but Mick was looking out the window at the wintery New York City streets. Ordering food for someone was a possessive act. It spoke of dominance and intimacy. It said, *I know what you want better than you do. I decide what happens to your body.* Or maybe Mick wasn't submitting to Griffin right now? Maybe he sincerely didn't know what to order here? Griffin was overthinking everything, looking for signs, for clues. He wished Mick would just say, "Wanna go fuck?" That would make things so much simpler.

When the waiter arrived, Griffin ordered for both of them. Pointless gesture probably, ordering food. He could barely swallow his water.

"So what have you been up to?" Mick asked, meeting his eyes again finally.

"I was down in New Orleans with Nora for awhile," he said. "Got cold here so I headed south in October."

"The Big Easy?" Mick raised his eyebrow. Griffin knew that look.

"It's okay. Apart from smoking a few cigars with King, I was on my best behavior. Didn't step one foot on Bourbon Street."

"What's her new place like?" Mick asked.

"It's nice. The Garden District is crazy. Every house is huge, old, and beautiful. And she only lives a couple blocks away from King."

"How's he?"

"Better than I've ever seen him. And Céleste is getting so big. She might have a crush on me. Don't be jealous."

Mick grinned. "I miss them all. How's Father S?"

"Søren is Søren. Loves teaching at Loyola. He says it's so much less work than being the only priest running a parish he feels like he's in semi-retirement. It's good for him though. He gets to spend more time with Nora."

"So Nora's good?" Mick asked.

"Nora's great. They all are. It's just . . ."

"What?" Mick asked.

Griffin looked left. He looked right. Then he leaned in and whispered, "Strange things are afoot at the Circle Eight."

Mick leaned in and whispered back. "What are you talking about?"

"I'm talking about Nora, Søren, and King. All three of them are acting weird, and they won't tell me why."

Mick furrowed his brow. "Good weird? Bad weird?"

"Good weird. Like Nora and Søren? They're in second honeymoon mode. They can't keep their hands off each other. I mean, they still fight like always, but it's different. When they fight it comes off like foreplay. I spent two months in the bedroom underneath Nora's. Thank God for earplugs."

"Second honeymoon is good, right?"

"It is. But it's more than that. They're keeping a secret, and King's in on it, too."

"Why do you say that?"

"I keep catching him and Nora together."

"Having sex?" Mick whispered.

"That wouldn't be weird. No, I catch them hugging all the time. Like these long serious hugs like someone just died."

"She's not dying is she?"

"I think she'd tell me if she was."

"Well, her mom died earlier this year. Maybe that's why she's crying so much?"

"Maybe. But that doesn't seem to be it."

"What do you think is going on?" Mick asked.

"I have one theory, but I don't know if you want to hear this."

"Gossip about the Nora and Father S? Of course I do," Mick said. "Spill it."

"I think Søren and King are boning again. Maybe."

Mick's eyes went huge. It was like looking at two quarters, bright and shining. "No way."

"Way," Griffin said. "King told me a while ago that he and the pope used to fuck in high school."

"Yeah, Nora told me that. But—"

"But I think they picked things up where they left off."

"Are you sure?"

"Not sure, but . . ." Griffin knew Søren and Kingsley had spent one night together while Nora was in Kentucky with her intern Wesley two years ago, but Griffin had chalked that up to Søren needing someone to wail on while Nora was gone. "We had a tree trimming party at King's, and afterwards me and Nora and Juliette all went upstairs to put Céleste to bed. I went back downstairs first, and when I got to the top of the steps I could see into the living room. Søren and King were kissing by the tree."

"Like kissing how?" Mick asked. "Just an 'oops, there's mistletoe and we're contractually obligated to kiss' kiss? Or like a real kiss?"

"They were kissing the way I kiss you," Griffin said. "I mean, the way I used to kiss you." He immediately wished he hadn't put it quite that way. Now all he could think about was digging his hands into Mick's hair, tilting his head back and holding him in place—hard—while he kissed him—deep. Mick looked at him with an inscrutable expression. Griffin could only hope Mick might be thinking the same thing . . .

"Anyway," Griffin continued quickly, "if they're sleeping together again, that might explain why Nora and King are acting so weird with each other. Sometimes they just look at each other and start laughing like they're in on some kind of joke that no one else is in on. But then Nora stops laughing and she starts crying, and that's when King hugs her and tells her it's okay. I think. My French is total *merde* these days, but I'm pretty sure he's telling her *tout va bien, nous sommes bien, nous sommes d'accord,* which means something like 'everything's fine, we're fine, it's all okay.'"

"What? What's okay?" Mick leaned in so far his elbows were on the table. Love, math, and gossip were the three universal languages. "Why wouldn't they be okay?"

Griffin sat back in his chair. "I don't know. I asked Nora about her and King and Søren and how odd they're acting, and she gave me a totally cryptic answer. She said I shouldn't worry my pretty little head about it. She said she and King had worked a deal out, they had an understanding, and although it was taking some getting used to for the both of them, everything was fine and dandy because all the cosmic tumblers had clicked into place and the universe was showing her its secrets. Or something like that."

"That is cryptic as fuck," Mick said. "What's that supposed to mean?"

"No idea, but I think she stole that last part from *Field of Dreams.* But it gets even weirder. Søren hugged me."

Mick pointed at him. "Bullshit."

"Okay, he didn't hug me. But he let me hug him, and he didn't even try to choke me to death for doing it."

"You're right. They have gone weird. Whew." Mick sat back. They both laughed. "I've been away too long. I missed all the good stuff."

Griffin almost agreed with him, almost teased him for being out of the country when all the interesting stuff was happening. He came within an inch of telling Mick it was his own fault for abandoning him. Teasing, of course. But not really. And since Griffin couldn't quite trust his motivations, he simply bit his tongue. Figuratively, of course. Mick was the masochist, not him.

"Well, you were in Rome doing cool, important stuff for school. But it's . . . it's good to talk to you again," Griffin said. "I was going a little nuts without you. I had all this gossip, and no one to tell it to."

"I've missed Nora gossip," Mick said. "She sent me some care packages while I was over there, but they didn't have any good gossip in them. Although one of them was postmarked from France. What's up with that?"

"Yet another Nora mystery. Driving me fucking nuts. She used to tell me everything."

"I know. And then you'd tell me everything she told you," Mick said. He laughed but then . . . he wasn't laughing anymore. "You know, I thought I'd hear from you."

"You said you wanted some time off," Griffin reminded him. "You said no calls, no texts, right? A real break?"

"Yeah, I did, didn't I?" Mick asked. "I thought you were mad at me."

"I wasn't happy with the situation, but I wasn't mad at you. And you can always talk to me."

Mick smiled at him and it seemed like he had something else to say. But the waiter decided just then to show up with their food.

They ate, both of them. A small miracle there. Mick had never been a big eater, but he clearly had an appetite. So did Griffin now that the butterflies had vacated his stomach. Mick took his phone out and showed Griffin pictures he'd taken in Rome. The Colosseum, the Trevi Fountain, the Pantheon. All landmarks. No selfies. Mick wasn't the sort of person who'd go around inserting himself into every photo he took. He had an artist's eye for the world. He wanted to see, not be seen. One of his more attractive qualities. One of millions.

"Did you go to Vatican City?" Griffin asked.

"I'm Catholic. Of course I did," Mick said, flipping through a few more pictures.

"Did you see Pope Francis there?"

"From a distance."

"Did you tell him you know a priest in New Orleans who wants to marry him?"

"I didn't, although I did send Father S a Pope Francis keychain."

"Did you get blessed by him or whatever?"

"Nope. He smiled and waved at a bunch of us, but he was surrounded by like twenty priests though. One of them was disturbingly attractive. Made me feel weird. I might have had a naughty altar boy fantasy about him," Mick said. Griffin made a mental note for future role-play reference.

"Speaking of disturbingly attractive priests . . ." Griffin pulled his phone out of his pocket. "You missed the most amazing Halloween party down in Nola."

He held out his phone and Mick took it.

"Holy shit," Mick said before bursting into laughter. "King dressed like a priest for Halloween?"

Griffin tapped the screen to slide to the next picture.

"And your priest dressed like Kingsley."

"Oh . . . my . . . God . . ." Mick breathed. "King and Father S swapped clothes?"

"See? This is part of the reason I think they're banging again. Or maybe it was just that one kiss. I swear I'd give my left arm to know."

"They look good. King makes a hot priest."

"And your pope looks like a fucking English duke when you put him in a Regency suit and boots. He put on his British accent for the entire night. I didn't even know he could do an English accent."

"His father was English, and he went to school over there."

"Mick, you should have seen it. Women were all over him. Nora and Juliette had to beat them off with a stick. I'm not kidding. Juliette picked up a stick and hit a girl with it, but the chick was a bisexual pain slut so it only made things worse. Juliette, by the way, was dressed like Nora. Leather corset, thigh boots, whip in her hand. Dominatrix goddess. It was glorious."

"Who's Nora dressed as? The Mad Hatter?"

The picture Mick had pulled up was of Nora wearing a large black top hat shoved down on her wild black curly hair.

"Not quite," Griffin said. "Sheridan flew down for the party, and that skinny little blond girl dressed as Axl Rose. And since she was Axl Rose, Nora was Slash. See?"

He flipped over to a pic of the two of them—Sheridan in her tight snakeskin pants, torn t-shirt, and feathered blonde hair, and Nora in black leather pants, a black pirate shirt open to the center of her chest, and a black top hat perched on her black wavy hair.

"That is the hottest thing I've ever seen in my life," Mick said.

"It gets better. This vid went viral when I posted it." He opened up YouTube. There was Little Miss Sheridan Stratford, star of stage and screen, doing Axl Rose's famous snake-hips shimmy on top of a table at Kingsley's house as "Welcome to the Jungle" blared in the background. "One million hits and counting."

"That is awesome," Mick breathed, watching the fifteen second vid again.

And again.

And again.

"I'm so glad Sheridan didn't get married to that vanilla dude," Griffin said.

"You and me both," Mick said, watching the video for the final time. Maybe. Sheridan and Mick had met one night at The 8th Circle and bonded over their shared love of sexual submission. When Sheridan came pouting for a threesome with the two of them, Mick had said, "Yes, please and thank you" before Griffin could even open his mouth.

Mick passed the phone back to Griffin. "So who were you for Halloween?"

"You really want to see?" Griffin asked.

"I don't know. Do I?"

Griffin flipped through his pictures until he found one Nora had taken of him. He turned the camera around and showed it to Mick.

Mick dropped his head down to the table for a few seconds before looking back up again.

"You went as Björk," Mick said. "You. Went. As. Björk."

"You have no idea how hard it was to find that damn swan dress in my size."

"You look fucking ridiculous in that."

"I'll have you know that in that dress I never felt more free or more beautiful in my life. I became that Icelandic fairy elf princess." Griffin pretend-tossed his pretend locks over his real shoulder. "I'm going to dress like Björk every day from now on until I die. In public."

"It's a good look for you. I approve."

"I'll need to borrow your eyeliner to complete the transformation."

"I brought it with me."

"You did?" Griffin asked, the laughter leaving him. The restaurant, which had been buzzing with the usual sounds of chatter and silverware, suddenly seemed to go silent.

"Well . . . yeah," Mick said as if confessing to a crime.

"Why? You just carry your eyeliner with you all the time now?"

"Not usually," Mick said.

"So . . . did you bring it just to wear for me?"

Mick blushed and crossed his arms over his stomach. He looked very young then, as young as he did when they first got together over two years ago. Eyeliner was their thing. If Mick was in the mood for kink and sex and lots of it, he didn't even have to ask for it. All he had to do was put on his eyeliner and wait for Griffin to get the hint.

"I don't know." Mick shrugged. "I thought . . ."

"What did you think?"

"I really thought you'd call me or text me or something while I was gone."

"Phone lines work both ways, Mick. And you're the one who wanted the break. I was trying to honor that."

"I know," Mick said. "I know you were."

They both fell silent. The waiter came and cleared away their plates. Griffin loved talking and hated silence. He fought his natural instincts to fill the void with chatter. He wanted to wait and let Mick find his words.

Finally Mick found them.

"Did you have sex with anyone while I was gone?" Mick asked. It wasn't the question Griffin expected, but he was ready to answer it.

"Yes," Griffin said.

"Nora?" Mick asked.

"Actually, no," Griffin said. "But she was there. You know she's working as a pro-domme down in Nola. She had a client—two clients, a couple. The husband is into cuckolding. He wanted Nora to tie him up and 'force' him to watch another man fuck his wife." Griffin raised his hands and put "forced" into finger quotes. Mick knew a lot about being "forced" to do "terrible" things he "didn't want" to do in bed.

"So you got paid to have sex?" Mick asked, sounding more impressed than shocked. "Like a male prostitute?"

"No, of course not. Nora took my money and donated it to Catholic Relief Services."

"Nora's a pimp."

"Hey, it's good work if you can get it. They were both very satisfied customers. Came back four more times. He's a Saint, by the way."

"A saint of what?"

"A New Orleans Saint. He's a linebacker on the football team," Griffin explained. Mick knew about as much about linebackers as Griffin knew about line dancing. "So . . . what about you? Did you see anybody?"

"Yeah. Kind of."

Griffin felt the "yes" more than heard it. Felt it like a punch in the gut.

"Girl? Guy?"

"Girl," Mick said. Griffin was embarrassingly relieved about that although it shamed him it did. Sex was sex. It shouldn't matter if Mick had it with a man or a woman. And yet the idea of anyone else inside his Mick . . .

"She's from Yorke," Mick said. "We've had some classes together."

"I see," Griffin said. "Are you two still . . ."

"No," Mick said. "It lasted about two weeks."

"Was it weird? Dating a girl?" Griffin asked.

"A little. It was nice at first. She's . . . she's beautiful. And normal for a change. That's not what I meant." Mick shook his head. "I really didn't mean it like that."

"You aren't the first person who's said I wasn't quite normal," Griffin said.

"She's not normal. I only mean she's . . . you know."

"She's not rich," Griffin said.

"Right."

"She's your age."

"She is."

"She doesn't drag you to parties you don't want to go to."

"No. She never did that."

"Well, she sounds like a huge improvement over me," Griffin said. "No wonder you asked for the break."

Mick rolled his eyes. "I didn't ask for the break because I wanted to date her. I didn't ask for the break because you made me go to a party. That wasn't it," Mick said. "That last party was horrible, yeah, but it was just the last straw. I was supposed to study abroad last fall, and you talked me out of going. Then I was supposed to go last spring, and you talked me out of going. Then I told you I was going this fall and instead of letting me go, you asked me to put it off one more year because you already made plans for us to go somewhere over fall break. And you asked me to transfer to Cooper Union so I could stay in the city all week instead of going back to Yorke. When I told you I didn't want to, you said I was being selfish. Selfish because I wanted to keep going to the school I'd been going to for two years and where I had professors I loved and had real friends for the first time in my life. And I didn't think that was selfish. I thought you asking me to leave my school so I could spend more time at home was selfish. Especially since you were never home anymore."

Griffin didn't say anything to that. There was nothing he could say to that. Mick was right. Completely and utterly right. He couldn't argue so he didn't argue.

"Do you think I actually wanted a break?" Mick asked. "If you think that, you should know I didn't. I didn't want it. I needed it. Because it was the only way."

"Only way for what?"

"Nora . . ." Mick began and met Griffin's eyes. "She told me a long time ago that the reason she left Father S was because there was someone she needed to be, and she couldn't be that person and be with Father S at the same time. And that's why I asked for the break from you. Because there was someone I had to be, and you weren't letting me be him."

"Good reason to leave someone," Griffin said, entirely without sarcasm. Now that he'd heard Mick say he didn't want a break at all, he could be magnanimous. "Were you . . . did you get to be you with this girl?"

"Pearl," Mick said.

"Pearl? Is she someone's grandmother?"

"Her parents are Brooklyn hipsters."

"They should be arrested for child abuse giving her that name."

Mick laughed. "Your name's Griffin. You can't talk."

"Hey, Griffin's a WASP name, not a hipster name. Totally different thing," Griffin said. He'd been legally required to play lacrosse in high school with a name like Griffin, but at least it wasn't a hipster grandma name. "So what's Miss Pearl like?"

"She was nice. I really liked her. But I was kind of terrified of being with her."

"Why? Because hipster is contagious?"

"Because she wasn't you." Mick gave him a nervous glance, but spoke again before Griffin could say anything. "So a month after we got to Rome, we went to Trivoli and we were there overnight and . . ."

"Right. It's okay. We were on a break. Even if we weren't, you know I'm okay with you being with girls."

"After a few days, she and I were out walking and she said something. She said, 'I thought you were a die-hard bug. Glad to know I was wrong about that.' I had no idea what she meant."

"B.U.G. Bisexual Until Graduation," Griffin replied. "I got called that in college, too. Maybe I'm still bi because I never graduated."

Mick laughed a little. "I told her I wasn't a bug. I was bisexual before college, and I was going to be bisexual after college. She said being bisexual is mostly a phase. Most people are all gay, straight, or lying."

"She's been reading too much Savage Love. What did you say to that?" Griffin asked.

"I said, 'I'm gay then.' "

Griffin smiled. "I guess that wasn't the answer she wanted."

"No, it wasn't. She tried to talk me out of it. She said the only reason I was hung up on you was because of your money and your family. I reminded her I'd asked you for a break, and that wasn't the sort of thing a gold digger usually does."

"She doesn't know you very well if she thinks you want me for my money. You obviously want me for my cock."

"Obviously," Mick said, smiling. The smile disappeared and he took a long deep breath. "I thought she was cool. We could talk art and stuff all day and all night long. And she was like me. Her dad's a teacher. Her mom's a nurse like my mom. We had a lot in common. It was . . . easy, being with her. Being with you isn't easy sometimes."

"I know it isn't. There's a little bit of pressure when you're with me, I guess."

"A little," Mick agreed. An understatement. Griffin's father was president of the New York Stock Exchange. His mother was a famed Manhattan socialite. Griffin had a part to play in his family and anybody with Griffin was expected to play that part as well. Griffin's mother had taken on the role of marriage-equality crusader. Not a week passed without her wanting Griffin and Mick to attend some function together. *Look, World. Look at my son and his boyfriend. Who could tell these beautiful young men they can't get married?* On top of that, Griffin had inherited The 8th Circle from Kingsley. The club was his responsibility and it took more of his time than Griffin ever dreamed it would. Wrangling wayward submissives and putting pro-doms into place and planning private parties and wooing new clients . . . Griffin had a new respect for Kingsley after all that. It was fun, empowering. And Griffin loved it. But what he hadn't loved was the time it took away from him and Mick. Mick hadn't asked to be the arm candy of the new King of Kink in New York. That wasn't what he'd signed up for over two years ago. Mick's resentment had built up quietly like junk hidden in an attic until the ceiling broke under the weight, and it all came crashing down.

"I'm sorry," Griffin said. "I asked too much of you. I should have taken better care of you and us. I love showing you off to the world."

"I'm not a watch. I'm not a new car. I'm just a nobody with social anxiety disorder."

"You're not a nobody. You're everybody, Mick." Griffin looked at him. "When I got the apartment I wanted a something small, because I didn't even want friends staying the night at our place. Just you and me. That's all I wanted. Our own little private kingdom. Somewhere along the way I forgot about that . . . I let people into our private world until there were so many people around I didn't even notice when you slipped out the side door. I asked you to transfer schools so we could spend more time together and completely forgot it was me who wasn't making time for you."

"It's not all your fault," Mick said. "I should have said something. I have a safeword. I could have used it to get your attention."

"You have my attention now. If you need to say anything to me . . . anything at all . . ."

"I do," Mick said. "I have something to say." Mick tucked a stray lock of hair behind his ear and without thinking Griffin reached out and touched Mick's ear.

"That's new," Griffin said. Mick had gotten his ear pierced while they were apart—an industrial-style piercing with a silver bar through the cartilage. Had Mick ever mentioned wanting to get a piercing before? Not that he recalled and Griffin would have recalled.

"I got it a couple months ago," Mick said. "I . . ." Griffin still had his fingers on Mick's ear. He caressed the lobe lightly. Mick seemed to be struggling for words. Good.

"I like it," Griffin said.

"Thank you." Mick whispered the words.

"You needed pain, didn't you?" Griffin asked.

Mick closed his eyes. "Yes."

"You were going to say something to me?" Griffin asked, his voice low.

"What I want to say to you . . ." Mick began. He seemed to have forgotten whatever it was he wanted to say. Talking was overrated anyway. Especially when Mick was right here, a foot away from him. Under the table their knees touched. Griffin took Mick's hand and put it on his thigh under the kilt. Mick kept his hand there. While they'd been apart, Griffin had fucked only the one person and even then it had been solely to distract himself from his loneliness. What he wanted—no, what he needed—was Mick back in his bed, in his collar, in his life.

"I wanted to say . . ." Mick continued.

"Say anything you want to me."

"Griffin?" came a voice from over Griffin's shoulder. "Griffin Fiske?"

Mick pulled away and Griffin nearly screamed. When he looked back over his shoulder he saw a woman approaching the table. It took five full seconds for him to put a name with the face.

"Hello, Bitzi," Griffin said, trying not to wince visibly. He forced a smile. "Long time no see."

"Too long. Too, too long," she said, bending over to hug him and kiss his cheek. A beautiful buxom blonde, she held a teetering glass of red wine in her hand. "How are you, darling?"

"Great. Just . . . great." She stood up and planted a hand on his shoulder to steady herself. Mick was giving him a look—that look. The who-the-fuck-is-this look. "Bitzi, this is Michael. Michael, this is Bitzi. Bitz and I used to hang out at some of the same clubs." He felt himself flinching every time he said her name. She was actually a Brandi, but her entire life she'd been insisting everyone call her "Bitzi." Some latent masochism, probably.

"Oh, that's not all and you know it," she said, pinching his shoulder.

"Ex-girlfriend?" Griffin continued. "Sort of?"

He'd fucked her half a dozen times, more or less, if he remembered correctly. It all happened in the span of one week, so maybe she considered that a relationship? As opposed to what he considered it: further proof he'd hit rock bottom.

"Oh, I was more than 'sort of' your girlfriend." She slapped his back a little harder than necessary. "Nice to meet you . . . I'm sorry. I didn't get your name."

"Harry," Mick said. "Harry Styles."

"You're cute," Bitzi said. "Are you Griffin's twink?"

"Jesus, Bitz," Griffin said. "How much have you had to drink?"

"Lighten up, Griff. It's Christmas Eve." She waved her hand in a dismissal. "You were so much more fun before you got clean."

"I OD'd," Griffin reminded her. "That's fun?"

"Well, when you were conscious you were more fun." She turned her attention to Mick again. Griffin tensed, ready to intervene if drunken Bitzi said anything else awful to him. "Do you party?" she asked Mick.

"Hugs not drugs," Mick said.

"You're precious," Bitzi said, the wine in her glass sloshing dangerously like a red wave on the ocean. "What are you? Fourteen? Fifteen?"

"Yes," Mick said. "Both."

"Bitz—" Griffin began but Bitzi waved her hand again.

"Oh, you know I'm just playing around," she said to Griffin. To Mick she said, "Your Griffin and I go way back. Ten years or more?"

"You two were together ten years ago?" Mick asked.

"We were," she said with a broad grin.

"Back when Griffin was on drugs?" Mick nodded. "Now it all makes sense."

Griffin snort-laughed. He couldn't help it. It just came out.

"Your twink's kind of a bitch," Bitzi said, the smile gone from her face.

"Sorry about that," Mick said. "But I paid a lot of money for this session, and he charges by the minute."

"Session?" Bitzi said, confusion clouding her already confused face.

"He's a power bottom, and I'm working the rough-trade beat now," Griffin explained. "You know, bad economy and all that."

"You want to go fuck?" Mick asked, raising his hand and tapping his imaginary watch on his wrist. "You're on the clock, Mister."

Griffin dropped his napkin on the table and lifted one finger in the direction of their waiter.

"Check, please!"

CHAPTER THREE

White Christmas

Once they were alone in the elevator, Griffin and Mick burst into laughter.

"Oh my God," Griffin said, half-laughing, half-groaning. "You don't talk much but when you do, it packs a helluva punch."

"I learned from the best," Mick said.

In unison they said, "Nora."

Mick leaned back against the elevator wall as it headed up to the thirty-seventh floor.

"Plus, she called me a twink," Mick said. "Only Alfred's allowed to call me your twink and only because he makes the fancy grilled-cheese sandwiches."

"Plus he's British. Even when they're insulting you it sounds classy."

"I still can't believe you had sex with her," Mick said, grinning to show he wasn't angry, only playfully horrified.

"I was so drunk," Griffin said, rubbing his forehead. "Like for a full week. And I was twenty, I think. Or maybe I was twenty-one. It's all a blur. That's my only defense."

"Her name is Bitzi."

"You fucked a Pearl."

"I know." Mick winced. "And I wasn't even drunk. I have no excuse."

"Forgive me?" Griffin asked.

"Always," Mick said.

"Always?" Griffin asked, cupping the back of Mick's neck. It felt strange touching Mick's neck and not feeling the leather of his collar against his hand. "You sure about that?"

Mick was a lot of things—intelligent, talented, submissive, artistic, sensitive . . . Aggressive he was not, but that didn't stop him from putting both hands on Griffin's shoulders and kissing him. It was a hard and hungry kiss and Griffin kissed him back twice as hard and twice as hungry.

"I guess you're sure," Griffin said against his lips. He had Mick's face in his hands and he looked into his eyes.

"I have a Christmas present for you," Mick said, a little breathless and glassy-eyed, just the way Griffin liked him.

"I have one for you too," Griffin said. "But I'm going to fuck you before I give it to you. How's that's sound?"

"Perfect. I'll give you mine before, during, and after."

"Before, during, and after? What kind of present is this?" Griffin asked.

Mick smiled at him. "You'll see."

Griffin kissed him again, pushing him up against the elevator wall, pinning Mick there with his full body weight.

"Fuck, I've missed you," Griffin breathed.

"I missed you more," Mick said.

Griffin grinned at him, put his mouth to Mick's ear, and whispered, "Prove it."

The elevator door opened and Mick smiled a seductive heated meaningful smile. Griffin couldn't wait to find out what it meant.

"Guess what?" Mick said.

"What?"

"I can."

Mick picked his backpack up off the elevator floor and stepped out into the hall. Griffin grabbed him by the hand, almost dragging him to their room—suite 37A.

Griffin opened the door and pulled Mick in after him, shutting it behind him and locking it. He slammed Mick's back to the door. Griffin's cock was already painfully hard. He hadn't had sex in weeks and hadn't had sex with Mick—the one person in the world he most wanted to have sex with—in over three months.

"If I don't get inside you soon, I'm going to die," Griffin whispered. "Literally. Bleeding to death on the floor. You don't want to kill me, do you?"

"If you don't get inside me soon, it won't matter. I'll be dead, too."

"Do you want me to hurt you?"

"After," Mick said. "Fuck me first."

Griffin held Mick by his chin and forced his face up. "What do we say when we want something?"

"Please fuck me, sir. Please?"

"Say 'please' again."

"Please?"

"Say 'sir' again."

"Sir . . ."

"Say 'fuck me' again."

"Please, please fuck me, sir."

Griffin could hear a note of desperation in Mick's voice. If Griffin's cock could talk, it would probably sound about like that.

"Bedroom. Now." Griffin clasped the back of Mick's neck hard enough to leave bruises and marched him from the door through the sitting area and into the bedroom. The concierge had brought all of Griffin's things up as requested. Griffin glanced around. Over ten years since he'd been in this room. Crazy . . . The room looked exactly as he remembered it—pale-blue and silver striped wallpaper, white curtains, ornate furniture and windows that looked down onto Manhattan. Per Griffin's request, the concierge had brought in a Christmas tree decorated with white lights and an angel on top. He didn't turn on the lamp by the bed. The lights from the tree alone lit up the bedroom, and it seemed as if a thousand stars were watching them.

"Do you have my collar, sir?" Mick asked between feverish desperate kisses.

"No. I left it at home." Griffin was already working on the buttons on Mick's vest. "I didn't want to jinx it."

Mick laughed. "You thought I wouldn't want you?"

"Even doms have insecure moments. And you did leave me."

"Only for a few months. Just so we could figure stuff out."

"What did you figure out?" Griffin pulled the vest down off Mick's shoulders and dropped it on the floor. He started in on Mick's pants.

"I figured out I wanted to be with you even if it hurts sometimes," Mick said as Griffin started at the bottom of Mick's shirt and unbuttoned his way to the top. "Because you're worth the pain. See?"

Mick didn't wait for Griffin to take his shirt off him. He pulled it off and dropped it on the floor next to his vest.

"Oh my God," Griffin said, his eyes flying open wide, his heart catching in his chest. Mick raised his right arm over his head so Griffin could see it all. "Mick . . . you got a gryphon tattoo?"

After that Griffin couldn't speak. He could only touch. The tattoo on Mick's right side was solid black. But though the color was simple, the design was elaborate. The head of the ornate mythical beast was on Mick's stomach and its body wrapped around his side and back. He'd had to raise his arm to show Griffin the wing that stretched almost vertically up Mick's side. With his fingertip, Griffin traced the outline of the gryphon—its proud head, its wings, its long tail that curled on Mick's back. He could feel Mick shivering from the light touch. It was easily the most beautiful tattoo Griffin had ever seen in his life, and it was on the most beautiful person he'd ever seen in his life.

"You did this for me?" Griffin asked.

"For us," Mick said. "And for me, sir. I needed the pain."

"This must have taken hours."

"Two weeks, three hours a day."

"You did the design?"

"Of course," Mick said. "It had to be perfect."

"It is perfect," Griffin breathed. "You're perfect."

"I pretended it was you," Mick said, putting his hand on Griffin's shoulder to steady himself as Griffin ran his hand over the tattoo. "It was easy. Felt like getting flogged by fire. I had to come after every session. I almost came during a couple times."

Griffin didn't laugh. He couldn't stop caressing the tattoo, especially the wings . . . the majestic wings etched along Mick's ribcage from hip to chest. The tattoo was still new enough Griffin could feel the raised edges of it.

"Is it healed?" Griffin asked.

"Yes, sir."

"Good." Griffin pushed Mick down onto his back on the bed and straddled his hips. He kissed Mick, but not on the mouth. He started at the throat and worked his way down Mick's chest, kissing and licking and biting. Mick wound his hands in Griffin's hair and the lights from the tree illuminated Mick's chest and arms. That wasn't enough naked flesh for Griffin so he pulled back and yanked Mick's shoes, socks, pants and underwear off in one near-violent motion.

Seeing his Mick naked on the snow-white bed was everything Griffin had wanted and dreamed of for three months right before his eyes. For a few seconds he did nothing but feast upon the image. They'd been lovers since Mick was a skinny, long-limbed skater boy who could barely get ten words out of his mouth around strangers. Since then, Mick had put on almost twenty pounds of muscle and looked like the young man he was instead of the scared teenage boy he used to be. But even Mick's broader shoulders and extra muscle didn't alter the air of vulnerability

Mick always wore around him like an invisible aura. Invisible, but Griffin could sense it. The scars from Mick's suicide attempt were still there, hidden under the wing tattoos on his wrists. And the damage his father had done to him by making him feel like a freak his whole life was still there, lingering under the surface just like the scars under the ink. Healed wounds were still wounds. Knowing that brought out Griffin's most fiercely protective and possessive instincts with Mick.

"Collar or no collar, I own you right now," Griffin said.

Mick gave him a look, that look, that fuck-me-until-the-world-ends look.

Now it was Mick's turn to say, "Prove it."

Griffin grabbed Mick, dragged him closer, and licked his cock from base to tip. Mick shuddered with pleasure underneath Griffin, which led to Griffin smiling up at him and saying, "I rest my case."

Lying on his side, Griffin wrapped an arm under Mick's right thigh, locking them together. He took Mick's entire cock into his mouth, sucking on it deeply, massaging every inch of it with his lips and tongue. Mick rewarded him with a sound that was somewhere between a gasp, a moan, and a cry. Griffin had missed that sound.

"You have permission to come," Griffin told him. "In fact, consider it an order. But take your time. I'm in no hurry . . ."

And he wasn't. He could do this all night. He loved having Mick's cock in his mouth. The only thing Griffin enjoyed more than giving Mick pain was giving him pleasure. And the only thing Mick enjoyed more than the pleasure Griffin gave him was the pain.

Being with Mick again brought Griffin's body back to life. For months he'd felt dormant, half-asleep. But now he'd woken up. His heart raced and his thighs clenched and his stomach tightened. Under his kilt, his erection throbbed and as the wool tickled him, it throbbed even harder. Mick's hips were moving against Griffin's mouth. His breaths were coming in short bursts. With his free hand Griffin reached up and pushed his palm into Mick's throat, not enough to cut off his air but enough to make him feel the pressure. It worked. Mick arched so hard his back came off the bed, and he came into Griffin's mouth with a rush of salt and heat.

Griffin swallowed every drop of him.

As Mick lay there panting between his slightly parted lips, Griffin kissed his hips and lower stomach.

"Don't move," Griffin said. Mick lifted his hand to give him a thumbs up. Griffin laughed. "Feeling good there?"

Then Mick gave him *two* thumbs up.

God, Griffin had missed Mick. Yes, the sex he'd missed, the kink, owning this gorgeous boy of his . . . but that right there, a tired, post-orgasm thumbs up that had them both giggling—that was love right there.

"You're insane," Griffin said. "You know that, right?"

"I haven't had any kink in months. I'm suffering from oxygen deprivation."

"Let's get you breathing again, shall we?"

Griffin threw his black leather duffel bag on the bed and unzipped it. From it he pulled an anal plug, a tube of lube, black leather wrist cuffs, a long bondage strap, a spreader bar, ankle cuffs, and a flogger (the vicious stinging kind).

"On your stomach, sub," Griffin ordered and Mick complied without hesitation. *On your stomach, sub* were four of Mick's favorite words.

It was jarring at first seeing the tattoo on Mick's back. His body was different now, and Griffin couldn't wait for his body and Mick's to get intimately reacquainted. But not quite yet. Griffin had a few things to do first.

Griffin applied a likely excessive amount of lube to Mick. They hadn't had anal in months. Better safe than sorry. Griffin may have taken an unnecessary amount of time with this step, but he couldn't get enough of touching his sub inside. He carefully inserted the anal plug to open Mick up. That was it for the gentleness.

Griffin yanked Mick's arms behind his back and buckled the leather cuffs on his wrists and ankles. With the bondage strap, Griffin tied Mick's wrists to the bed frame. He cuffed Mick's ankles to the spreader bar—a two-foot spreader. Perfect. Griffin picked up the flogger and struck the center of Mick's back. Then he did it about a hundred more times.

Griffin didn't aim for Mick's new tattoo, but he didn't actively avoid it either. The tattoo was healed but still sensitive. He couldn't help it if he loved the sounds Mick made when his agony and ecstasy intersected.

When Mick's back and shoulders glowed a bright red, Griffin dropped the flogger. He sat at Mick's side and kissed the welts. And since Mick didn't have his collar on, he kissed the back of his neck.

"You want me inside you?" Griffin asked into Mick's ear.

"As soon as possible," Mick replied in a low and desperate voice. "Sir."

Griffin sat up and pulled his tuxedo jacket off.

"Sir?"

"Yes?"

"Will you leave the kilt on?" Mick asked.

Griffin smiled down at Mick. Sometimes he could pull off the stern scary dom-thing that Nora and Søren were so good at. But not now. Nothing could stop him from smiling.

"You're as bad as Nora," Griffin said.

Mick grinned back. "That's not true."

"It isn't?"

"No. I'm as *good* as Nora."

"Better," Griffin said.

"I'm better than Nora?"

"Oh yeah, she doesn't put out for me anymore." Griffin winked at him and Mick laughed. And that was the best. The two of them. Alone. Laughing together. Together laughing. Now it was Christmas.

Griffin bent and kissed Mick's naked shoulder while he eased the plug out. Then he pulled up his kilt and rubbed lube all over his erection. With such an enjoyable task he usually took his time, rubbing and stroking and making Mick watch and wait. Not tonight. Tonight he finished fast, more eager now than he'd ever been to be inside Mick.

Eager as he was, Griffin moved slowly as he pushed the tip of his cock into Mick, penetrating him with a long, controlled stroke.

Griffin groaned loud and long as he sunk into Mick. Mick released a sigh. Griffin could feel the tension Mick had amassed during the beating now leaving his body.

"You did miss this, didn't you?" Griffin asked as he pushed into Mick again meaningfully. "You missed my cock in you."

"So much," Mick said. "Every inch."

"How many inches?"

"Eight and a half," Mick said.

"You sure? We better count." Griffin pulled all the way out. "Count."

"One," Mick said as Griffin pushed in just the tip.

"Two." Griffin tilted his hips just slightly.

"Three." Not slamming into Mick at this point was taking every ounce of self-control Griffin had.

"Four," Mick said with a grunt as Griffin's cock pushed passed his G-spot.

"Five . . ." The grunt turned into a groan as Griffin went deeper. His thighs were hard as steel as he tried to steady himself.

"Six." Griffin gripped Mick's hip and squeezed it. He shifted his knees and lowered his mouth to Mick's neck.

When Mick counted seven, Griffin bit the back of his neck. When Mick flinched from the pain, Griffin pushed in as far as he could go. Almost.

"Eight," Griffin said for Mick. Then with one more brutal thrust, he said, "And a half."

The counting lesson over, Griffin gave in to his need and fucked Mick like his life depended on it. He rode him with long strokes, strong thrusts, full and possessive pushes, all the while caressing Mick's sore back, rubbing the still-burning skin. It still wasn't enough for Griffin. He pulled out again and unstrapped Mick's ankles from the spreader bar and pushed him onto his back.

"Knees up," Griffin ordered and Mick obeyed, bringing his knees to his chest so Griffin could fuck him face to face. They hadn't had sex in months, but this wasn't the sort of thing one forgot how to do. It was so easy to be with Mick, so natural. Religious people, the kind not like Nora and Søren, sometimes called the sort of sex he and Mick had "unnatural." They didn't understand that this was the most natural thing in the world for them, joining their bodies together, being with each other and in each other. What was more natural than their bodies following their hearts?

Griffin bent low and kissed Mick on the mouth, a deep kiss with mingling lips and tongues and breaths.

"I've missed making love to you," Griffin said.

"Is that what this is?" Mick asked.

"I love you so it has to be."

"I was scared you'd stop loving me," Mick said and Griffin knew exactly what he felt. "I got the tattoo because I was afraid I wouldn't have you anymore."

"That's the one thing you never have to be afraid of. Never." Griffin touched Mick's face with his fingertips, touched his hair which was always so soft. They kissed again for a long time as Griffin moved inside Mick. The kiss only ended when the need to come grew too great for Griffin to hold off any longer. Clutching Mick by the shoulders, Griffin rode him with deep strokes. Mick was panting again. Sometimes if the angle was perfect and the mood was right, Mick could come solely from anal penetration. To help him along, Griffin held Mick's cock in his hand and lightly massaged it.

There were no words for the sight of Mick lying on white sheets with his eyes closed, his arms tied to the bed and his head thrown back. Griffin pressed his lips to his exposed throat and came hard with a series of quick short thrusts. Beneath him, Mick whimpered from his own orgasm. The tension was unbearable, all tight knots and straining muscles. Then it was over. Done. Griffin collapsed onto Mick's chest. Mick went still underneath him. His only move was to wrap his legs around Griffin's lower back, his favorite place to rest them.

Griffin felt Mick's chest move. He was laughing.

"What?" Griffin asked.

"I think I got come on your kilt," Mick said with a sigh. "Sorry about that."

"I hope you did," Griffin said. "I'd be disappointed if one of us didn't."

"Pretty sure you're not going to be disappointed."

Griffin flipped the kilt up and saw a telltale white stain.

"Good boy," Griffin said, giving Mick a quick kiss before pulling out of him and disentangling their limbs.

Mick rolled out of bed and headed to the bathroom for the post-sex cleanup routine. While he was gone, Griffin found his gift for Mick and set it under the tree. He pulled the covers down on the bed and relished the night ahead sleeping with Mick spooned against him. If Mick was planning on staying the night, that was.

Griffin stripped out of his socks and tuxedo shirt and pulled on a black T-shirt from his overnight bag. When Mick emerged from the bathroom he wore nothing but the ankle and wrist cuffs. He seemed in no hurry to take them off.

"I have your Christmas present," Griffin said.

"It's not Christmas yet," Mick reminded him as he sat on the bed. If Griffin was ever going to be put in a spaceship all alone and sent rocketing across the Milky Way never to return to earth and he could only take one photograph with him, it would be a picture of Mick sitting on a white bed wearing black leather ankle cuffs and wrist cuffs and nothing else. Except maybe his collar. That's all he was missing.

"I got my present early. Now you get yours."

He nodded at the tree and Mick walked over to it somewhat warily.

"It's not something big, is it?" Mick asked. One of the first requests Mick had ever made of Griffin was "no more big presents." No sports cars, no original Picasso paintings, no ski lodges in Aspen. Normal presents. Socks. Goofy t-shirts. A new skateboard. Griffin had reined in the urge to buy Mick every awesome thing on earth. But this gift was different. This gift had cost him nothing and everything at the same time.

"Just a little something," Griffin said. "It's a little weird. But I wanted you to have it. I've been holding onto it for a long time."

"How long?" Mick picked up the slightly weathered envelope from under the tree and brought it back to the bed.

"I've had it about ten years."

"Wow," Mick said sitting back down on the bed cross-legged. "Are you sure this is for me?"

"It is. You'll see. Open it."

Mick gave him a curious look but he did as he was told. He gingerly tore open the envelope and pulled the letter out.

"Read it out loud," Griffin said. "I don't even remember what is says, it's been so long."

Once more Mick gave him a look, a little skeptical, but he did as he was told.

Dear Whoever Is Reading This,

I'm in love with you.

Griffin saw Mick's eyes flash at him, more curious now than ever. He kept reading.

I don't know who you are yet, but I'm going to keep this letter until I meet you. Two nights ago I was at my friend King's house and he caught me snorting coke in his bathroom. He kicked me out. I went back to my place and called a bunch of "friends" over. They trashed the place so badly I had to get a hotel room while professionals came and cleaned up my mess. My life is a mess right now. I keep trying to quit drugs and quit drinking. I'm not doing a very good job of it. Now I'm here in Suite 37A at the Waldorf-Astoria, hung over and a little sick to my stomach. King came to see me here. He wasn't mad at me, just worried. Apparently he went through a rough time like this when he was twenty-eight and was pretty sure he wasn't going to live to be thirty. He asked me if I had anything worth living for. Anything I wanted to do or be or have that I wanted more than I wanted drugs. King told me something I didn't know about him. He said he wanted to be a father someday. When he was tempted to go back to the bad place where he was ten years ago, he'd think about the kids he didn't have yet but would someday have. He had to take care of himself if he wanted to be alive to meet his own children. I thought about it. I don't really want kids. My brothers are the breeders in the family. So I told King I wanted you.

Who is "you"? King asked.

You is someone I can be in love with, I told King. I wanted someone to be in love with and someone to love me back. Someone I can put a collar on and own the way Søren owns Nor. I saw her curled up on his lap two nights ago in his music room. He was reading to her and she had her eyes closed but you could tell she was awake because she was smiling. I was so jealous of them and what they had that I decided to go get as fucked up as possible until I stopped thinking about what they had that I didn't. King asked me if I'd give up drugs and drinking to have what they had. If King could offer it to me would I give up the partying in trade? I know he couldn't do it but he wanted to know if I would. I told him yes. King gave me a few sheets of hotel stationary and told me to write a letter to the person I wanted to be in love with, the person I wanted to own someday and tell him or her all this (by the way, if I haven't told you already, I'm bi, but if you're reading this you probably already know that).

So here I am writing you to say I'm going into rehab tomorrow. Second time I've tried it but maybe second time's a charm. This time I'm not going to leave early. I'm doing this for me, definitely. I'm sick of feeling sick all the time. But I'm doing it for you, too, even though we haven't met yet. At least I don't think we have. I'm going to seal this letter up and keep it. I'll give it to you someday because I have to believe you exist and you're out there, and I'll find you.

When I find you I'll be healthy and alive, and I'll be able to take care of you. Because that's what I want most is someone to love and take care of and spoil. And maybe someone to wear a collar for me and sit at my feet and listen while I read something to you. Or I don't have to read. We can just talk. Or we can just be. Or we can do whatever you want to do because if I love you as much as I want to love you, then I want to make you happy. Just tell me what to do and I'll do it. King says I'm a natural dominant, but for you, because I love you, I'll do anything you want me to do.

Love,

Griffin Fiske
Waldorf-Astoria
Suite 37A

Griffin waited, not speaking. He watched Mick fold the letter up and slip it back into the envelope. He set the envelope on the white table by the white bed. He stood up and walked over to Griffin who looked up at him. There was a moment, a long one, where they only looked at each other without saying a word.

Still not speaking, Mick went down on his knees and rested his head against Griffin's thigh. Griffin bent over and laid his cheek against the center of Mick's back.

"I was terrified," Griffin said as he traced the edge of the gryphon tattoo with his fingertip again. He would never tire of doing that.

"Of what?"

"Of you being away from me for three whole months. You being across an ocean without me in a foreign country. I could handle missing you that long, but I hated the thought of you being on your own. What if someone tried something with you? What if someone tried to hurt you, and I was four thousand miles away?" Griffin would never forget slamming Mick's dad into a wall. That hadn't been the first time Griffin had to get physical with someone because of Mick, and it hadn't been the last either. "I kept talking you out of going because I didn't want you somewhere I couldn't take care of you. It was wrong of me to guilt trip you into staying when you had to go. I just want you to know that. I'm sorry. I was wrong. I won't do it again, and if I try to do it again, tell me, and I'll stop. Deal?"

"It's a deal."

"And if I do that, you won't leave again, right?"

"I can't," Mick said. "You're a permanent part of me now. You can take off a collar. You can't take this off." He laid his hand over the gryphon on his stomach. "I need what you give me."

"I give you what you need."

"You do."

"So we're doing this?" Griffin asked, his heart clenching like a fist in his chest. "This forever thing? I'm not asking you to marry me. I'm just saying no more breaks. If something's broken, we fix it. We don't throw it out."

Griffin felt Mick nodding against his leg. "I don't regret going to Rome, but three months apart was more than enough for me."

"Okay," Griffin said. Mick sat back up and looked at him. "We're in it to win it. No more breaks. You and me and for always. Sound good to you?"

Griffin held Mick's chin in his hand.

"Sounds perfect."

"Do you want to stay the night with me here?" Griffin asked.

"I want to stay the night with you everywhere."

"We'll start with here tonight. Get back in bed. I want to violate you some more."

"Can we do something first?" Mick asked.

"Maybe. What is it? I might be feeling generous."

"I have to go get something."

Mick started to stand up but Griffin put a hand on his shoulder and pushed him back to his knees.

"Crawl," Griffin ordered.

Mick's breath caught in his throat and his pupils dilated. Typical sub. A slut for rug burn.

He watched Mick crawl from the chair over to his backpack and back again.

"Give it here," Griffin said, holding his hand out. Since he'd had to crawl on his hands and knees, Mick carried his eyeliner pencil in his mouth. He dropped it in Griffin's palm.

"Sit up," Griffin ordered. "And hold still."

Griffin uncapped the pencil and angled Mick's face into the light.

"Go easy on me," Mick said as Griffin carefully lined Mick's eyelids. "Jared Leto, not Adam Lambert, okay?"

"I'll make you look like Ozzy Osbourne if you try to tell me what I can do to you again," Griffin said, putting on his most stern dominant voice as he finished his work. Mick looked beautiful as always, but now he looked like *his* Mick again, the Mick who lived on his knees for Griffin.

"Ozzy who?" Mick asked.

"Oh, you're getting it now, sub."

"Is that somebody from long, long ago?" Mick asked. "Like your childhood?"

"Keep cruisin' for a bruisin,' pain slut. I have the misery stick with me, and I'm not afraid to use it."

Griffin pushed Mick onto the bed.

"Use it," Mick said. "I'm out of practice submitting. You'll have to beat me back into it."

Griffin grinned at him, that demonic sort of grin he used when attempting to terrify subs.

"Challenge accepted."

Five minutes later and with the aid of a sheet and his bondage strap, Griffin had Mick tied to the headboard of the bed in a kneeling position. Mick was sitting on his heels with his hands over his head. His entire back, from neck to thighs, was on beautiful display.

Griffin took a thin flexible cane two feet in length and flicked it against Mick's back under his right shoulder blade. Mick flinched. Anyone would. Nothing stung quite like a cane. But Griffin didn't want Mick simply flinching. He wanted him in pure agony. So Griffin flicked the cane again. Right onto the very same spot he'd hit before.

Then he did it again.

And again.

Over and over Griffin flicked the same sensitive spot under Mick's shoulder blade. Ten times. Twenty times. His pale skin turned pale red, then bright red, then a blazing burning scarlet. Griffin could sense Mick recoiling, twisting in his bonds, instinctively trying to move away from the relentless assault on that one little part of his back. And yet Griffin could hear Mick's labored breathing, a sure sign of arousal.

"Nora taught me this trick," Griffin said, still flicking that same spot. "I don't need to hurt every square inch of you. Just the same square inch over and over again. You're going to have the ugliest bruise on your back tomorrow. Just in this one spot. You'll feel it every time you move. Does it hurt?"

"So much."

"Good," Griffin said.

There was a time and a place for mercy during a BDSM scene.

This was not the time.

This was not the place.

Griffin kept striking the same spot until finally Mick let out a sound of pure agony. He'd buried his mouth against his arm and released a sort of strangled scream.

But Griffin struck the spot again.

"Yellow," Mick said, his voice strained.

"Oh my God . . ." Griffin chuckled. "The pain slut cries mercy. I never thought I'd live to see this day."

Griffin placed his hand over the spot he'd been torturing for the last ten minutes. Mick's skin burned to the touch. And when he kissed that spot it burned against his lips. Mick groaned. It might have been from pleasure and it might have been from pain, but Griffin didn't care. To Mick they were one and the same.

"You're a sadist . . ." Mick said, audibly wincing.

"That's the nicest thing you've ever said to me, slut."

Griffin slapped Mick hard on the ass because of course he did. Why wouldn't he?

Speaking of asses . . . Griffin grabbed the lube off the bedside table. When they both were wet enough, Griffin pushed back into Mick. Once he was fully embedded, Griffin pulled his t-shirt off and pressed his naked chest to Mick's naked back. With his hands on Mick's hips, Griffin raised and lowered him on his cock.

"Now do you remember how to submit to me?" Griffin asked into Mick's ear.

"Yes, sir . . ." Mick breathed.

"You're my property even when you forget you are," Griffin said. "You belong to me whether you like it or not."

"I like it," Mick said.

"You like this, too." Griffin pushed in deeper. It wasn't a question. They both already knew Mick did. "Even if you didn't like it I might still do it to you. Why?"

"Because you own me."

"I own you. Your body belongs to me. Every . . . single . . . beautiful . . ." Griffin wrapped his hand around Mick's erection, "inch of it."

Mick came in Griffin's hand. It was sudden, but not unexpected. Pain was by far the most effective aphrodisiac where Mick was concerned. Nothing worked quite as well as a long, sustained beating.

"Sorry, sir," Mick said between breaths.

"Don't apologize to me. Apologize to the housekeeper who has to clean your come off the headboard."

"I'll write a note to her," Mick said.

"Yeah, I know where you can stick it."

Mick laughed but the laugh stopped when Griffin pushed up and into him again. Mick might have had his orgasm but Griffin was only getting started.

He fucked intently, vigorously, and mercilessly. Mick would never again forget who was in charge in this relationship. And if for some reason he did, Griffin would remind him.

"I could go all night," Griffin said into Mick's ear. "I think I will."

He pulled out of Mick and untied him from the headboard. Griffin stripped out of his kilt and crawled into bed.

"I should make you lie on your right side," Griffin said as he dragged Mick to him. "I could make you feel that bruise with every stroke. But then I wouldn't get to see your ink. Decisions, decisions . . . I'll be nice. You know, since it's almost Christmas."

Griffin put Mick on his left side. With a pillow he propped up Mick's right leg. It was the easiest way to open him up so Griffin could comfortably fuck him for as long as he wanted to, which was forever.

As he thrust in and out of Mick slowly, Griffin kissed the shoulders and neck and back he loved so much. His hand rested on Mick's tattoo, Griffin on gryphon.

"That's why," Mick said, his voice still a little breathless.

"What's why?" Griffin asked.

"Why I got the tattoo right there," Mick said. "The first time we had sex, I was on my side like this and that's where you put your hand. It's my gryphon landing pad."

"Don't make me laugh when I'm fucking you. My cock will do weird things."

"Weird things? Like what? Start a band? Go on a shopping spree? Write a haiku?"

"That's it. You're in so much trouble." Griffin shoved Mick onto his stomach and held him down on the bed, a hand on the back of Mick's neck. With rough strokes, Griffin fucked Mick hard, hard enough to make the bed rock. Luckily it was a padded headboard.

Griffin gave everything he had to his Mick. His love, his lust, his desire and hunger, his grief over the break-up, his joy over the reunion, his need to own Mick—truly own him and have him and keep him safe and happy and treasured until the end of time.

When he came at last it was with Mick's name on his lips and his lips on Mick's shoulder. He rolled onto his back and Mick stretched out on Griffin's chest.

"I have so much come inside me," Mick said.

"Merry Christmas." Griffin kissed the top of Mick's head. "I'll let you take a shower. But not yet. You have to stay here for a few minutes."

"Yes, sir. Happily. And wetly."

"Is wetly a real word?"

"It is now."

Griffin wrapped both arms around Mick. He'd let him go. Eventually. Maybe.

"What are we going to do tomorrow?" Griffin asked. "I guess your mom is expecting you back home."

"She sort of is. I think she missed me while I was gone."

"I guess I can share custody. You know . . . we could pick your mom up and go to the ski lodge. Lucas and the kids are all sick so they aren't coming this year. There's plenty of spare rooms. Although your mom and Aiden could just shack up. He thinks she's hot . . ."

"My mother is my mother. She is not hot."

"She is a stone cold fox. She looks like Jennifer Connelly."

"Who?"

"She was the chick in *Labyrinth*. Aiden totally wants to be her Goblin King."

"You're creeping me out so much right now."

"He told me you and I had to get back together so he could continue to woo your mom. He wants to woo the fuck outta her."

"Now I know why Nora tells Father S she hates him all the time."

"It's meant to be. They're both divorced, same age. They both have kids about the same age, both cute as hell."

"Can you just beat me some more if you're feeling this sadistic?"

"If your mom and Aiden get married, then my half-brother will be your step-father, and that'll make me your uncle."

"That's it. I'm going back to Rome." Mick tried to escape Griffin's arms but Griffin wouldn't let him go.

"No. You never get to leave me again. Especially not if we're going to be family."

"Wings," Mick said, invoking his safeword. Griffin ignored it.

"Call me Uncle Griffin."

"I have a few other names I'm tempted to call you first."

"Don't be rude. Not my fault your mom's a MILF, and my brother's got a middle-aged-man crush on her."

"He's forty-five."

"He wears Merrells and khakis. He's middle-aged."

"I'm going to tell him you said that."

"Don't you dare. He still gives me the worst wedgies."

"Just don't wear underwear anymore," Mick said.

"You," Griffin tapped him on the end of the nose, "are a genius. Now go take a shower before we do more damage to these white sheets."

Mick sat up and looked at the bed. Wet spots everywhere.

"I think it's too late. We're going to have to burn them."

"In that case, we might as well get them even wetter."

Griffin pushed Mick on his back and kissed him and kissed him and kissed him. He kissed Mick's neck and chest and licked his collarbone end to end. He bit Mick's hips and stomach, then flipped him over and ran his tongue and lips from Mick's neck down his spine to the very base and back up again. With his whole body he worshiped Mick's, every part of it, with his hands and mouth and skin on his skin.

They were tangled up with sheets and legs and arms, with tongues and fingers and teeth. Finally they stopped and Griffin held Mick to him so tight it hurt them both.

"No more leaving," Griffin said in his ear.

"Never," Mick said and Griffin could hear the anguish in his voice. "It hurt to leave you. But I don't regret it. Is that weird?"

"No." Griffin ran his hand through Mick's hair. "That's just life. You do what you have to do. Even if you have to do it, it's not easy. I had to go to rehab to get clean. It wasn't fun. I couldn't wait to get out. I don't regret it. Not for one second. It made me into the man I am today, the man who is here with you, not somewhere else—like a cemetery."

"I can't believe you wrote me a letter before we even met."

"You were with me in rehab," Griffin said. "Just an idea. I didn't know who you were yet, but you gave me something to look forward to, a dream to hold on to. You kept me there working at getting clean when that was the last place I wanted to be."

"I love you," Mick said. "You know that, right? I did say that tonight, right?"

"I know." Griffin kissed him on the lips softly. "Now go take a shower before the bed is one big wet spot."

Mick laughed. "You coming with me?"

"You get it warmed up. I'll be right there."

Mick got out of bed and headed for the bathroom. Griffin stretched and stood up. He heard the comforting sound of the water turning on and Mick getting into the shower. It was the beautiful sound of life going back to normal.

He walked to the window and looked out on the city. It had started to snow again. From the thirty-seventh floor the city looked like a fairy-tale kingdom. The skyscrapers looked like castle turrets. The snow looked like falling stars.

From his overnight bag he pulled out his phone and snapped a picture of the cityscape and sent it to Nora.

Merry Christmas! he captioned it.

Nora wrote back seconds later.

Nora: **My beautiful city. I hope it misses me.**

Griffin: **I'm sure it does. I know I miss you.**

Nora: **Speaking of missing, what's the news with my angel?**

Griffin: **Good news. I have a sub again.**

Nora: **YES!**

Nora: **I told you so.**

Griffin: **Exactly what I wanted for Christmas.**

Nora: **I have a present for you if you want it.**

Griffin: **I want ALL the presents.**

Nora: **My present is a secret I'll tell you. I have a sub now, too. Collared and everything.**

Griffin: **Serious? Never thought that would happen. Who's the lucky guy and/or girl?**

And when Nora replied with a looooong text message that included a name he knew, Griffin nearly fainted. Because that name was . . .

"MICK!" Griffin yelled. But Mick was in the shower.

Griffin dropped the phone on the floor and ran naked into the bathroom almost wiping out on the wet tiles in his haste to get to Mick. He wrenched the shower door open and stepped inside. Then he grabbed Mick by the shoulders.

"MICK!"

"What the fuck?" Mick demanded. He pushed wet hair out of his eyes.

"Oh my fucking God . . . Mick. You'll never believe it."

"WHAT?"

"I found out what's going on with Nora and King and why she keeps going to France every couple of months and crying and King keeps telling her it's okay and why Nora and Søren are like in second honeymoon mode." The words came out in a wild joyful rush.

"What? What is it?"

"Nico. King's son. She's fucking King's son Nico. Not just fucking him. She collared him. She owns him. They're in love." Griffin was holding Mick's shoulders so hard he was almost shaking him. Then he did shake him.

"Wait. Nora did what? Are you shitting me?"

"No! She just told me. Apparently he took care of her after her mom died, and the usual happened but it wasn't the *usual* usual because Nora collared him afterward. Kid must be real fucking good in bed if Nora collared him and risked Kingsley's wrath. Not just that though. I was right. King and Søren are together again. Like *for real* for real. Which is why Søren's so happy and horny all the time, and Nora's so happy and horny, because she has a sub now and it's . . . oh my God, it's insane. Søren has King and Nora. Nora has Søren and Nico and King has Juliette and Søren and it's like the sexiest love hexagon ever."

"Five people. That's a love pentagon."

"I don't have time for a geometry lesson when Nora collared King's son. All the cosmic tumblers are clicking into place and the universe is showing me its secrets!" He yelled that last part, which he stole from Nora who stole it from *Field of Dreams*. Seemed the right thing to do.

"This is the best gossip in in the entire history of gossip," Mick said, almost hooting with laughter. "Why is Christmas so awesome this year?"

"Because you're here," Griffin said, holding Mick by the back of his neck. "You're here and I'm here. And Nora's fucking King's son Nico and Søren's fucking King and I'm fucking you and that's fucking awesome."

He shook Mick again. But only a little.

"Good fucking Christmas," Mick agreed once Griffin stopped shaking him.

Griffin kissed him until they both dissolved into laughter yet again.

Not just a good fucking Christmas.

Best fucking Christmas ever.

ABOUT THE AUTHOR

Tiffany Reisz is the author of the internationally bestselling and award-winning Original Sinners series for Mira Books (Harlequin/Mills & Boon). She lives in Kentucky with her husband, author Andrew Shaffer.

Like Tiffany Reisz on Facebook: www.facebook.com/ littleredridingcrop

Follow Tiffany Reisz on Instagram: @tiffany_reisz

Visit www.tiffanyreisz.com to subscribe to the Tiffany Reisz e-mail newsletter and receive the free Original Sinners novella, *Something Nice*

Printed in Great Britain
by Amazon

43263196R00169